MAYA, THE BLINDFOLDED

HER MISTAKE...SHE TRUSTED HIM.

PRASAD BAG

FOR MY PARENTS....

Contents

Acknowledgements

My Sincere and Humble Thanks to,

My wife – Shraddha, for her encouragement to write this novel. For my Kids – Atharv and Arnava, for their curious questions about plot and characters.

My consulting Editor, Sudhir Raja, for his dedicated work on this novel and his humble suggestions about my linguistic corrections.

My Dear Friends, Uday Tambekar and Sampada (Sanu) Tatwadi, for their valuable feedback for this novel.

Ashwini Kurdukar and Rohan Sonawane , for their valuable contribution while making this novel.

And to all my friends and family who directly or indirectly encouraged me to write this novel.

1

Chapter 1

—♡—

"Maya, it seems you are not focusing on your work," Kapoor was angry.

'How could I make such a stupid mistake?' Maya felt ashamed. Her eyes began welling up.

"Sorry, Sir!" She apologized.

"Do whatever but fix this error immediately! I need a fully tested enhanced version of this encryption program by the end of the day tomorrow." Kapoor got up from his chair and stormed out of the conference room.

Mrs. Pinto gave a stern look at Maya. She hurriedly followed Kapoor and murmured, "I told you, Sir, these days, she is not focused on her work."

*****

It was evening again in Mumbai. The sky had a reddish-orange hue. The departure of the Sun left behind bright yellow patches on the horizon. The wind had changed its direction, flowing inwards from the coast. Streets were illuminated by pale-yellow streetlights.

Working-class Mumbaikars were busy returning to their homes. But the day at 'KKSwTech' was still going on. The KKSwTech was a subcontractor company of 'HM-Tech,' heavy machinery manufactured company. The KKSwTech had developed an advanced encryption software program for 'HM-Tech' to encrypt drawings and other documents for security purposes.

Recently, KKSwTech received a new order from HM-Tech to enhance the encryption program to encrypt the new types of documents.

The technical team at KKSwTech Pvt. Ltd worked day and night to develop the enhanced version of the encryption program. The software was ready in record time, and now it was time for its presentation to KKSwTech's founder and CEO, Ashok Kapoor.

Maya Gomes, a development team lead, was chosen for the presentation. In her early twenties, Maya had a darker skin tone with an attractive round-shaped face. She had a straight nose and beautiful black eyes.

It was Maya's first presentation to Kapoor.

She worked rigorously on the presentation and changed it numerous times for its perfection.

*****

Kapoor was sitting at the one end of the big oval table. Mrs. Pinto, Maya's immediate boss, was sitting to his right. She was a plump lady in her late fifties with gray hair. Two other department heads were seated at the left of Kapoor.

The room's lights went off, and the projector started streaming bright whitish-yellow light beam on the front screen.

"These are the new types of machine drawings of our client, 'HM-Tech.' Accordingly, we have made changes in our encryption software." Maya pointed the white cursor to the colored diagram on the projector screen.

"Let me pass the first drawing document through encryption software .." White cursor moved across the screen several times,

"..and... vola! See, The same document is converted into its encrypted version."

Maya tried to open the document with other software, but the it did not open.

"As you see, I can't open it with any other software."

All were keenly looking at the screen.

"Does the entire document encrypted?" Mrs. Pinto asked.

"Yes, Ma'am."

"But still, there are some numbers and letters are in their original form. "Kapoor's dense voice boomed in the dark.

"Why are they not encrypted?" He asked without taking his eyes off the screen.

Maya slumped. She was unaware of the issue. She turned back and looked keenly at the screen.

"This drawing document looks different. Our encryption software is not developed for this drawing document." Maya said in a low voice.

Kapoor quickly started flipping the pages from the given printouts. The sound of rapidly flipped pages was cutting the silence of the room.

"Where did you get the original versions of these documents?" Kapoor asked while turning pages. Other semi-lit faces turned toward Kapoor.

"From the folder named Version2.0 that you gave me, Sir," Maya answered. Her eyes were still scanning the document on the screen.

Kapoor signed heavily. Others exchanged glances with soft laughter.

"Maya, you worked on documents from the Version2.0 folder. Recently we received new documents, and those are kept in folder Version2.1. You know it." Kapoor said in a loud voice.

All eyes turned toward Maya.

'Oh, God! How could I have made such a stupid mistake?' Maya blamed herself. She gasped and remained seated with her head down.

Awkward silence took control of the room.

"Maya, it seems you are not focusing on your work." Kapoor was angry.

'How could I make such a stupid mistake?' Maya felt ashamed. Her eyes began welling up.

"Sorry, Sir!" She apologized.

"Do whatever but fix this error immediately! I need a fully tested enhanced version of this encryption program by the end of the day tomorrow." Kapoor got up from his chair and stormed out of the conference room.

Mrs. Pinto gave a stern look at Maya. She hurriedly followed Kapoor and murmured, "I told you, Sir, these days, she is not focused on her work."

*****

Maya came to her desk with drooped shoulders. She removed her golden bracelet from her hand and kept it on the table. She sat on the chair and closed her eyes.

In a few minutes, she logged into her computer. The computer screen came alive, and a blue 'desktop' appeared. Maya began moving the computer mouse around, clicking frequently, and as a result, various windows popped up on the screen.

Suddenly, her mobile rang.

"Hello?" Maya answered the phone, but her eyes were still glued to the computer screen.

"Ma'am, I'm on the way to your house. Please tell me what work I have to do today." A female voice came through the speaker. It was Suman, her housemaid.

Maya quickly took her eyes off the computer screen and turned her chair toward the cubicle wall.

"Suman?! Where have you been since the last two days? No calls, no messages. You didn't even answer my phone calls." Maya whispered in a severe tone.

"Sorry, Ma'am. My son, Sameer, was suffering from a high fever. I was busy with him. Also, my husband..."

"Alright, alright...." Maya cut Suman off and relaxed back in her chair.

After a few thoughtful seconds, she said,

"Purchase some vegetables on your way home."

"Okay, Ma'am."

"Prepare some pasta and vegetable soup."

"Okay, Ma'am."

Maya's desk phone rang. The phone's LCD screen displayed 'Kapoor' in black.

"Suman, I have to go now..." Maya hurriedly disconnected the call and quickly picked up the desk phone.

"Yes, Sir... Okay...Sure...I will be there." Maya said respectfully.

She stood up from the chair, tucked her mobile into the back pocket of her jeans, and started walking hurriedly toward the corner cabin.

*****

"May I come in, Sir?" Maya asked from outside the cabin door.

"Yes, come in." Kapoor's authoritative voice came from inside.

Maya entered the cabin. She saw Mrs. Pinto was already in the cabin.

"Sit, Maya." Kapoor pointed toward an empty chair next to Mrs. Pinto.

Maya sat down and had a quick glimpse of Mrs. Pinto's face.

'Hmm..it seems Mrs. Pinto is not in a good mood.' Maya realized.

"Mrs. Pinto was telling that last week you refused to do one urgent work." Kapoor initiated the conversation.

"Yes, I refused because I had to attend my cousin's wedding in Goa. The leave was approved by Mrs. Pinto, herself." Maya replied promptly.

"It was an urgent client requirement, Sir! We must respond to our client's requests promptly." Mrs. Pinto grunted and looked straight into Maya's eyes.

"But Sir, it seems, of late, I have been criticized about my work on purpose, and..." Maya's voice rose.

"That's not true, Sir. I treat all my team members equally." Mrs. Pinto replied sharply.

"Why do you think Mrs. Pinto does not treat you fairly?' Kapoor relaxed at the back of the chair and asked calmly.

'Go ahead, Maya. This is the chance to settle your score with Mrs. Pinto. Everyone in the office knows she has a grudge against you, and she always targets you.' Maya's inner voice said.

"That I am not sure, Sir. But my guess is ...." Maya took a few seconds to gather her thoughts. "I guess... I'm not like other team members."

"Like how?"

"Like, I don't pamper her ego..."

"These are all baseless accusations, Sir." Mrs. Pinto intervened with an elevated voice. She promptly stood from her chair, "With your permission, Sir, I would like to leave now. I have more important works to do." She said in irritation.

"Okay, Mrs. Pinto, please carry on," Kapoor said.

Mrs. Pinto gave a stern look at Maya and reached to the cabin door. She forcefully pulled the doorknob and walked out of the cabin. The door closed with loud sound than usual.

Maya also stood from her seat.

"Sit down, Maya." Kapoor said.

Maya sat back in the chair.

"Look, Maya, you cannot refuse work. This is not acceptable."

"But Sir, Mrs. Pinto..."

"I know, I know Maya, you feel Mrs. Pinto targets you but bear with me for one more month. Then, I will transfer you to another team, okay?"

"Okay, Sir." Maya wanted to say more about Mrs. Pinto's unprofessional behavior, but she kept quiet.

Kapoor turned to his computer screen. Maya stood from her chair and walked toward the cabin door.

"Anyways, the mistake that happened today during the demo should not happen again."

Kapoor's eyes were reading from the computer screen.

"Yes, Sir."

"How much time would you need to upgrade the encryption software ?" Kapoor suddenly looked at Maya.

"Two days, Sir,"

"Only two days?" Kapoor was surprised.

"Yes, Sir!"

"How can you be so sure?"

"I have written the software. I am positive, Sir !" Maya replied confidently.

"Okay, then. What should I say? You have written the software; you know it better. Good Luck!"

*****

Suman opened the main door of Maya's apartment with her set of keys and entered. She lifted the over-stuffed bag of vegetables and proceeded to the kitchen.

She kept the bag onto the kitchen platform and wiped the thin layer of sweat off her forehead. She took a deep breath and let one glass of cold water run down her throat.

After drinking water, Suman began retrieving the vegetables from the bag. She took a knife and a chopping board from the drawer and started slicing lettuce. The touching sound of the knife blade on the chopping board filled the air.

'Sameer's fever should be gone by this evening.' Thoughts began running in her mind.

'What if his fever does not reduce by this evening? Should I take him to another doctor?' Suman reached for the next vegetable.

'Oh, no! I forgot to tell Sameer's father about dosages of medicines.' Suman exclaimed, and she suddenly felt an intense pain in her finger. She looked down and found one cut on her middle finger. The blood began gushing from it, and the white chopping board turned red in a few seconds.

Suman quickly opened the tap. She put her bloody finger under its water, and the doorbell rang.

Suman closed the tap and came out of the kitchen. She opened the main door. The old Suzy was at the door.

"Oh, hello, Suzy auntie. Come in." Suman welcomed Suzy.

"How are you, Suman?" Suzy smiled and walked in her baby steps.

"I am okay, auntie."

"You seem to be very busy nowadays. You have forgotten your neighboring Suzy auntie." Fake anger appeared on Suzy's wrinkled face.

"No, it's not like that, auntie. Nowadays, I come to work in the afternoon. That is usually your nap time." Suman hid her injured finger behind her back.

"I sleep minimal these days. Please do come as you used to before. "

"Okay, auntie, I will come, for sure. Do you need something?"

"I need a cup of milk." Suzy extended her right hand toward Suman and handed her one empty cup.

"Okay, sure," Suman took the cup and went inside the kitchen.

While Suman was on her way to the kitchen, Suzy got a glimpse of Suman's reddish finger. Her wrinkled face turned straight.

"What happened to your finger?" Suzy asked worriedly.

Suman was bearing the intense pain from her finger.

"What happened to your finger, Suman?" Suzy asked again.

"Nothing much, auntie, just a small cut." A loud male voice came from the kitchen.

'Oh…My God! It seems Bhagat's ghost possessed Suman.' Suzy realized, and she rushed to the kitchen.

Suzy saw a man standing near the kitchen platform as she entered the kitchen. His back was at Suzy. Suzy's stony eyes observed him keenly and realized that he was short and fat. His hair was silver-white, and he was wearing a blood-stained white shirt and pants. He was pouring milk into the cup.

"Yes, This is Bhagat! " She confirmed to herself and nodded her head positively.

Suzy quickly moved toward the kitchen platform. She picked up the knife from the chopping board and stabbed the man at his back.

"Aaaahh...!" The man screamed in pain. While bearing the pain, he slowly turned and faced Suzy. Suzy saw the man's face was black, and his eyes were bigger than usual.

"I told you, Suzy, leave from my land... immediately... otherwise...." The man stammered in pain.

"Otherwise, what Bhagat?" Suzy shouted in anger.

Suddenly, Bhagat started laughing. "Heh...Heh...Heh..." His entire body was shaking. Suzy could see dripping blood from his red teeth.

"Bhagat...Why are you laughing." Suzy shouted again.

"Hahaha... ha ha...." Bhagat laughed. "It's my land, Suzy. I was murdered for this land. I'm not going anywhere, but I will definitely drive you all from here."

"Bhagat, you will not succeed," Suzy screamed.

"I will succeed, Suzy. You won't be able to stop me. Ha..Ha..Ha.."

"Oh, is that what you think? Wait! I will show what I can do." Suzy leaped toward Bhagat.

Bhagat dodged her and got out of the kitchen. He came into the hall and quickly moved toward the main door.

"Heh... heh... heh..., you can't do any harm to me, Suzy. You are too old. Heh... heh... heh!"

Suzy, too, followed him outside the kitchen. She noticed his feet were floating a few inches above the ground.

She saw Bhagat open the main door latch and get out the main door in the blink of an eye.

*****

Suzy followed Bhagat through the stairs, and in a couple of minutes, she was on the ground floor. She came out of the building entrance and looked for Bhagat in all directions.

At a distance, she saw someone sitting at the bench near the main gate.

Suzy slowly walked toward the bench and realized Suman was sitting on the bench. Suman was panting and breathing desperately. Her face was ashen. Her eyes were tightly closed, and her body was shaking uncontrollably.

"My dear, Bhagat's ghost has got into you, but don't worry, I am going to force it out of you," Suzy shouted from a distance. Suman did not reply. She swept her shaky hand across her forehead to get rid of sweat.

"Suman..." Suzy shouted again. "Suman..Don't worry...I am coming at you."

Suzy took one more step toward Suman.

"Suzy... Suzy..." A voice came from behind.

'Oh...This is Bhagat's voice..' Suzy recognized. She quickly turned around. Her suspicious eyes began scanning everywhere.

"Suzy... Suzy..." Bhagat's voice came again from a different direction.

'Hmmm... now he is playing hide and seek with me.' Suzy thought.

"Suzy... Suzy..." The voice came again.

'OH! This time Bhagat's voice came from the Suman's bench." Suzy realized. She looked at the bench and saw Bhagat sitting in Suman's place.

Suzy was surprised for a moment. But the next moment, her face turned red. She started inching at Bhagat.

"He, he... He, he... He, he..." Bhagat laughed menacingly.

In a couple of minutes, Suzy was standing in front of Bhagat.

"He, he... He, he... He, he...Suzy go away from my land; otherwise, I will teach you a lesson...He, he... He, he... He, he." Bhagat again laughed menacingly. Suzy saw his teethes were red and dipped in blood.

"I will teach you a lesson, Bhagat!" Suzy roared. The fire was ignited in her eyes. She sprang toward Bhagat. Bhagat dodged her, and Suzy fell to the ground.

"Ha, ha, ha... ha, ha, ha." Bhagat taunted Suzy with his laughter. Suzy's anger reached to next level. She attacked Bhagat again.

"Heh... Heh... Heh...., you are too old, Suzy. You will never overpower me, never! Heh, heh, heh!" Bhagat sprinted toward the main gate.

" I am not going anywhere, Bhagat. Go away, and don't dare to return." Suzy shouted at the top of her voice.

Suzy saw Bhagat reach the main gate and gave her a nasty look. His black tongue was utterly out of his mouth like a sneak out of a hole.

Suzy shouted again, "Go away!" but Bhagat did not move further. He just stood there with poison spewing eyes and a cruel smile on his face.

"Go away!" Suzy shouted furiously.

"Suzy... Suzy..."

Suzy heard Bhagat's voice from behind. She quickly turned around.

"Suzy... Suzy..."

Suzy heard Bhagat's voice from another direction. Suzy sharply turned toward voice like a needle moved toward the magnet. Her desperate eyes did not see anything.

"Screeeeeeeeech!" The sound of breaks came from the road. Suzy looked at the road. A truck barreling down the road jolted Suman at full speed. Suman tossed through the air like a football.

"Aaaahh...." Suman screamed before hitting the ground.

"Suman!" Suzy scrammed and rushed in a great hurry toward the road.

She walked out of the main gate and reached the fallen Suman.

Suman's head was severely hit on the ground. Blood started gushing from her wound like water spurting from a cracked coconut.

Suzy froze on the spot. Her shocked eyes kept staring at fallen Suman.

Suman remained unconscious in a pool of blood.

*****

Maya's cab stopped opposite Ruby Park. She paid the fare in a hurry and came out of the cab. Without caring about vehicles from both directions, she darted toward the Ruby park. Vehicles suddenly stopped and honked loudly. Maya's ears did not sense the honked horns. She rushed through the main gate in a great hurry.

'Ruby Park' was the two-storied building situated half-mile away from the main road. It was surrounded by the dense foliage of Mango and Banyan trees. It was one of the buildings in a quiet middle-class locality in Worli's Tagore Nagar. One under-construction building work was going at the backside of Ruby Park. The vehicles passing through the two-lane road running outside Ruby Park were mainly from that under-construction building.

Once entered through the gate, Maya began running toward the building. A group of people was standing in the building compound. As Maya's eyes caught the ambulance standing near the building entrance, her legs suddenly halted.

Suman was being loaded into the ambulance on a stretcher. Her eyes were closed. The blood in her hair had become dense, and that caused them to clump.

Maya looked at Suman and suddenly burst into tears.

Soon, the ambulance started. Maya's looked at the leaving the ambulance with teary eyes.

Maya turned toward the building entrance once the ambulance disappeared down the road. Suzy was sitting on the bench near the building entrance.

Maya went to Suzy and sat beside her. She lightly kept her hand on her shoulder. Suzy did not sense it. Her eyes were staring blankly at the place where Suman had been laid.

"Auntie?" Maya's somber tone broke Suzy's trance. She looked at Maya with lost eyes. A few strands of her white hair were floating in the wind, and Her body was shaking slightly.

Maya looked at Suzy for a few seconds and asked softly, "What happened, auntie?"

In response, Suzy's eyes again turned toward the spot where Suman had been laid. Maya, too, looked in the same direction with a perplexed look.

"Did you see anything? The other guy said that a truck hit Suman. Is that true?"

Suzy nodded slightly.

"Really? Where did that truck come from?" Maya, in her anxiety, shook Suzy's body slightly. Suzy's weak body shook, but she kept staring at the spot where Suman was laid.

The curtain of blurriness formed in front of Maya's eyes. She took out a lace-edged handkerchief from her purse and wiped the tears that were eager to flow down her cheeks.

Suzy slowly raised her hand toward the place where Suman had been laid.

"What's the matter, auntie?"

"Suman was possessed !" Suzy said calmly. She lowered her hand but kept staring at the place.

"What you mean Suman was possessed? Don't say such things, auntie. I am getting scared."

"Fear is an illusion that controls your mind," Suzy said in a plain tone.

"What you mean possessed ???"

Suzy slowly turned her head at Maya. She looked into her eyes and said firmly, "Bhagat's ghost had possessed Suman."

"What?!" Maya almost shouted and quickly sprang up like a released spring.

"Yes, Bhagat! Our previous landlord. This building, RubyPark, is standing on his land. I heard he did not want to sell this land, so he was brutally murdered. He was stabbed multiple times in his chest with a long knife."

"Oh... really?"

"Yeah... I spoke to him."

"With whom? with Bhagat?"

"No...with Bhagat's ghost."

*****

The sky's color was changing to a yellowish-orange. The dimly lit evening slowly turned into a dark night, and shadows blended into the surroundings. The wind started blowing more intensely, carrying dry leaves and dust particles with it.

Suzy's emotionless eyes suddenly appeared angry.

"You don't believe what I said, right? Like the others, you too think I am mad, don't you?" Suzy shook Maya's shoulders roughly and asked in an elevated tone.

To avoid Suzy's strange gaze, Maya looked in the other direction. She could still feel the heat from Suzy's eyes.

"I can see ghosts. I clearly saw Bhagat's ghost in Suman." Suzy said firmly.

Maya did not reply.

"You still don't trust me, right?" Suzy growled with the high chin. A strange smile formed on her face.

"It's getting dark, auntie. Let's go upstairs." Maya said hesitantly.

"No! First, tell me, do you believe me or not?" Suzy almost shouted in her feeble voice. Maya felt the heat in Suzy's words.

"Yes, I believe you. You may be right. Something must have happened to Suman. Otherwise, how could she end up in front of the speeding truck." Maya said.

Suzy's eyes returned to normal. A faint smile appeared on her face

"Come on, let's get upstairs, auntie." Maya helped Suzy to stand.

In a couple of minutes, they began walking toward the building entrance. Suzy had a faint smile on her face.

*****

The building's entrance was around fifty feet from the compound wall. The wind-driven, slowly moving trees cast different shaped shadows between the compound wall and the building entrance.

One banyan tree was standing opposite the entrance near the compound wall. A single streetlight was standing adjacent to the compound wall. The yellow glow from the streetlight illuminated the top of the banyan tree. The banyan tree, compound wall, and streetlight stood in straight line.

Maya and Suzy entered the building's dark entrance. It was dark inside the lobby.

'Oh... it seems the ground floor passage light is off.' Maya thought.

"Be careful, auntie." Maya tightly holds Suzy's upper arm.

They began climbing the stairs.

After climbing a few stairs, Maya saw the weak rays of streetlight were streaming in through the staircase's broken window. The rays helped cut through the darkness slightly.

They were greeted by flickering tube-light on the ceiling as they reached the first-floor passage.

'Oh, damn! This tube is about to go out too.' Maya thought.

She pushed the partially opened main door of Suzy's apartment. They entered the apartment and slowly reached Suzy's bedroom.

Maya laid an exhausted Suzy down on the bed.

"Can you please put on the fan?" Suzy asked.

"Sure." Maya switched on the ceiling fan. Suzy's gaze fixed on the rotation of the fan. Fan's pane slowly picked up the speed.

"Take some rest, auntie," Maya said.

"Maya?"

"Yes, auntie?"

"You still don't believe that I can see and talk with ghosts, do you?" Suzy's gaze was still fixed on the rotation of the fan.

"No, it's not like that, auntie." Maya walked closer to Suzy. "I think... if God exists, then ghosts and other evil spirits exist too." Maya said, and at the next moment, she wondered what she had just said.

"Yes, well said, Maya." Suzy gloated. While keeping her smile, she said, "There are two types of powers, good and evil. God possesses positive energy, while ghosts, demons, and evil spirits have negative energy. You are right; if you believe in God, you must believe in ghosts, demons, and evil spirits as well...Remember, there is a different world around us that we all can not feel. Only few can feel it, sense it...after all .. the reality is also one type of illusion." Suzy said convincingly.

"Okay, auntie. Don't think too much. Take rest ." Maya's assuring words relaxed Suzy further. Maya began walking out of the bedroom.

"Hope Suman is okay." Suzy appeared worried.

"Let me find out," Maya said. She quickly dialed Suman's number.

"Hello... Hello?"

"Hello." A gruff male voice came through the speaker.

"Hello, I'm Maya. Suman works at my place. How is she now?"

"She is critical. The Doctor just took her to the surgery."

"Oh, okay. May I know who this is?"

"I'm her husband, Keshav."

"Don't worry, Keshav. She will be alright."

"..."

"Let me know if you need anything. If you want me to come there, but the hospital's atmosphere makes me nervous." Maya said in a shaky voice.

"No problem, madam. I have my people here." Keshav said meekly.

"I'll send some money too. Let me know if you need more."

"Okay, madam. Thanks."

Maya disconnected the call.

"Suman is being operated upon. Hope she gets better soon...Okay, auntie, I will leave now." Maya said while keeping her mobile in her bag.

"Stay back; we will have dinner together."

"Sorry, auntie. I have a lot of office work to finish. Please have your dinner on time."

"Is mom not at home?"

"Yeah, she has gone to Goa to attend my cousin's wedding. She will be back in few days."

"Will you return late from the office tomorrow and the day after as well?" Wrinkles formed on Suzy's forehead

"Yeah, maybe."

"Okay, now, open this cupboard and take out the book, with a black cover, from the first shelf." Suzy pointed her finger toward the wooden cupboard.

Maya unwillingly opened the cupboard and took out the book.

"Take it and read it as soon as possible," Suzy said.

'Holy Chants,' Maya read the book's title, embossed in golden ink. She opened the book and turned to page one. Its musty smell reminded her of the smell of old books from her college library.

"What's this about?" Maya curiously flipped a few pages.

Suzy got up from bed in slow motion and went close to Maya. Her old, powerless eyes gave Maya a severe stare.

"That world will be nearer in the next two days," Suzy said in a low voice.

"Which world?"

"That world!" Suzy slowly raised her right hand toward the ceiling. Maya was clueless. She momentarily looked at the ceiling and kept staring at Suzy's face.

"That world exists between ours and hell. Ghosts and spirits from that world will be here in the next two days." Suzy whispered in a shaky voice with bulged eyes.

"What?" Maya's voice raised. She quickly glanced at the entire room. She began feeling uncomfortable.

While keeping her middle finger on her dry lips, in a hushed tone, Suzy continued, "Shhhhh!!! In fact, it has already started coming closer to us during the last few hours. As I told you earlier this evening, I saw Bhagat's ghost in Suman." Suzy said in a firm tone.

"Oh..." Maya blinked rapidly for few times with widened eyes.

"Bhagat's ghost wants us to leave this building and ultimately his land. Otherwise, He is going to kill everybody here. Make sure you don't get wounded and bleed in the next two days. Otherwise, through your blood, Bhagat's ghost will possess your body and kill others." Maya could not believe her ears. She missed the heartbeat, and her handgrip on the book tightened. She was scared to death.

"Oh... o.. okay..okay." Maya stammered.

"If he attacks you, chant the verses on page number 45 in this book. That will keep you safe." Suzy's assuring words did not reduce Maya's growing uneasiness.

"Okay, I will, but I must leave now," Maya said.

.

*****

Maya entered her apartment in a great hurry and closed the door without turning back. It was dark inside. She switched on the light and kept the book on the TV stand. She sat on the wooden stool next to the shoe rack and started untying her shoelaces.

As she heard her mobile's ring, she retrieved it from her backpack. The lit-up screen was showing Michael's picture. A sweet smile appeared on Maya's face. She touched the green icon of an old rotary dial phone from the screen.

"Hi, Michael..." Maya said.

"Hi, you reached home?" Michael's voice came through the phone's speaker.

"Yes, a few minutes ago."

"How about Dinner?"

"Sorry, Michael! I have urgent work to finish." Maya apologized.

"Okay, no problem, by the way, what are you having for dinner?" Michael asked.

"I will order something."

"Is everything okay?"

"Why?"

"You seem upset."

"..."

"Maya?"

"Something happened today."

"Oh, what happened?" Michael asked eagerly.

"My maid, Suman, met with a road accident."

"Oh my God. How is she now?"

" I just spoke to her husband. She is undergoing surgery."

"Oh, that sounds bad."

"...."

"Maya?"

"..."

"Maya, are you okay?"

Maya put her head down as her mind was overwhelmed with thoughts.

'Should I tell Michael? Will he believe me, or will he think I'm crazy?' Thoughts were racing in Maya's mind.

"Go on, tell me what happened?" Michael insisted softly.

Maya did not reply.

"Maya?" Michael said lovingly. His comforting tone melted Maya.

"Suzy auntie said, before the accident, she saw Bhagat's ghost in Suman."

"Bhagat's Ghost? Who is Bhagat?" Michael asked in a displeased tone.

"Suzy auntie told me, Bhagat, who owned the land on which our building, 'Ruby Park' is standing, was murdered for this land. He doesn't want anybody on his land; otherwise, he is going to kill all of us." Maya explained.

"Okay, calm down, Maya. We will talk about this when we meet. Should I bring you some food?" Michael asked politely.

"No. It's okay. I'll order something. Bye."

Maya disconnected the phone and turned toward her bedroom.

"Keep the book in an easily accessible place." Suddenly, a loud voice came from the main door.

Maya's heartbeat raced. She instantly looked back and saw Suzy was standing at the main door. The flickering tube light from the passage was creating a much taller shadow than her figure. The shadow came stretching till Maya's feet in the hall.

"I said, keep the book in a place where you can easily find it," Suzy said in a loud quivering voice. Her tone was authoritative.

Maya realized she did not close the main door properly when she came in. It was opened wide with its own weight and a little push from the wind.

Maya took a deep breath and approached the door. "Don't worry, auntie, I will keep the book at an easily accessible place. Goodnight."

*****

Maya freshened up and sat down in front of her computer.

Soon, the room filled with the sound of the tapping of keys. Maya's hands were busy typing keys, and the wall clock's hands were busy, running with the time.

After around an hour, Maya's mind started showing signs of fatigue. Her stomach reminded her about its emptiness. She shut down the computer and dialed the Pizza shop's number.

After a few seconds wait, a voice came through the speaker, "Hi, how can I help you?"

"Hi, I would like to order a pizza...". Maya began giving her order.

*****

The clock was showing 11 P.M.

"Ting...tong!!" The doorbell rang.

Maya came out of her bedroom and rushed toward the main door. She pressed the button on the door camera unit. The camera screen came to life. It showed a dark silhouette of a face was standing in front of the door, under the floor's flickering tube light.

While Maya was watching the dark face keenly and suddenly, "Pizza delivery." a loud voice came through the camera speaker. Maya jerked back. Her heartbeat suddenly increased.

She took a few deep breaths.

After some moments, She looked one more time at a dark silhouette of a face on the camera screen and opened the door.

"Good evening, madam, here's your pizza." The delivery guy was standing three feet away from her. Maya looked at his unusually dark face. He slid a pizza box in front of her. Maya maintained the distance with him and took the box with her hands. She could feel the warmth of the pizza inside.

"I already paid," Maya said while closing the door.

"Thank you, Ma'am!" The delivery guy's sound faded as the door closed.

Maya rushed to the bedroom with a warm pizza box in her hands.

Maya opened the pizza box on the table next to her monitor and sat in her chair. She hungrily pulled apart a slice of pizza, took a large bite, and ravenously pushed it inside her mouth.

After a couple of slices more, Maya's stomach became happy. She grabbed a bottle of water from the corner of the table and had a few gulps.

After another slice, She went to the kitchen for ketchup. She saw very little ketchup at the bottom of the bottle.

"Ahhhh...It's almost empty..." She irritated.

She came out of her apartment and rang Suzy's doorbell.

While waiting for the door to open, she looked up at the flickering tube light. With each flicker, the tube light was making a desperate attempt to breathe.

Maya rang the doorbell once more.

The door finally opened. Suzy's wrinkled face appeared through the grills of the inner door. Her eyes were red. Maya was taken aback and stuttered.

"Sorry to disturb you, auntie. I am all out of ketchup and was wondering if I could borrow some from you." Maya said apologetically.

Suzy opened the outer door and turned around.

While walking inside, she said, "It's in the kitchen drawer. Help yourself."

Maya went into the kitchen and found the ketchup bottle in one of the drawers.

She picked the same, and while she was walking back toward the main door, she noticed Suzy's bedroom door was partially opened. A reddish-orange hue was visible from inside.

'Is auntie still awake?' Maya asked herself.

Maya's curiously walked toward Suzy's bedroom. As she cautiously inched closer to the bedroom door, her ears started picking strange whispering sounds from inside. She waited at the door for a few seconds and slowly pushed the door inside.

"Auntie...?" She called out meekly. Her tone was asking, 'Auntie, are you still awake?'

The door slowly swayed open. The smell of burning candles suddenly rushed into Maya's nose. A nasty expression formed on her face. She coughed a bit and instantly covered her nose with her palm.

With a palm on her nose and a nasty expression on her face, Maya saw a big white-colored star painted on the floor. The red, yellow, orange, and blue colored lit candles were placed in the smaller inner triangles of the star. Maya squinted with surprise. The reflection of the burning candles appeared in her eyes.

Maya saw Suzy was sitting on the ground in front of the lightened star. She was continuously mumbling and oscillating back and forth. On hearing Maya's voice, she suddenly turned around and looked at her with a blistering gaze. Maya scared.

"Come in, Maya... come in... sit here," Suzy said in a deep voice.

Maya went inside and sat next to Suzy. Her face mirrored her fearsome state of mind.

"Who were you talking to, auntie?" Maya asked with a shaky voice. Her eyes were scanning at Suzy, burning candles and a big white start.

In response, Suzy stared back at her and said casually, "...with your uncle, your Robert uncle has come to visit me today. Do you want to ask him anything?"

'Oh, Lord...! I made a mistake by coming here.' Maya thought. Her body began shaking slowly. She desperately wanted to get out of the room.

"No, auntie, I am going .." Maya said in a low voice.

"You do not trust what I say, right ?" Suzy asked with a smile on her face.

Maya did not reply. She kept looking at Suzy.

"You want to know more about your childhood?" Suzy asked. Maya kept quiet.

Suzy closed her eyes in intense concentration and asked in a deep voice,

"Robert, please tell about Maya's childhood events."

A few minutes passed. Suzy nodded and said," Okay...Okay...I will tell her about these things".

Next moment Suzy opened her eyes and told Maya about her childhood events.

Maya was stunned. She did not know how to react. Her entire body was shivering.

"You want to know the solution to your current problem?" Suzy asked. Maya gave Suzy a blank look.

"Yes, I know, you want the solution to your problem." Suzy smiled and turned toward the star. She closed her eyes in intense concentration and asked in a deep voice,

"Robert, please tell us the solution to Maya's current problem."

Maya looked at Suzy in disbelief. Her palms increased the grip on the ketchup bottle. The silence in the room was torturous to her.

After a few minutes, Suzy obediently nodded and said, "Okay, I will let her know."

Suzy opened her eyes and looked straight at Maya.

"Robert says your boss is not good to you."

'Only Michael and Sarah know about this, and they do not know auntie. How does auntie know about it? 'A thought flashed in Maya's mind. Her eyes widened, and her heart began pondering rapidly.

"Soon, you will be In trouble because of your boss," Suzy said, and she again closed her eyes.

After a few seconds, Suzy nodded with closed eyes, "Okay, okay. I will tell her that too." Suzy opened her eyes and looked straight into Maya's eyes.

"Robert says, he sees Bhagat's ghost around. He can get into anybody through their blood and use them to kill others. Bhagat's ghost is particularly looking for you."

"Looking for me?" Maya felt shackled and rooted to the ground. All of a sudden , her heart began pondering heavily.

"Yes, he is. He wants you and your mother to leave this building. He doesn't want anybody to be on his land." Suzy continued in her deep voice.

Maya could not take more. She gathered all her strength and ran out of the room.

*****

Maya entered her apartment with a thumping chest. She was breathing heavily, and her body sweated profusely.

She dialed Michael's number.

"Hello...Michael Suzy auntie can communicate with ghosts. I just saw that." Suzy said excitingly.

Michael thought for a second and asked in a light tone, "Do you believe in all these things, Maya?"

"This is a fact, Michael! Suzy auntie can communicate with ghosts."

"Really? "Michael laughed.

"Michael, believe me. Suzy auntie can actually talk with ghosts." Maya stressed her point.

"How do you know?"

"I just saw her talking with Robert uncle's ghost."

"Robert uncle?"

"Her husband. He died a couple of years ago."

"No way, Maya. That cant' be true." Michael continued in his light tone.

"No, Michael, it's true. Some time back, she asked about my childhood to Robert uncle's Ghost, and he told all the events correctly. Some of those events were known only to me. That's why I am sure auntie could speak to ghosts." Maya's convincing tone made

Michael think for a few seconds.

"And who told you that Bhagat's ghost wants you to leave the Ruby Park?"

"Bhagat told himself to Suzy auntie."

"You mean the real Bhagat?"

"No. Not real Bhagat."

"Then?"

"His ghost !"

"Come on, Maya! How can anyone possibly talk to ghosts?"

"Yes, Michael, Suzy auntie could talk with ghosts and spirits. Today Suzy auntie saw Bhagat's Ghost possessed Suman before her accident." Maya said assertively. Michael sensed the high degree of confidence in Maya's voice. He was surprised to see the aggressiveness in her response.

After a few awkward seconds, he asked,

"So, are you saying Bhagat's ghost will come to kill you?"

"Yes." Maya's voice turned soft.

Michael stunned.

He took a deep breath. Maya waited for a few seconds for Michael's reply and continued anxiously,

"Suzy auntie gave me a book earlier."

"Which book?"

"Book name is 'Holy Chants.' She said if Bhagat's Ghost attacks me, then I must chant the verses on page number 45, and that will keep me safe."

"hmm, m..."

"You think I'm nuts, right? I knew you won't believe me." Maya said in a soft tone.

"No. No. It's not like that. but..."

"Bhagat's Ghost is still around here, Michael! He can take control of anybody's body through their blood, and then he kills anybody who he wants to kill." Maya said anxiously and disconnected the call.

She came to her bedroom. She switched on the night lamp.

A dim blue light replaced the darkness of the room. A thin layer of sweat appeared on Maya's forehead.

All of a sudden, she felt thirsty. She grabbed the water bottle from the table and emptied it.

She was breathing heavily. She laid down on the bed, and slowly, her tired mind slipped into a deep sleep.

*****

Maya's eyes opened suddenly. It took a few seconds for her eyes to adjust to the dim blue light of the room. She looked at the wall clock. It was showing 2 A.M.

Suddenly, a dark figure passed in front of her.

"Oh! Who is in my bedroom?" Maya screamed silently. Her heart started beating like a drum. Her body began shivering, and her lips were trembling. She cringed under the bed-sheet and closed her eyes tightly. Sweat began pouring out from her each pore.

In a few seconds, she heard the sound of furniture moving from the hall.

'Who is moving furniture in the hall?' Maya was breathing heavily. She had tremors in her hands and fingers.

She tried to open her eyes, but fear was tightly controlling her closed eyes. She remained in bed, shaking with fear. Her ears were alert to pick up the slightest sound from outside.

Soon, the sound of moving furniture stopped, and she could hear the sound of running tap water.

'In which bathroom the tap is open?' Maya opened her eyes. The sound of running water came for a few more minutes and stopped abruptly.

'It must be the middle bathroom.' Maya guessed.

After a brief pause, the sound of running tab water came again.

'Who is turning the tap on and off?' Maya's fear and confusion reached a peak. Her heart was palpitating.

The sound of running water stopped again.

Maya waited for a couple of minutes and took the bed-sheet off her face.

Her entire body was shivering in fear. She got up from the bed and slowly went out of the bedroom.

As she entered the hall, she was surprised. The hall was bathing in yellow light.

'I did not switch-on this light. Who did then?' Maya stared at the yellow light for a few seconds. Her eyes slowly scanned the hall from one corner to another corner.

The couch, chairs, and furniture were askew. It had shifted from its original position.

"Oh! Who moved this furniture? " Maya asked herself with eyes full of surprise.

She slowly moved toward the middle bathroom with weak legs and fear in her eyes. She saw the middle bathroom door was slightly open. The bathroom light had illuminated the floor outside the bathroom.

While passing by, Maya looked to her right at the kitchen. It was neat and clean. Every item in the kitchen was at its place.

She reached the bathroom door and pushed it. It opened partially. A bucket under the tap was full of water, and a thin stream of water was still streaming into the bucket. She got inside the bathroom and turned the water off.

While returning to her bedroom, she passed the kitchen. She peeped inside again, and she was shocked from her core. All the shelves and drawers in the kitchen were wide open. Many vessels were out on the kitchen platform. Other utensils were on the floor. The refrigerator door was wide open. The kitchen was in a messy state.

Maya looked at the mess with bulging eyes. She was shocked beyond belief.

'I just passed by, and everything was fine. Who did this? Am I living in two different worlds at the same time?' Maya thought with pondering heart.

She rushed back to her bedroom. She lay down on the bed and covered her face with a bedsheet. But underneath, her eyes were wide open. She was breathing heavily.

After a couple of minutes, through the bedsheet, she saw a shadow approaching her bed. She closed her eyes tightly. Her heart began thumping again. Her blood became cold.

Suddenly, she heard the sound of the door opening and closing. Her heartbeat went through the roof.

'Which door is it? Is it the door of the middle bathroom again ?' Maya wondered quietly.

"Ahhhhh... it's the bathroom door of this bedroom itself!" She realized with a thumping heart.

Maya uncovered her face and looked toward the closed bathroom door. The bathroom light was spilling through the gap between the door and its frame.

"Hello? Anybody inside?" Maya asked in a shaky voice. She was breathing heavily with eyes shot with fear.

She waited for a couple of minutes but did not hear any sound from the bathroom.

"Hello? Anybody inside?" Maya asked again. No reply.

She wiped the sweat from her face and walked gingerly toward the bathroom door. She pushed the door open, and she was stunned.

Maya saw a short, fat man in blood-soaked white clothes sitting on the bathroom floor. His face was black, and his tongue was red.

"Why are you here, Maya?" He asked in bellowed voice.

'Oh... this must be Bhagat's ghost!' Maya recognized, and she scrammed at the top of her voice.

"Aahh... aaaaa!!!"

*****

2

Chapter 2

"I see Bhagat's ghost every day, and it calls me Maya... Maya... Maya."

"How does he look?"

"He is short and fat. His face is black. His hair is white, and his mouth is bloody. He wears a white shirt and white pants, but there are bloodstains all over."

"When did you first see this Bhagat's ghost?"

"It's been a while now."

"Did he call you today?"

"Yes."

"Was he louder today?"

"Yes."

"Hmmm... these are typical symptoms." Dr. DeSuza said calmly.

"Symptoms ? symptoms of what ?" Maya confused.

"Bhagat's ghost is your hallucination, Maya." Dr. DeSuza looked straight into Maya's eyes.

"What do you mean? I see him every day. He talks with me. Even Suzy auntie saw him many times." Maya said excitingly. She felt a fluttery feeling in the belly.

"Did Mrs. Suzy speak with you about Bhagat's ghost?"

"Yes, She only told me Bhagat's whole story."

Dr. DeSuza took a deep breath and leaned forward toward Maya.

"I know what you are talking about, Maya. But Listen to me; Bhagat's ghost is not real. Just ignore him." Dr. DeSuza's said softly. Suddenly, Maya felt connected to his calm and composed demeanor.

" I feel Bhagat is very much real."

"You need to ignore him. Otherwise, he will haunt the rest of your life."

Maya thought for a second and said in a shaky disbelieving voice, "No, I can't. He feels so real."

"I repeat Maya, he is not real. Just ignore him." Dr. DeSuza stressed his point.

"But I just can't!"

"You have to. Otherwise, these symptoms will get worse." Dr. Said firmly.

He pulled his prescription pad out in front of him. Before he began writing, he raised his head and said,

"I will write down medicines. You need to take them regularly."

Maya wanted to ask many more questions about Bhagat's ghost, but she could not.

A couple of minutes passed by in silent contemplation. Maya could only hear the faint sound of Dr. DeSuza's scribbling on his prescription pad.

"Has Mrs. Gomes accompanied you today?" Dr. DeSuza asked without raising his head.

"Yes."

"You may wait outside, and please ask Mrs. Gomes to come in." Dr. DeSuza continued writing on the prescription pad.

*****

Michael parked his white sedan in front of Dr. DeSuza's clinic. He turned off the engine and quickly got out of the car with the keys in his hand. He began walking toward the clinic door.

'I am late... shit! Damn, this morning traffic.' Michael was irritated. Suddenly he realized he had not locked the car. Michael quickly turned back toward the car and pressed the lock button on his key fob.

"Beep... beep." The car responded with a couple of honks and blinking headlights.

Michael approached the receptionist's desk.

"Hi. I was supposed to be here with Mrs. Rita and Maya Gomes. We had an appointment with Dr. DeSuza at 11 A.M. Sorry, I'm late. "

"Yes, Maya is still in the session with the Doctor, but Mrs. Gomes is waiting there." The receptionist pointed to Rita, seated on a couch in the reception area.

Michael sat beside Rita.

"Sorry, I am late." Michael murmured.

"No worries." Rita said.

After some time, the receptionist's phone rang.

"Yes, Sir," she answered briefly. She hung up the phone and turned toward Rita and Michael.

"The session is over. You may go in now."

"Thank you," Michael said.

Michael and Rita walked to the doctor's cabin. Michael was about to push the cabin door, but it opened from inside. It was Maya, heading out.

"Hi, When did you come?" She asked surprisingly.

"Sometime back. Wait there. "Michael pointed toward the couch.

"Okay." Maya nodded. She slid through the narrow gap between the door frame and Michael.

"We will be back soon," Rita said to Maya.

Michael entered the doctor's cabin, and he instantly realized the visible freshness of the cabin. Everything was in white, the furniture, the curtains, the paint on the wall. The tube light's white light added freshness to the room's overall freshness.

"Doctor, this is Michael." Rita introduced Michael to Dr. DeSuza, a slim man in his late forties. Michael perceived the intelligence on Dr. DeSuza's round face.

"Good morning!" Dr. DeSuza stood and gave Michael a firm handshake. While seated back on his ergonomic black leather chair,

Dr. DeSuza pointed to the empty chairs in front of him.

"Please be seated."

"Doctor, what has happened to Maya?" Rita asked eagerly while being seated on the chair.

While twirling his pen between his fingers, Dr. DeSuza took a few seconds to gather his thoughts and leaned forward again.

"Mrs. Gomes, Maya is suffering from hallucinations. It is a type of mental condition."

"Mental condition?!" Rita's eyebrows raised. She suddenly felt expanding heaviness at her core. She looked at Michael in surprise.

"Doctor, we have been together for the last three years, but I have never seen any signs of a mental condition in Maya," Michael said anxiously.

Dr. DeSuza nodded in an understanding manner.

"I get it, but the signs may not be that clear. Let me ask you, Does Maya say things that are not related to anything at that moment?"

Rita went into flashback mode.

"Yes, for the past few months, on numerous occasions, Maya's behavior has been disorganized and uncoordinated. Once, she was cutting onions in the kitchen, and suddenly, she went into her bedroom and started reading a book, leaving the uncut onions behind. In another incident, she was talking to me in the kitchen and abruptly went to the hall." Rita said.

"Has she ever had any episodes of delusions?"

Michael and Rita looked at Dr. DeSuza with straight faces.

"Delusion means... a firm belief or opinion that is contradictory to reality." Dr. DeSuza explained.

Michael flashed back.

"Yes... I think Maya is a firm believer that Suzy auntie, her neighbor, could talk with ghosts." Michael memorized.

"Any hallucinations?" Dr. DeSuza asked.

"Hallucinations?"

"It is a kind of apparent perception of something that is not present."

"Bhagat's ghost!" Michael exclaimed in disbelief.

"What about Bhagat's ghost?" Rita asked anxiously.

"She did not tell you about Bhagat's ghost?" Michael turned at Rita and asked in surprise.

"No.." Rita shook her head.

"Bhagat's ghost! Maya told me that she had seen Bhagat's ghost many times, and she had spoken to it as well. She says that Bhagat's ghost gets into our body through our blood." Michael said excitingly.

He paused for a few seconds and asked anxiously,

"But what about her neighbor Suzy auntie? Maya says Suzy auntie had seen the Bhagat's ghost as well."

The doctor took a deep breath and reclined on his leather chair.

"I know Mrs. Suzy. She is my patient, too, and recently she has also been diagnosed with hallucinations. In the previous session, She talked with me about Bhagat's ghost." Dr. DeSuza said calmly.

Michael and Rita were shocked. A sad silence filled the room. The sound of the window AC suddenly appeared unusually loud.

"Oh! So, it was Suzy auntie's hallucinations that made her see Bhagat's ghost manifest in Suman!" Michael slumped back into the backrest.

"Yes! Bhagat's ghost is Mrs. Suzy's hallucination. Mrs. Suzy must have spoken to Maya about Bhagat's ghost, and that has triggered Maya's hallucinations about Bhagat's ghost." Dr. DeSuza explained.

"Oh !" Rita said worriedly.

"So Maya will always have hallucinations about what's been told to her?" Michael asked.

"Can't say. Maybe or maybe not." Dr. DeSuza shrugged his shoulders.

"and will she experience hallucinations all the time?" Rita asked with a confused face.

"Once she starts taking medications, not all the time. But we can't say for sure that she will not have hallucinations at all. She will still have it, but irregularly. Also, it depends upon the patient to patient."

Tears filled in Rita's eyes. She controlled her emotions, but her throat choked up. She coughed lightly.

Dr. DeSuza offered her a glass of water.

"Doctor, what is the treatment for Maya's condition?" Michael asked worriedly.

"She needs to take medications daily, without fail. "

"Will She able to go to the office and be able to perform her duties?" Rita asked in a shaky voice while keeping a glass of water on the table.

"If she takes the medications regularly, then why not? But keep in mind, it's going to be a long treatment." Dr. DeSuza concluded.

*****

After few days, at around 9 A.M, a police jeep entered the KKSwTech building complex. Inspector Jadhav got down from the jeep and headed to the KKSwTech office on the 5th floor.

"Good morning, Sir!" A constable greeted him at the office entrance.

"Morning... where is the body?" Inspector Jadhav asked.

"This way, sir." The constable quickly walked a few steps ahead of him through empty cubicles.

"Here, sir." The constable pointed his hand toward a dead body lying in a cubicle, a few feet away from him.

Inspector Jadhav saw a narrow yellow strip strung across the cubicle entrance. A photographer was taking pictures of the body from different angles. The flashes from his camera were momentarily illuminating the area near the cubicle. A forensic expert was busy consolidating forensic evidence from the floor, walls, and furniture with a brush and other tools.

Inspector Jadhav bent and crossed under the yellow strip. While approaching the body, he took off his police cap and held it in his hand.

The Inspector observed the deceased was a slim lady in her late fifties. There was a lot of blood around that had flown from the deep wound on the lady's back head.

"Hello inspector, I am Ashok Kapoor, the owner, and CEO of KKSwTech," Kapoor said from the other side of the yellow strip.

"Do you have a minute to talk?" Inspector Jadhav asked while shaking his hand with Kapoor.

"Sure, let's go to my cabin," Kapoor said promptly and began walking toward his cabin.

Inspector Jadhav followed Kapoor.

"What is the name of the deceased?" Jadhav asked while entering the cabin.

"Mrs. Pinto."

"Who saw the body first?"

"Our office boy, who is usually the first to reach the office in the morning. He called me." Kapoor sat on his office chair and gestured Inspector Jadhav to sit opposite.

"What was the time when he called you?" Inspector Jadhav asked while sitting down on the chair.

"Around 8 A.M."

"Then what did you do?"

"I came here immediately, saw the body and..."

"At what time did you reach here?"

"...around 8:40 A.M."

"Okay."

"I saw the body lying in the cubical and immediately called the Police."

Inspector Jadhav thought for a few seconds.

"Is that Mrs. Pinto's cubicle?"

"No...that cubicle belongs to our another employee, Maya Gomes."

"Then what was Mrs. Pinto doing there?" Inspector Jadhav raised his eyebrows.

"Mrs. Pinto was Maya's boss, so I guess she might have some work with Maya."

"Hmm...how were the relations between Mrs. Pinto and Maya?"

"Unfortunately, not that good."

"and what was the reason?"

"Maya thought that Mrs. Pinto was targeting her personally to harass her. There was some bad blood between them."

"Alright, what were the office timings for Mrs. Pinto?"

"She usually used to report at 10 A.M."

"And at what time does she usually leave the office?"

"She used to work late hours."

"How late?"

"Till 10 P.M. or sometimes till 11.30 P.M."

"Who was the last person to leave the office yesterday?"

"Give me a minute. I can find out that information from the key-card records."

Kapoor quickly logged into his computer.

"Do you have closed-circuit cameras?" Inspector Jadhav asked while glancing all over the cabin.

"Sorry, what?"

"closed-circuit cameras, CCTV cameras?"

"Yes, we do, but at present, the CCTV has been down because of a software glitch," Kapoor answered without taking his eyes off the screen. He typed some more.

"Oh!" Kapoor's face turned serious. He touched his throat and turned his head toward the wall.

"Who was the last person to leave yesterday?" Inspector Jadhav asked suspiciously. He tried to look at the screen with a wrinkled brow.

Kapoor remained quiet for a few seconds.

"Who was it ?"

"Maya Gomes."

One constable came into the cabin and gave a small transparent plastic bag to Inspector Jadhav.

"Sir, we found this near the body."

There was one thin golden bracelet inside the bag. Inspector Jadhav carefully looked at the golden bracelet and passed the bag to Kapoor.

"Do you recognize this golden bracelet?" asked Inspector.

Kapoor looked at it keenly. "This seems to be Maya's bracelet."

The Inspector stood up hurriedly and asked with solid eye contact, "Where can we find Maya Gomes now?"

"At her home. She is not well. Why?"

"As you said, she was the last one to leave the office yesterday. We have a few questions for Miss Gomes."

*****

Maya's eyes opened as the alarm erupted in the morning. The previous day was very hectic for her in the office. She was a busy whole day and returned home late in the night.

Maya did not feel like getting up from the bed. She was feeling feverish. She remained in the bed, and her mind drifted to sleep again.

*****

"Maya... Maya... Maya..." Maya heard the whispering voice. She opened her eyes partially and saw a faint figure sitting in front of her bed, on the chair. She tried to open her eyes further, but sleep weighed down her eyelids and took control of her mind.

*****

"Maya... Maya... Maya..." Maya heard the whispering voice again in her sleep. She opened her eyes and saw a faint figure again, sitting on the chair in front of her bed.

"Maya... Maya... Maya..." She heard the voice again. This time the faint figure appeared more evident to her.

'Oh... it's Bhagat's ghost... sitting in front of me.' Maya suddenly realized. She missed her heartbeat. She quickly got up from her bed. Her lips were trembling.

"Maya... why are you still on my land?" Bhagat grunted. Maya felt tremors throughout her body. She tried to go out of her room, but she fumbled and fell partially.

"Ha... Ha... Ha... Ha..." Bhagat laughed. His black tongue came out of his mouth. Blood was dripping through his teeth.

Maya got up quickly and ran toward the bedroom door. While she was getting out through the door, she heard Bhagat's words from behind,

"Maya...You must leave my land."

Maya dashed outside and sat down by the dining table. She was panting heavily. Beads of sweat appeared on her forehead. While breathing heavily, she stared at the partially open bedroom door.

'He will come out from it at any moment now.' Maya murmured. The door moved slightly due to the wind, and Maya felt a chill creep over her. With fearful eyes, Maya kept her gaze fixed on her bedroom door... waiting for Bhagat's ghost to come out.

Nobody came out of the bedroom door.

"Good morning, Maya," Rita said from the kitchen.

Maya came to her senses. Maya heaved a sigh of relief and reclined into a chair.

"Good morning, Mom," She replied.

Doorbell rang. Rita opened the door. There were one police inspector and two constables at the door. Rita took a step back.

"Miss Maya? "Inspector Jadhav asked.

"Maya, come here. The Police are here to see you." Rita called Maya from the main door.

'The Police?' Maya wondered. She sensed an urgency in Rita's voice. She hurriedly got up from the table and walked into the hall.

"Miss Maya? "

"Yes."

"Miss Maya, I am Inspector Jadhav. I am in charge of Mrs. Pinto's murder case." Inspector Jadhav introduced himself.

"What?! Pinto ma'am been murdered?" Maya was shocked. She covered her mouth with her palm. Momentarily, she lost her balance. She took the support of the couch's arm to stand and sat on the couch.

Inspector Jadhav sat on the chair opposite her, and the two constables stood behind him.

"Yes...this morning, Mrs. Pinto's dead body was found in your cubicle. Miss Maya, yesterday did you have a discussion with Mrs. Pinto in the office?"

"Yes, we had a work-related discussion, nothing unusual." Maya took a deep breath and said in a sad tone.

"Miss Maya, you were the last person to leave the office yesterday."

Inspector Jadhav paused for a few seconds and looked strangely at Maya.

"So tell me, Miss Maya, How did Mrs. Pinto's dead body end in your cubicle?"

"I don't know. Why are you asking me?" Maya's voice raised.

"Miss Maya, there's no need to raise your voice." Jadhav raised his voice too.

"Then why are you questioning her, inspector?" Rita asked politely.

"Who are you?"

"I am her mother, Mrs. Rita Gomes. "

"See, Mrs. Gomes, I am just doing my job. The murder victim, Mrs. Pinto, did not have good relations with Miss Maya, and Miss Maya was the last person to leave the office yesterday." Inspector Jadhav explained.

"Yesterday, I just had a routine work discussion with Pinto ma'am in her cabin. She did not even come to my cubical." Maya said in a steady voice.

"While leaving the office yesterday, was Mrs. Pinto still at the office?"

"Yeah, I saw her cabin lights were on."

"If she was in her cabin at that time, then how did her dead body end up in your cubicle?" Inspector Jadhav asked again.

"I don't know what Pinto ma'am was doing in my cubicle," Maya answered in irritation.

Inspector Jadhav gave one small transparent plastic bag to Maya.

"Is this yours?

Maya carefully looked at the golden bracelet from the plastic bag.

"Yes, this is mine," She recognized the bracelet.

"We found it near Mrs. Pinto's body." Inspector Jadhav looked straight into Maya's eyes. His sharp eyes scrutinized Maya's facial expressions.

Maya returned the bag to Jadhav. She looked at her empty wrist and remembered. "Yesterday, I removed it and kept it on my table. It's my habit. I forgot to put it back." She said in a low voice.

"Okay, Miss Maya." Inspector Jadhav sighed and stood.

On his way out, he went closer to Rita while giving her a sharp look." Ma'am, we will soon find out if your daughter is trying to mislead us." Rita did not reply. Inspector shifted his piercing stare toward Maya and said in his loud voice,

"...and if we find that she is lying to us, We will be going behind bars for a long time."

*****

Rita and Maya were in a shocking state for some time.

"What is this about Maya?" Rita asked in a surprised tone.

"I am also not sure, Mom..let me call..."

Suddenly, she heard her mobile ring. She picked up the phone.

"Hello, Maya. How are you doing?" Kapoor's booming voice came through the speaker.

"I was not feeling well last night. But I am okay now...Sir, I just heard about Mrs. Pinto, actually what exactly ....."

"Can you come to the office now?" Kapoor cut-off Maya in between.

"Now? Is it urgent?"

"Yes..."

"Okay..."

"Great! See you at the office." Kapoor disconnected the call.

Maya looked at the clock,

'Oh, it's 11 A.M. I'd better hurry up and get to the office.'

Maya wore a white t-shirt and dark blue jeans. She tied her hair into a tight, high ponytail and applied light make-up to spruce up her tired face. She kept her mobile in her jeans pocket and flung on a small knapsack.

Rita saw Maya going to the main door and followed Maya swiftly to the door.

"Where are you going in such a hurry?" Rita asked in a worried tone.

"Oh... I forgot to tell you, Mom, It was Kapoor Sir's call, and he asked me to come to the office urgently." Maya replied quickly while putting on her socks and shoes.

"You have not been keeping well since last night. Is it that urgent for you to go?" Rita wondered.

"Not sure, Mom. He didn't specify anything." Maya opened the main door.

"Hmmm... but if it's not that urgent, why don't you stay at home and take a rest instead?" Rita suggested.

"I am fine, Mom. Bye." Maya quickly moved toward the stairs. While descending the stairs,

"Maya, have a breakfast and go." she heard Rita's voice, followed by her coughing sound.

"It's okay, Mom. I am not hungry." Maya called from halfway down the stairs.

*****

Maya quickly walked out of the building's compound and reached the bus stop on the main road. She was faced by an insanely long queue, stretching nearly a quarter of a mile from the actual bus stop. Maya sighed deeply and joined the line.

Within five minutes, the bus came and stopped in front of it. The bus was already full of passengers. Only the first few people from the queue could set foot on the bus through its narrow door; others struggled at the door.

The bus conductor looked at the struggling passengers to get inside the bus.

"Board the next Bus." He shouted and forcefully pulled the old cord from the bus ceiling.

"Ting, ting!!" Bell rang in the driver's cabin. It was the signal for the driver to 'Go!'.

The driver started the bus immediately, and the last passenger was still hanging on the first step of the foot board, struggling to get into the bus, business as usual.

Two more buses arrived and followed the same ritual.

Maya became impatient. Upon seeing the next bus leaving the same way, she came out of the queue and waved to an approaching cab. The black and yellow cab stopped near her.

"Mumbai Central Station!" Maya said while getting into the cab.

The cab started.

After a few minutes, Maya asked the driver, "Can you please drive a bit faster? I'm in a hurry."

"Okay." The driver said, and he stepped on the accelerator. The cab sped up with a jerk.

*****

Maya arrived at the Mumbai Central train station and was greeted by another long queue at the ticket counter.

'Oh! I forgot my travel pass at home.' Maya realized. She looked at the queue from start to end, which crept forward at a snail's pace.

Unwillingly, she stood in the queue. The loudspeaker above the ticket counter was continuously blurting announcements about incoming and outgoing trains. Maya listened to the unpleasant tone of the loudspeaker reluctantly. Each passing minute only made her more impatient.

After waiting patiently in the queue for more than fifteen minutes, it was her turn at the ticket counter.

"One return ticket to Churchgate." Maya slid a currency note through the narrow slot in the window. In return, she received her ticket with some change. Maya glanced at the ticket and made sure its details were correctly printed on 'To Churchgate' in the middle and 'Return' in its right corner.

Maya descended the railway bridge and reached the platform, which, as usual, was choc-a-bloc with people. She quickly merged into the crowd and headed to the section where the ladies' coach would arrive.

It was hot and humid. People had more and more sweat beads rolling down their faces as the muggy minutes went by. Many women were fanning themselves with their small handkerchiefs. Some men wiped their foreheads with their shirt sleeves. In that sultry weather, everyone was anxiously looking to their left, anticipating the arrival of the train.

In a few minutes, the train arrived. It had three times the number of people it could carry. Before the inside passengers could alight, the boarding passengers pushed themselves in. There was friction between entering and exiting passengers who crossed each other. As a result, many of the existing passengers' crisply ironed shirts were crushed into wrinkle-filled relics. Some lost the upper buttons of their shirts, while others had their hair ruffled up right back to its early-morning state.

Maya was also part of that human tornado and got herself into the ladies' compartment. She was pushed from all directions, and her feet stamped upon by other passengers. She gently pushed them aside. She held the handle that hung from the ceiling rods with one hand and her bag with the other.

The train started.

Maya gripped one of the grab-handles, hanging from the ceiling, tightly, making sure she could keep her balance and at the same time withstand the squeeze from the rest of the passengers.

In a few minutes, the train gained speed, and a cool breeze made its way through the tiny gaps between the tightly packed people and reached Maya. The touch of the cool breeze on the sweaty body gave Maya relief. Unconsciously, her eyes drooped while her body was gently lulled by the train's vibrations.

*****

"Maya!" Sarah's voice came from behind while Maya got off of her cab.

Sarah was a slim, medium-heighted , fair-skinned girl with an attractive smile on a beautiful oval-shaped face. She was dressed in a crisp white T-shirt with a colored print on the front, black jeans, and a small brown leather purse slung over her shoulder.

They both entered the office. Maya went to her cubicle and found it was sealed. She headed for the conference room.

Maya entered the conference room and switched on the lights. She grabbed the water bottle from the table. She sat back in her chair, took a deep breath, and finished the bottle in seconds.

After a few minutes, the conference room door opened with a loud sound.

Kapoor came in, sat on the chair in front of Maya, and opened his laptop.

"Hello, Sir."

Kapoor did not give a response. Maya felt odd.

"Hello, Sir." Maya greeted again.

"Yesterday, somebody murdered Mrs. Pinto. You were the last person to leave the office. Also, your bracelet was found near Mrs. Pinto's body. Did anything happen between you and Mrs. Pinto?" Kapoor came straight to the point.

Maya was surprised. She did not like Kapoor's tone.

"No, Sir! " Maya shook her head in denial.

"Mrs. Pinto's body was found in your cubical. Police think there must be something happened between you and Mrs. Pinto, otherwise how her body end in your cubical?" Mrs. Kapoor leaned forward on the table and looked straight into Maya's eyes.

"Nothing happened between Pinto ma'am and me, Sir," Maya said firmly.

"Look, Maya, I know you. You will not do such a thing. But if anything happened accidentally, then please tell me. " Kapoor said.

'NO... NO... NO...' Maya cried to herself on the inside but couldn't speak out.

"I repeat, Maya. If anything happened accidentally, please surrender to the police. Don't worry; I will help you to get the bail ." Kapoor said in a slightly raised voice. His voice scared Maya at her core, and her heart started palpitating in fear. She couldn't bear it anymore.

"No, Sir. As I said to the police, nothing happened between Pinto ma'am and me. Now, if you excuse me, I am not feeling well. I would like to leave." Maya said in a firm tone. She stormed out from the conference room and ran toward the entrance door.

*****

Sarah was returning from the cafeteria to her cubical with a mug of coffee in her hand when she saw Maya rushing out through the glass entrance door. She noticed Maya's troubled face.

'Why was Maya rushing out of the office, and why did she look so upset?' Thoughts bothered Sarah's. Then she saw Kapoor standing outside the conference room.

Sarah quickly followed Maya, who didn't wait for the elevator. She headed straight for the stairs.

"Maya... wait... waaaait!" Sarah shouted from behind, but Maya began descending the stairs quickly.

"Maya... Maya!" Sarah called again and followed her down.

When Sarah reached the ground floor, she saw Maya had already gotten into a cab.

"Maya?!" Sarah started running toward the cab, but before reaching close enough, the cab started. Sarah could see Maya's sad face through the cab's glass window.

Sarah took her mobile and dialed Maya's number. It kept ringing and finally got disconnected.

"Shit!!!" Sarah irritated and dialed again. This time too, it kept ringing and got disconnected. Sarah tried a third time, and at last, Maya answered.

"Maya, what happened in there? Why did you leave the office so abruptly?"

"..."

"Maya?" Sarah heard Maya's crying sound.

"Maya, tell me, please. What happened between you and Kapoor, sir? Why are you crying?"

"..."

"What did Kapoor Sir say to you?" Sarah nearly shouted. Maya said tearfully,

"I think, Kapoor Sir suspects that I have done something wrong to Mrs. Pinto. I'm the one behind Mrs. Pinto's murder."

"What???" Sarah exclaimed in shock. Her loud gasp and exclamation made many a passer-by turn around a look.

' Is Kapoor sir out of his mind? How can he make such an allegation?' Sarah wondered. She remained in a state of shock for some time.

*****

Sarah dashed through the office entrance door, breathing heavily, panting and huffing. Her dramatic entry attracted many eyes from the floor. She went straight into the conference room, where Maya was seated earlier. The space was empty. She quickly headed to Kapoor's cabin.

Kapoor was speaking on his desk phone. Sarah stood in front of Kapoor, steaming with anger. Sarah's stormy entry made Kapoor pause his conversation for a second, and he looked at her. Daggers of anger were flying out from Sarah's eyes. Kapoor ignored her and got back to his phone conversation.

Sarah maintained her angry posture and did not flinch. A volcano of anger was bubbling inside her.

After a few minutes on the phone, Kapoor put down the receiver.

"Yes, Sarah?" Kapoor said casually, gave her a glance, and turned his gaze back to his computer screen.

"I just spoke with Maya. She said you suspect her in Mrs. Pinto's murder?" Sarah said in one breath.

"Not me, Police suspects," Kapoor said sharply. His confidence made Sarah think for a second.

"How can you suspect your employee?" Sarah looked straight into Kapoor's eyes.

"Maya's relations with Mrs. Pinto were never good," Kapoor said firmly.

"Having a bad relationship with a Mrs. Pinto does not mean that Maya killed her!" Sarah almost shouted.

"When a person's reputation is at stake, they'll do anything. Mrs. Pinto was not that strong a woman. As per her post-mortem reports, she was walloped on her head." Kapoor paused for a second to let Sarah digest what he had just revealed.

"No... no! I still don't believe that is possible. Maya cannot murder anybody." Sarah said firmly.

"How can you ignore the evidence?" Kapoor said in a low but firm voice.

"What evidence?"

"Mrs. Pinto's body was found in Maya's cubical. Her golden bracelet was found near Mrs. Pinto's body."

The next moment, Kapoor's desk phone rang.

"Hello, ...just a minute," Kapoor answered. He put his right palm on the receiver and turned to Sarah.

"I don't know anything more, Sarah. Evidence is against Maya. I am going to suspend her."

"Sir... sir... please don't make any hasty decisions."

"I never take any decisions in a hurry," Kapoor said firmly.

"Okay, Sir. Please give her some time." Sarah said desperately.

Kapoor looked at Sarah's face and thought for a moment. While returning to his call, Kapoor said conclusively,

"Better she hurries up. She doesn't have much time."

*****

That evening, Michael and Sarah went to Maya's house.

"She has shut herself in the bedroom ever since she returned from office," Rita said worriedly at the main door itself.

"Let me talk to her." Sarah gently patted Rita on her shoulder, went straight toward Maya's bedroom, and knocked on the door.

"Maya! It's me! Open the door. Maya!!" Sarah repeatedly knocked on the door.

"Maya, open the door," Michael shouted too and knocked on the door.

Maya opened the door briefly and walked back into the room. Michael, Sarah, and Rita followed her inside. The room was quite dark as the blinds had been drawn. Rita switched the light on. Maya sat on a chair. Sarah sat next to Rita, while Michael preferred to stand.

"Are you Okay, Maya?" Michael asked softly.

Maya looked at Sarah with a blank face. Her eyes were swollen.

"What's the matter, Maya? Why do you look upset?" Rita asked.

"Nothing, Mom. I just overslept." Maya replied woefully.

"Your eyes are swollen." Rita kept staring at Maya's swollen eyes.

"Mom, don't worry. I told you, I overslept." Maya said more intensely and tried to hide her face from Rita.

"Maya! Don't lie to me. Tell me, what happened?" Rita said in a shaky voice. Maya kept quiet with her head down.

"Maya?" Rita asked again. Her emotions took over, and her voice became teary.

"Maya, didn't you tell her?" Sarah jumped into the conversation. Maya shook her head.

"Maya, you should have told auntie about what happened at the office today," Sarah said assertively.

"Yeah, I should have, but I was agitated and didn't feel like speaking to anybody." Maya looked back at Sarah.

"Oh yes, I understood that... when you did not answer my first few calls." Sarah said. Maya raised her head and looked at Rita.

"Sorry, Mom."

"Sorry for what? Maya. I'm getting worried. Please tell me." Rita appeared visibly concerned.

"Auntie, it's an office matter," Michael said in a low voice.

"What office matter? I have never seen Maya this upset before." Rita retorted.

"Auntie..." Sarah glanced at Maya, who was looking down. She took a few seconds to gather her words. She wanted to explain, what had transpired, in as few words as possible. Rita was looking eagerly at Sarah.

"There's nothing much to worry about, auntie. Uhhh... you know, Kapoor Sir? The owner and founder of KKSwTech." Sarah began her explanation.

"Yes, I know Kapoor, Sir. Maya has mentioned him many times in the past. He seems to be a nice man. I also had the chance to meet him once. What about him?" Rita continued in her worried tone.

"It's not as much about him... it is about a misunderstanding he has about Maya."

"What misunderstanding?

Maya could not hear anymore. She leaned forward with a jerk.

" Kapoor sir suspects I did something to my boss, Mrs. Pinto, at the office, because of which, they found her dead in the morning...."

"Jesus Christ!!" Rita said. She couldn't believe what she was hearing. A strange fear gripped her mind. She went close to Maya.

"I am sure you are not involved in any of this. How can Kapoor Sir accuse you of something you haven't done? And how do the others believe in any of that?" Rita asked in an elevated and tensed voice. She looked at Michael and Sarah.

"Off-course not, auntie. None of us believe that Maya has done anything like that."

"Oh, Lord!" The shock on Rita's face was palpable. She walked back slowly toward the bed with drooped shoulders and sat next to Sarah, totally lost.

A few awkward moments passed by, and the doorbell rang.

"Let me see who's at the door." Rita went out of the bedroom with fear still ripe on her face.

"Maya, You will have to produce your own evidence to prove you are innocent. And in the meanwhile, we can apply for anticipatory bail. My mom knows Advocate Deshpande; I will talk to him and make the arrangements." Michael said.

"Thanks a lot, Michael!" Maya said in a courteous tone.

"No worries."

Maya came near the window. Nervousness had her mind and body in a firm hold.

"Don't worry, Maya. I believe, in my heart, you are innocent, but you have to prove your innocence by hook or by crook." Sarah came closer to Maya and said softly.

"Do you think I will ever be able to prove my innocence?" Maya asked with pain on her face.

"Off-course, Maya, you certainly will." Sarah's encouraging tone did not help Maya. She just kept looking outside the window.

Sarah's phone rang. She went outside the room to answer the phone.

Maya was lost in her web of thoughts and kept looking at the lonely road outside the window.

Michael went to Maya. He gently patted on her shoulder and said,

"Maya, don't worry; we will prove your innocence."

*****

The doorbell rang continuously for a few seconds, getting more frantic with each instance.

"Maya, open the door," Rita called from the Kitchen.

Maya opened the door and was taken back. Inspector Jadhav with two men constables and two stout lady constables were at the door.

"Ma'am, we have a warrant against You. Come with us to the police station." The inspector, Jadhav, showed the warrant. Maya took the warrant paper with shivering hands. Her eyes welled up full of fear.

"What's the matter, Maya? Why is the police here again?" Rita came out of the Kitchen and asked worriedly.

"I... d... don... don't know, Mom." Maya stuttered without taking her eyes off the warrant. Her tongue felt paralyzed with fear.

"Why are you here again, Inspector?" Rita asked.

"We have a warrant against Ms. Maya for murder."

"What???" A chill went up Rita's spine.

"That's not true. I haven't committed any murder." Maya shouted in disbelief; her whole body was trembling.

"Is this your bracelet Ma'am?" Jadhav showed Maya a transparent plastic bag with a gold bracelet inside it. Maya took the plastic bag and looked at the gold bracelet with disbelief in her eyes.

"Yes...this is my bracelet. You have shown this before." Maya admitted meekly.

"We found it near the dead body of Mrs. Pinto. Any idea how it got there?" Inspector Jadhav asked in a stern voice.

"As I told you before, I had removed it and kept it on my table. I do that many times a day. But yesterday, before leaving the office I forgot to collect it from my table. I don't know how it got near Mrs. Pinto's dead body." Maya said anxiously.

"Ma'am, you must come with us to the Police Station." The inspector ordered.

"No... No. I am not going anywhere." Maya turned around and quickly started walking inside.

"Wait, Ma'am. We have a warrant; you have no choice." The inspector raised his voice. But Maya rushed to her room.

"She is innocent. My daughter hasn't killed anybody. These are all lies." Rita cried as she lamented.

"Go bring her back at once." The inspector ordered the lady constables, who speedily followed Maya to her room. They got hold of her before she could lock herself in.

"No, no, leave me... leave me alone," Maya shouted while crying. The lady constables held her from both sides and began shoving her toward the main door.

"No... No... let me go at once." Maya tried to escape fiercely from the grip of the constables, but they just held her tighter and took her along with them.

"Maya... Maya." Rita came after Maya and the constables.

"Don't worry, Maya. Everything will be alright. God is with us! God is with us!"

*****

Police took Maya into custody for questioning. She was bombarded with similar questions. Repeatedly. Again and again.

After two weeks, she was transferred to judicial custody.

There she became the victim of other cellmates' constant taunts and nasty waves of laughter. Her teary eyes turned swollen, and her fear-dipped face transferred into a straight face.

She waited desperately to get bail.

*****

In a few days, Maya got the bail. As per bail conditions, Maya was not allowed to leave the city, and she had to report immediately to the Police Station when called.

*****

3
Chapter 3

—♡—

After one month, the doorbell rang. Maya opened the door.

"Happy Birthday!" Michael said energetically from the door.

A sweet smile emerged on Maya's face.

"This is for you." Michael handover her the think square cardboard box.

"What is it ?" Maya asked in surprise while glancing at the box from all angles.

"Open it." Michael came inside the hall and sat on the couch. Maya put the box on the table and opened it.

"Oh, Cake!" Maya saw the round chocolate cake in the box. 'Happy Birthday, My Dear Maya, Love from Michael.' was stylishly written in white icing.

"Thanks ..Michael," Maya said while closing the box.

"Who is it, Maya? "Rita came from her bedroom. She was dressed to go out.

"Oh! Michael!"

"Hello, auntie."

"Mom, Michael, bring the cake for me," Maya showed Rita the cake box with her hand gesture.

"So nice of you, Michael. " Rita said.

"Okay, I am going to market to bring some food items for the Maya's birthday celebration," Rita said while opening the main door.

"Hope you are coming in the evening for the celebration," Rita looked at Michael.

"Yeah, auntie, I will be here."

"Good...Bye." Rita said, and she stepped out of the main door.

Once Rita left, Michael lovingly looked at Maya and said softly.

"Maya, I want to tell you something."

Maya noticed the sudden change in Michael's voice. She instantly looked at him. Michael's eyes talked with her eyes. She smiled and turned her head down in shyness. She waited for this moment for a long time. She knew what Michael was going to say, but she asked lovingly in a soft voice,

"What?"

"I want ..want to say, Maya..aah.." Michael was gathering the courage to speak.

"What? tell me." Maya asked eagerly with love in her eyes...

"I want to tell you, Maya..." and suddenly, Maya's phone rang. Michael became upset. Maya closed her eyes momentarily. She sighed deeply and picked up the phone.

"Hello...again...? Now? ..but I told you everything...oh...no..." Maya said in an irritated tone. "Okay, I will be there in a short time," She disconnected the phone and looked sadly at Michael.

"Who was that?" Michael asked.

"Call was from the police station. They are again calling me for questioning." Maya sighed.

"Again? How many times they are going to question you? "

"I have to go, Michael," Maya said in a sad tone, and she turned toward her bedroom with dropped shoulders.

"I will come with you," Michael said promptly while getting up from the couch.

"It's okay, Michael, I will manage. You may have to go to the office, right ?"

"Yeah ..but I can be late..no worries." Michael's optimistic tone pleased Maya.

"Okay..give me a few minutes. I will get ready." Maya went inside.
*****

On the way to Police Station, Maya's mobile rang, but she did not realize it. She was lost in her web of thoughts.

"Maya, your phone?" Michael reminded her while driving,

She looked at the number on the phones' screen and said,

"Unknown number."

In a few minutes, the phone rang again. Maya looked at the screen and let it ring.

"Who is it ?" Michael asked.

"Unknown number."

The phone rang again in a few minutes.

"Who is it?" Michael asked impatiently.

"Again, unknown number.."

"Answer it ..see who is calling ."

Maya took the phone.

"Hello?"

"I have the evidence that can prove your innocence. "The strange sound came from the phone's speaker. The unknown caller was using a voice scrambler to disguise his voice.

"Who are you, and how do you know me?" Maya asked.

"I know you very well, Maya, and I know you are innocent." The caller continued in a strange voice.

"I don't know what you're talking about."

"I have kept the evidence in the brown envelope in the letterbox at the ground floor lobby of your building. Go and grab it now."

"Why are you helping me?" Maya asked suspiciously.

"Consider me as your friend."

"Why should I believe you?"

"You don't have other option, Maya, but to believe me. I am your last chance to get evidence of your innocence. Go and grab it."

Maya thought for a second and asked while biting her inside lip.

"Now?"

"Yes, as I suspect I am being followed by people who are against you. Good Luck."

"Wait...the letterbox is not..." Before Maya could complete her sentence, the call got disconnected. Maya tried the number again,

'The number you dialed is not a valid number.' Maya heard the automated message.

'Who was that guy?' Maya started thinking. She changed her sitting position with a crossed leg.

"Who was it?" Michael asked impatiently, But his words did not get through Maya's ears. She was lost in her maze of r thoughts.

"Maya? Who was it?" Michael asked again, loudly. But still no reply from Maya. She was deeply lost in her web of thoughts. Michael touched Maya's shoulder,

"Maya?"

"Yeah..." Maya snapped out of her trance.

"Who was it? What about the letterbox?" Michael asked eagerly.

"I have no idea who that guy was. He said he has kept the evidence of my innocence in a brown envelope in our building's letterbox."

"Evidence of your innocence?" Michael smirked. "He must be kidding."

Maya thought for a few seconds. She looked into Michael's eyes and said firmly,

"Let's go home, Michael, and check the letterbox."

"Really? You believe in this crap?" Michael was surprised.

"Yes, let's go, Michael." Maya was determined.

Michael nodded unwillingly and made the next U-turn.

*****

It was a cloudy evening. A cool breeze was flowing through the atmosphere. The black clouds formed far in the Indian ocean had traveled on the monsoon winds to pay their annual visit to India.

Suddenly, the sound of roaring tires interrupted the surrounding silence of Ruby Park. A car speedily approached the road, and the sound of screeching brakes echoed in the engulfing silence.

The car stopped in front of Ruby Park. Its taillights glowed like shining rubies.

Maya and Michael got down from the car. The sound of slamming the door echoed through the eerie silence.

They passed through the main gate and walked toward the building.

They entered the building entrance. It was dark in the lobby. Maya went straight to the letterbox, located at the corner of the lobby. The letterbox was old and rusty.

Maya cleaned the dust off the letterbox.

"Who else lives in this building?" Michael asked.

"Only my family and Suzy auntie." Maya pulled the letterbox's doorknob.

"So, there are only two families that live in this whole building?" Michael askcd in surprise.

"There are two apartments each on the second floor, but they are locked. They are owned by a single family, and they live abroad." Maya said. She again pulled the doorknob of the letterbox. The door did not open.

"Let me try." Michael came forward. He took out his mobile from his pants pocket and turned the torch from it.

"Hold it this way." He gave the mobile to Maya. Michael looked at the letterbox from all angles in the little rays of torchlight. Michael pointed his finger to the letterbox door and said, "It's locked. " Maya bent forward and keenly looked at the tiny rusted lock on the letterbox door in the narrow light beam.

"Yeah." She said in a low voice.

"Do you have the key to this box?"

"Let me check." Maya dialed Rita's number. "Mom... Do we have the keys to the ground floor letterbox?"

"We haven't used that letterbox for a long time, Maya. The postman delivers our letters straight to our apartment." Rita explained.

Maya disconnected the call. "No. We don't have keys." She looked at Michael and shook her head.

"Hmm... let's break it then," Michael said conclusively.

He went back into the open space between the main gate and building.

It had started raining. Flashes of lightning were followed by cracks of thunder in the sky.

Michael picked up a tennis ball size stone and returned to the lobby.

He hit it hard on the letterbox door. After a few strong hits, the door was smashed. However, it was not beaten enough to break. Michael held the smashed door edge and pulled it.

"Aaahh..." Michael roared.

The door partially bent. Michael focused the torch through the newly formed gap between the bend door and its frame. The yellow rays of torchlight showed the brief portion of the brown envelop.

"Look, It's a brown envelope. The caller was telling the truth." Michael said excitingly.

"Really? Let me see." Maya exited. She pushed Michael aside and peeped through the gap.

"Yes, it seems to be an envelop." She said.

"Let me take it out. " Michael said, and in excitement, he slightly pushed Maya aside and retrieved the envelope.

"Let me see!" Maya was excited. She was breathing heavily. She grabbed the envelope from Michael's hand.

"Yeah... it's a brown envelope." She checked the envelope upside down and looked at Michael with a twinkle in her eyes, but she noticed blood on Michael's finger. Happiness from her face suddenly vanished.

"Michael, you are bleeding." Maya's face turned gloomy.

Michael looked at the wound, "It's just a small cut, don't worry." He said casually.

"Sh... show... show me the wound!" Maya stammered. She came close to Michael and looked at his bloody finger. Her face turned grave.

"It's alright, Maya. It's just a small cut. Don't fret too much. I will be fine." Michael said in an assuring tone.

Maya did not reply. She stared at him.

"What?" Michael asked with a smile.

Suddenly, his smile vanished.

"Oh! You think that Bhagat's ghost will get into me through this?" Michael showed his bloody finger.

Maya's mobile rang.

"Why did you want the key to the letterbox?" Rita's voice came through the receiver.

"Somebody has slipped an envelope into the letterbox."

"Who put the envelope in that old, rusty letterbox?" Rita asked in irritation.

Suddenly, Maya felt Michael standing behind her.

"I will call you back, mom." Maya disconnected the call and turned around. At that moment, lightning flashed in the sky, and Michael's face illuminated momentarily. His eyes were wide open, and he was peculiarly staring at Maya.

The thundering sound followed.

"Michael? You startled me! " Maya stumbled. Michael laughed weirdly. His laugh echoed in the darkness of the lobby.

"Stop laughing, Michael; you're scaring me," Maya said in a shaky voice. Her heart began pounding while looking at Michael's newly acquired look.

"Michael, why are you staring at me?"

"To scare you, Maya, hee...hee...hee..." a deep voice came through the darkness of the lobby. Maya looked keenly in the direction of the voice. Suddenly, Bhagat's ghost appeared from behind Michael.

"Oh!" Maya missed the heartbeat.

"He..He...He.." Bhagat's ghost entered into Michael, and Michael convulsed furiously.

"Oh, it seems Bhagat's ghost got into Michael's body." Maya realized. She took a step backward. Slowly, Bhagat's full face emerged on Michael's. Maya missed her pulse.

Michael's teeth changed as sharp nails, and their color was dark red like a carnivore that had just taken a bite out of its prey. There was a trickle of blood from the corner of his mouth.

"AHHH... No... no...!" Maya screamed. Her shaky palm dropped the envelope on the floor.

"He, he, he... he, he, he... heh, heh, heh!" Bhagat's face again flashed on Michael's face.

Maya's body began trembling.

On seeing Maya's condition, Bhagat's laughter got louder. Maya saw eerie wickedness in his eyes.

Slowly Bhagat began inching closer to her.

"Nooooo!!! Nooooo!!!" Maya let out a fearful scream.

While blubbering, Maya ran upstairs toward her apartment. Michael tried to grab her, but Maya was quick enough to escape from him. His hand brushed against her upper arm. Maya felt the cactus had rubbed on her upper arm.

"Ahh...." Maya screamed in pain.

She ran speedily on the stairs toward her apartment. Michael was close behind, but Maya's sudden burst of fear-propelled athleticism worked in her favor. She sprinted to her first-floor apartment.

*****

Maya raced into Rita's bedroom and locked the door from inside.

It was dark inside. Maya switched on the yellow light and looked at the bedroom door to ensure Michael had not followed her. She was trembling with fear, and her whole body was shaking. Her face was wet mixture of sweat and tears. A few strands of her hair were stuck on her face.

After a few seconds, she heard a loud thumping on the door from outside. The weak doorknob was vibrating from the thumps.

'If Bhagat's ghost ever attacks you, read chants from page 45 from this book.' Suzy's words echoed in Maya's mind. She took a few deep breaths and pulled a chair toward the wardrobe. She opened the wardrobe and climbed on the chair. Her shaky hands desperately began searching through the shelves.

She pulled one book. Read its title and fiercely flung it to the ground. She repeated the same steps for all other books.

The sound of bumps on the door was becoming loud with each passing second.

"Where did I keep it, damn it?" Maya murmured desperately while searching frantically.

All the books from the upper shelf were strewn on the floor in a few minutes. Maya looked at the dark empty shelf in disappointment. She got down from the chair.

She sat on the bed and held both her hands tightly on her head.

'Where the hell did I keep that book?' Maya stressed hard.

The sound of bumps on the door became more vociferous. Every bump made Maya's heart thump faster. Maya realized that the weak doorknob would fall out anytime.

'It must be here, must be here.' Maya thought and again started searching vigorously in the room.

"Thud... thud... thud..." The doorknob became loose, and it was about to break at any moment!

Something suddenly struck Maya. She quickly ran toward Rita's writing table and forcefully pulled out its drawers, one by one. First drawer, nothing! Next drawer..no luck, next drawer...no luck! Finally, she opened the last drawer, and in a moment of relief, she saw a book with a black cover. Maya read the book's title, embossed in golden ink, 'Holy Chants.'

She picked the book and began turning the pages frantically. She stopped at page 45. By now, the bumps on the door grew to their most vigorous.

As she initiated the reading of chants, the doorknob broke. It hopped into the room, and the door swung open. It slammed against the wall by force.

'Thud!' a loud noise echoed in the room.

Maya saw Michael was at the door. He looked wildly at Maya and sprang toward her.

'Let me start reading the chants loudly.' Maya thought.

Maya began chanting. Her fear-influenced tongue was struggling to say the chants.

Upon hearing the first two phrases of the chants, Michael slowed down. Maya felt confident. She continued her chanting more vigorously.

Michael halted in his tracks and retreated. Maya's confidence grew further, and her chanting became louder.

"Arrrrrgghhhh!!!" Michael screeched. Maya saw Bhagat's face appear momentarily on Michael's face.

He turned back and walked out of the bedroom toward the hall. Maya followed him, chanting loudly, constantly.

Michael had cupped his ears tightly. He was walking in toward the hall as he was in a daze. Looking at Michael's incapacity, Maya kept up the barrage of verses.

Michael picked the glass jar from the dining table on his way to the hall. The jar was full of water. In pain, he raised the jar like a ball to throw at Maya. Maya held the book in her left hand and picked the knife next to the cake box. She kept throwing verses at Michael in a loud voice.

Michael threw the glass water jar at Maya, which she dodged sharply. Jar hit the wall, and water spread all over the wall. The broken pieces of jar scattered on the floor.

Maya moved aggressively and stabbed Michael on his upper arm.

"Arrrgggh... aaahhh!!!" Michael cried in pain. Blood started flowing from his upper arm.

He fell down to his knees, covering his ears and continuing to wail in pain.

Suddenly, Maya saw smoke emerge from Michael. In front of Maya's eyes, the curtain of smoke formed, and it flew toward the main door. She tried to look hard through the smoke but could not see anything.

Maya kept looking at the smoke with wide eyes. Suddenly, she felt her legs had lost all their strength. She dropped herself on the couch like a sack of potatoes. Her eyes closed with tiredness.

*****

The rain was pouring heavily. The intense lightning in the sky was obediently followed by loud thunder. The wind was flowing speedily, pressing hard against each obstacle. Leaves of the trees were struggling hard to remain attached to the branch.

The wind picked the brown to envelop from the wet floor of the lobby. With its force, the envelope flew outside in the open space. Before rain could make it completely wet, the wind blew the envelope further in the open drainage, passing parallel to the compound wall.

The flow of drainage water gabbed the envelope like prey. A wet envelope began flowing on the drainage water and quickly disappeared in the flow.

*****

The next day, around 5 P.M., Maya and Michael were sitting at the Police Station.

"Shall we mention the mysterious caller and the evidence in that envelop?" Maya whispered in Michael's ears.

"First you tell me, what happened to you yesterday evening at the letterbox? You suddenly became aggressive and attacked me." Michael whispered back.

"I don't know. After I saw the blood on your finger, I saw Bhagat emerge from behind you..."

"You mean Bhagat's ghost?"

"Yes... I saw Bhagat's ghost enter your body. Then, your face turned into Bhagat's face. I felt so scared." Maya shuddered just thinking about the experience.

"Hmmm... after seeing my blood, you assumed Bhagat's ghost would get into me, right? You had the same hallucination again." Michael sighed deeply.

"Shall we mention about the mysterious caller and the evidence of my innocence or not?" Maya asked again.

"What will we say? Are we going to say that yesterday, late in the evening, we went to the letterbox and found the envelope containing evidence disappeared? Do you think the Police will believe us?".

"Hmmm." Maya thought for a moment. "The mysterious caller's number is not working anymore. However, we need to let the Police know that the caller does exist. He gave us the evidence of my innocence, but now that is missing."

"The Inspector wants to see you both inside." A constable came from inside and told Maya and Michael.

Michael and Maya went inside the inspector's cabin. Inspector Jadhav indicated to them to be seated on the empty chairs in front of him.

"What happened to your arm?" Inspector Jadhav asked Michael while looking at the bloody bandage on his upper arm.

"Nothing much, Sir...Just a small accident." Michael replied.

Inspector Jadhav stared at the bandage for a few seconds and turned to Maya,

"Miss Maya, I called you yesterday, but you did not come to the Police Station." Inspector Jadhav asked curtly while sitting in his chair.

"Sorry, Sir. On the way here, I got a call. The caller said he had left the evidence of my innocence in my building's letterbox. So, we immediately turned back toward my house and..." Maya said excitedly.

"Wait..wait...for a second, who called you?" Inspector Jadhav squinted and leaned forward.

"Not sure, Sir, it was an unknown caller."

"Unknown caller?" Inspector Jadhav's voice raised, and wrinkled formed on his forehead.

"Yes, Sir."

"Hmmm..." Inspector Jadhav sighed deeply and reclined comfortably back into his chair.

"So, as said by your unknown caller, did you get that envelop that was supposed to prove your innocence?" Inspector Jadhav asked.

"No, Sir. We saw the envelope, but at the end, we could not able to get a hold of it." Maya said.

"Okay, let me get this straight, the evidence was there, but you did not get it?" Inspector Jadhav asked thoughtfully.

"Yes, Sir!" Maya nodded.

Suddenly, Inspector Jadhav's face became serious. He again leaned forward on the table and asked,

"Do you read lots of suspense novels, Ms. Maya?"

"No, Sir."

"Then why are you telling me this unknown caller's wild story." Inspector Jadhav was irritated.

"No, Sir. It's not a story. It really happened to us ..and.." Maya said eagerly.

Inspector Jadhav gestured with his hand for Maya to stop talking,

"Enough!" He raised his voice. Maya became quiet.

Inspector reclined back into his chair again. After a few thoughtful seconds, he asked,

"Okay, now tell me in detail all your activities on the day when Mrs. Pinto was murdered?"

"Sir, I already told you many times, in detail, about what happened that day, but you keep asking me the same thing repeatedly," Maya said in a helpless tone.

"Yes, we got some more lead, so I am asking you again; tell me in detail, what exactly happened on that day?" Inspector Jadhav's asked in a sharp tone.

Maya sighed deeply and again began telling the details of that fateful day.

*****

Michael started the car, and his mobile rang.

"Hello? Oh... okay. I will be there in half an hour." Michael disconnected the call in a hurry.

"Who was that?" Maya asked curiously.

"There is an issue in our production system at the office. I need to go to the office immediately."

"Alright."

Michael started the car.

After a few minutes of a drive, he asked Maya,

"Where should I drop you?"

"Ahh..." Maya looked through the windshield keenly to figure out their exact location.

"You can drop me at the next light." Maya pointed toward the tiny red dot at a distance.

At the light, Michael pulled the car aside. Maya got out of the car. Michael waved and sped off.

Maya started looking for a cab.

After a couple of minutes, her mobile rang.

"Hello,"

"Did you get my envelope?" The mysterious caller's strange voice came through the speaker.

"Yes, and No," Maya said.

"What do you mean?"

"I took the envelope from the letterbox, but I don't have it now."

"Why not?"

"Something happened..."

"What happened?"

"I can't tell you that," Maya said while waving to the cabs.

"..."

"Hello?"

"..."

"Hello? Can you hear me ?" Maya checked if the call was still on.

"Yes, I can hear you. Now listen to me carefully."

"Okay..." Maya kept waving at the cabs.

"I will deliver one more packet at your doorstep in some time. Make sure you get that one. It too contains the evidence of your innocence."

"Wait...wait... by what time will I get that envelop?... Hello...hello..." The call got disconnected.

"Shit!! He did not let me finish." Maya irritated. She dialed Rita.

"Mom..are you at home?" She asked with pondering heart.

"No..I just came in the market." Rita said. "..but why are you.."

"Okay, mom, I will call you back" Maya suddenly disconnected the call.

'Shit...shit...I have to reach home as earliest as possible.' Maya murmured in irritation started waving to the cabs.

For a few minutes, Maya waved desperately for all the cabs who went in front of her. But not a single cab stopped.

In desperation, she crossed over to the middle of the road. She stood there and started waving at incoming cabs.

Finally, one cab stopped.

Maya entered the cab in a hurry and said in a hyper tone, "Take me to Ruby Park, Worli...fast!"

*****

The weather was cloudy. A man in a hoody came to the floor. Under the flickering tube light, he checked the apartment number of Maya's apartment. He kept a brown-colored thick cardboard packet in the front of the main door and rang the doorbell. There was no response from inside. The door did not open.

The man waited for a minute and rang the bell again. He waited more and rang the bell a third time. While he was waiting, he heard the sound of the neighboring door being opened. The man ran off before the neighboring door could open completely, leaving the packet behind.

Suzy came out from her apartment and wondered, 'Who was that?'. She came to staircases and looked upstairs and downstairs.

While returning toward her main door, she noticed the packet in front of Maya's main door.

'It seems Maya has received packet through the courier service.' Suzy thought and took the packet inside.

*****

Maya hurried back to the apartment but could not find any packet in front of her main door.

'Where the hell has that packet gone? Did the caller lie?' Maya wondered. She looked around and saw Suzy's main door was partially open.

Maya entered Suzy's apartment and came into the hall where Suzy was watching TV.

"Hello, auntie, did you see a packet in front of my apartment?"

Suzy lowered the volume of the TV.

"Yes," Suzy said, and she pointed her finger toward a thick brown-colored packet on the TV table.

"This is the packet that was in front of your main door."

"Thank you, auntie." Maya took the packet and began looking at it from all sides.

"Is Rita not at home?" Suzy asked.

Maya did not give a reply. She was busy examining the packet keenly.

"Maya?" Suzy asked loudly.

"Yes, auntie?"

"Is Rita not at home?"

"Yeah, she has gone to the market."

"Oh, okay. If you want, you may wait here till Rita returns." Suzy said and turned up the TV's sound volume. Maya sat on the couch and began watching TV too.

Some time passed, but Rita still did not return. Maya continued watching TV. Her eyes were watching the moving colored images on the screen, but she was lost in her web of thoughts.

A few more minutes went by.

'Oh... it has been a while now, and Mom has not returned yet. I am dying to know what's in this packet.' Maya thought. Her right leg was continuously vibrating. She made a few sidelong glances while holding the packet in her hand.

'Forget it... let me open the packet here itself.' Maya's impatience got the better of her.

"Auntie, do you have a blade or a knife to open this packet?" Maya asked Suzy.

"Yes, I do," Suzy said. She stood slowly from her chair and went into the kitchen with her baby steps.

In a few minutes, she came back with small a knife of the narrow blade.

'Here it is..." Suzy handed Maya the knife.

"Thank you, auntie," Maya said happily. She cut open the package on one side, and her phone rang.

"Go ahead, answer the phone. Give me the knife, and I will open the package for you." Suzy offered the help. Maya gave the packet and the knife to Suzy and answered the phone.

"Hi...where are you?". Michael's voice came from the speaker.

"I am at Suzy auntie's place." Maya moved toward the window.

"What are you doing there?"

"You won't believe it, that mysterious caller called again and said he is going to deliver another package at my doorstep."

"Did he leave the package?"

"Yes, he did, but before I could reach home. Suzy auntie picked it up..."

Suzy began cutting tape on the packet. After a few cuts,

"Ahhh!". Suzy cried softly in pain. She cut her palm while opening the packet.

Suddenly, Suzy saw movement to her right. She turned and saw Bhagat's ghost, standing in front of her, at a distance.

"Smmmhhhh... Smmmhhhhh... Smmmhhhhh" Suzy could hear Bhagat's breathing sound.

Suzy quickly looked at her wound and instantly looked back at Bhagat. He smiled. His smile blew Suzy with fear.

She screamed, "Maya!!"

Maya heard Suzy cry out in pain, and she immediately turned. Upon looking at Suzy's red hand, she said on the phone,

"Michael, I will call you back." Maya disconnected the call and ran toward Suzy in great hurry and fear.

"Oh my God, it's bleeding!" Maya shouted on seeing blood on Suzy's palm.

Suzy's eyes widened with fear, "We must stop the blood flow. Go to my bedroom, take out the medical kit from the wardrobe, and bring it here. immediately." She ordered Maya. Her face was indicating urgency.

Maya ran to Suzy's bedroom and opened the wardrobe door. Her hands began rummaging through the wardrobe for the medical kit.

"It's in the upper right corner. Bring it here at once." Suzy shouted desperately from the hall.

Maya got the medical kit and brought it in front of Suzy. In those few seconds, Suzy repeatedly shouted, "Bring the box here. Open it quickly, open it quickly."

Maya dipped a cotton ball in liquid antiseptic and applied it to Suzy's wound.

"Ahhhh...ouch!" Suzy exclaimed.

Maya held the cotton ball over the wound for a few minutes till the initial wave of blood subsided. Blood stopped oozing. Maya began to apply a band-aid on the wound.

"Thank God you put the medicine on time on the wound. Otherwise, things would have ended very badly." Suzy said in a thankful tone.

"The bleeding has stopped now, and the band-aid has also been applied. There is no need to worry." Maya assured Suzy while closing the medical kit.

Maya took Suzy to her bedroom. She gave her a glass of water and helped her to lay down on the bed.

"You take rest, auntie. I will be outside till Mom come. Call me if you need." Maya said in a soft voice. Suzy nodded.

*****

Maya came into the hall and called Rita.

"How much longer, Mom?"

"I will be there in a short time," Rita replied.

"Okay... come soon," Maya said, and she sat on the sofa. She cut off the remaining sticky tape on both sides of the packet. She opened the package with a tingling hand and retrieved one brown-colored envelope from it. She felt her tension unexpectedly released. Her eyes went up, looking heavenward,

'Thank God! Thank God! Yes! Finally, I got the evidence of my innocence.' Maya kissed the brown envelope happily.

She Kept the envelope in her hand; in a slumped posture, she watched TV for some time.

"I can't wait any longer. Let me open it." Maya said to herself excitingly." She tore the mouth of envelop and put her hand inside it. She retrieved one pen drive from it.

While looking at the pen drive with stunning eyes, she suddenly felt the movement behind her. She quickly turned back and was startled. It was Suzy standing at a distance.

"Oh...Suzy auntie. You scared me!" Maya said in a soft tone. She kept her hand on her thumping heart.

"What's the matter, auntie? Why are you standing there?" Maya asked curiously.

Suzy did not reply. She simply gave Maya a blank stare. Looking at Suzy's emotionless eyes, Maya felt strange.

"Say something, auntie?" Maya stood from the couch with a stiff face.

"Heh... heh... heh." Bhagat's ghost appeared behind Suzy, dressed in bloody, white clothes.

'Oh my God! It seems Bhagat has possessed auntie through her wound.' Maya wrapped her arms around her belly. She was stunned.

"I told Suzy to get off my land, but she did not listen. Now, look what I'm going to do to her. Ha...Ha...Ha...!" Maya saw Bhagat's ghost enter Suzy, and her body shook as she had been electrocuted. Maya's face turned pale with fear. She kept looking at Suzy with wide-open eyes and a quivering heart.

In a few seconds, Suzy had a devilish smile on her face. She was looking hungrily at Maya.

"What... what... happened, auntie?" Maya asked with fear coursing through her body. She began moving closer to the window.

Suzy's evil smile broadened further. Maya's fear peaked.

Suzy started laughing loudly.

"Hee...Hee...Hee...Hee...Hee...".

Maya came near the window. Suzy followed her.

"Please stop laughing auntie. I m scared!" Maya shouted. Suzy came nearer to Maya.

Suzy laughed louder, and suddenly Bhagat's face emerged momentarily in Suzy's face. Maya's heart began beating fast, so fast that she pressed her hand against it to make sure it didn't burst out of her chest.

"Ahhh..No.." Maya shouted in fear, her jaw clenched, and Suzy pushed her with power toward the window. Maya fumbled. The pen drive from her hand thrown outside the window and landed on the road.

'Oh..No. I must get that pen drive.' Maya saw the pen-drive on the road. She ran toward the main door, but with a sudden burst of athletic speed, Suzy stopped her.

'How did she move so fast now?' Maya wondered. A few minutes back, she saw Suzy was very slow in her movement, and now Suzy's unusual agility made Maya gasp with surprise. She held Maya's hand with hers and pushed her onto the couch, and leaped on top of her.

Maya saw Suzy continue to laugh and bring her hands toward Maya's neck. Maya tried to get up but was pinned down by Suzy's force. Suzy was laughing, and suddenly Maya again saw Bhagat's face instead of Suzy's.

"Maya! Leave my land. Go away! Go away!" His voice was grudgingly scary.

Fear crippled Maya. She felt Suzy's clutching hand on her throat, like an iron grip. She started feeling breathless. Her tongue stuck out of her mouth, and her hands, upper body, and legs began convulsing.

After an intense struggle, Maya managed to wriggle free. Suzy lunged at her from the couch, and Maya dodged her. She coughed severely and ran fast toward the main door, maintaining her balance. She was about to open the main door, but Suzy grabbed her from behind.

Maya wrestled with Suzy and finally opened the inner of the two doors. She then pushed Suzy inside and opened the outer grill door. She had almost slid one of her legs through it when Suzy grabbed her other leg and tripped her into the passage.

Suzy sat on Maya's chest and tried to strangle her again.

"Maya! Go away! Leave my land. Leave! Leave now!! Ha..Ha..Ha.." Suzy's laugh appeared more menacing in the light of the flickering tube-light.

"Ahhh! Ahhh!" Maya screamed loudly, and with a valiant push, she pushed Suzy off her chest. She was quickly on her feet and saw Suzy was too up as quickly. With rasping breaths, Maya ran toward the stairs.

"Maya! Get off my land. Go away!! "

Suzy took off and caught up with Maya at the beginning of the staircase. She pounced on Maya like a panther does on its prey. Maya swiftly moved to the side, and Suzy missed her. Suzy began an uncontrollable roll down the stairs.

"Auntieeee...!" Maya scrammed.

While looking at Suzy fall, Maya felt everything spinning around her. Sudden darkness appeared in front of her eyes. She began feeling dizzy, and she suddenly collapsed on the floor under the flickering tube light. Flickering white light was falling on her motionless body.

*****

The pen drive on the road was stamped under the tires of many ongoing vehicles.

Soon, Rain started. The Smashed pen-drive broke into pieces. It turned into the trash and washed away in the rainwater.

*****

A Police Jeep entered the Ruby Park compound in the dusk. The people were standing in small groups near the building. Inspector Shinde from Worli police station stepped out of the Jeep in crisply ironed uniform with three constables. As people saw approaching policemen, they cleared the path for them.

"Which floor?" Inspector Shinde asked one of the constables walking two steps ahead of him.

"First floor!"

While entering the building, Inspector Shinde spotted the ambulance waiting near the main gate. The three constables, followed by Inspector Shinde, began ascending the staircase.

Before reaching the first floor, they saw Suzy's dead body covered with a white bedsheet. A few elderly women were sitting on the staircase, keeping a safe distance from the body.

While looking at the body, Inspector Shinde said to constables, "You guys go upstairs in the apartment and wait there." The constables continued up the staircase.

Shinde bent forward slightly and pulled the white cover partially off Suzy's body to look closer. He looked more closely at Suzy's head wound and the surrounding pool of blood.

While observing the body, his attention suddenly went to the beginning of the staircase. He got up and started walking up the stairs. On the way, he turned and looked back at Suzy's dead body repeatedly.

Soon, Inspector Shinde entered Suzy's apartment and walked toward the hall.

Cloudy weather wasn't allowing enough sunlight in the hall. In the dimly lit room, he saw Maya sitting on the couch with a grim expression on her face. Her eyes were dull and wet. Rita was sitting to her left, and Rita's right palm held Maya's left palm tightly.

Michael was sitting on the right of Maya, and his left hand was softly placed on Maya's shoulder.

Inspector Shinde came to Maya and looked at her for a few seconds. The constable standing nearby whispered, "Sir, this is Maya ma'am; the old lady fell down the stairs in her presence."

Inspector Shinde glanced around the entire hall. He pulled a black foldable chair and sat down in front of Maya's couch. He slowly took out his record book while looking at Maya, Rita, and Michael. Maya felt Inspector Shinde's presence and opened her puffy eyes.

After opening his record book, Shinde turned toward Maya. He noticed the thin layer of tears in Maya's eyes was eager to flow down her cheeks. He cleared his throat, bent forward toward Maya, and said in his thick voice, "Miss Maya, I'm extremely sorry about Mrs. Suzy."

Maya took a deep breath and wiped her tears.

Inspector Shinde gave Maya a few seconds and said, "I have a few questions for you." He started flipping pages of his notebook. Suddenly, He stopped and asked softly, "I will note down your answers for my reference. I hope it's okay with you?"

Maya sniffed and nodded. Inspector Shinde settled on a blank page.

Inspector Shinde raised his head and looked straight into Maya's eyes. Maya could not look directly at his eyes for long and turned her head toward a small figurine of Jesus Christ on the table next to Shinde.

"Since when did you know Mrs. Suzy?"

"Since childhood," Maya said in a flat voice.

"How was your relationship with her?"

"Good. Suzy auntie was like a family member to us." Maya felt a knot in her throat, but she controlled it. Newly formed tears quickly made their way down her cheeks.

Rita patted Maya gently on her shoulder. She let her eager tears flow but muted the sound of her cry.

An awkward silence filled the room.

Inspector Shinde patiently looked at Maya. The three constables were standing behind Shinde like his bodyguards and were staring at Maya with their blank faces.

"I'm sorry, Miss Maya, but I have to continue with my questions." Inspector Shinde said politely.

Maya cleared her throat. She made a deliberate effort to control her emotions and said in a broken voice, "Sorry, please continue."

Inspector Shinde stared at Maya. After getting confirmation from her face that she was in a state to talk, he bent forward and continued with his questions.

"You were the last person to meet Mrs. Suzy, right? In fact, you were there when the accident happened, weren't you? "

Maya nodded her head positively.

"Can you tell us, in detail what took place?"

Maya felt as if the event were being projected on the front wall, like a screen, and she started describing them.

"I came here to collect my package. I collected it, but I waited here since my Mom was not home. I asked Suzy auntie to give me a knife or a blade to open the package. She went to the kitchen and came back with this knife." Maya pointed to the small knife kept on the front teapoy. Inspector Shinde put on the transparent plastic hand gloves and picked the knife. He saw the dry blood on the edge of the knife's blade.

"Okay. Carry on, Miss Maya." Inspector Shinde kept the knife on the teapoy and removed the hand gloves.

"While opening the package, I received a call from Michael. Auntie took the knife from my hand and asked me to answer the call. I handed the knife to auntie. While answering the call, I went toward the window and then..." Maya suddenly stopped talking abruptly. Her eyes were still looking at the apparent 'screen' in front of her.

"There was blood oozing from her palm. When I looked at her, she shouted, 'We must stop the blood. Go to my bedroom, and bring the medical kit from the wardrobe, and bring it here at once ".

Maya paused for a few seconds and took her eyes off the 'screen.' She turned her gaze to the floor.

"Then?"

"I fetched the medical kit, put some medicine, with a cotton ball, to her wound, and covered it with a Band-Aid. I took her to her bedroom. I put her on the bed and came out into the hall. I started watching TV and after a few minutes...." Maya slipped back into a trance.

"Then what?" Inspector Shinde asked.

Maya continued staring at the 'screen,' but fear appeared in her eyes. Her face turned reddish, and her breathing became labored. She went into a trance.

"And then what?"

Maya did not respond. She was lost in her trance. Inspector Shinde, the constables, and Rita looked at each other with baffled looks. Shinde waited for a few seconds and asked again, loudly, "And then what, Miss Maya?"

This time Inspector Shinde's loud words pierced Maya's brain, shattering her trance. She snapped back to reality. She looked at Shinde with bulged eyes.

"And then what?" Inspector Shinde asked again, this time a bit more politely.

"...I saw Suzy auntie standing behind me at some distance, and she suddenly started laughing." The fear became more and more evident in Maya's eyes, and she started fumbling while speaking.

"Her... her... her smile... was different; it was... it was... weird and... and... there was something evil... evil... about it." Maya was mesmerized by the scenes playing out in her mind.

"What did you do after that?"

"I was scared and told her to stop smiling, but she kept on smiling. Then after a couple of minutes, her smile turned into a laugh. She began laughing loudly, which scared me even more. I tried to run out toward the main door, but she grabbed me. Her agility and speed were unbelievable. Whenever I had met her before, her movements were slow. Sometimes they were terribly slow. But this time, however, she grabbed me so swiftly that it shocked me."

Inspector Shinde, all constables, and Rita were looking gravely at Maya.

After a brief pause, Maya started speaking rapidly, "Somehow, I escaped from her iron grip and went toward the main door. I managed to open both the doors and ran toward the staircase. I was about to start descending the stairs when she tried to grab me from behind. She leaped toward me, but I dodged her. She could not balance herself, slipped, and tumbled down the stairs at great speed."

Maya's emotions reached their peak. She burst out crying loudly. Rita held her tightly and rubbed her back.

Inspector Shinde continued writing. One of the constable made a call on his mobile, and the other started reading his messages. The third constable, Tawade, remained standing at his position.

While jotting down his notes, Shinde raised his head and ordered the two constables, "Send the body to the hospital for a post-mortem."

"Yes, Sir." Both the constables saluted him and left immediately.

*****

It took a while for Maya to calm down. She rested her neck on Rita's shoulder and closed her eyes.

"Miss Maya..with in one or two days you need to come to police station and record your witness. " Inspector Shinde said while closing his notebook.

Maya nodded.

Shinde stood and took his mobile out from his pocket and turned toward the window. He looked outside the window while the call was connecting.

"Yes, Sir. I am at the scene Sir...Yes... Yes... Okay, Sir... Okay, Sir..."

"Sir..." Inspector Shinde heard a voice from behind. He turned, and his head jerked back. He immediately pressed the mute button on the phone and said in an urgent tone,

"Oh, Tawade! You are bleeding. How did this happen?"

Tawade's left arm was red. Blood was streaming down from his upper left hand to his fingers. He tried to stop the blood, but a few blood drops had already been made to the floor.

"A small nail was sticking out from the bathroom door, and my hand accidentally brushed against it. It's alright; it's a small wound." Tawade said in pain.

"That's not a small wound, Tawade. You need to immediately apply for medicine." Inspector Shinde said in an urgent tone. He got back to his phone and babbled, "Sir, I will call back in some time."

While disconnecting the call, he came to Maya and asked, "Miss Maya, do you have any medicines to apply to his wound?"

Maya opened her eyes. Constable Tawade's red arm was in front of her eyes. She became alert. Her eyes bulged momentarily. She quickly got up and wiped her face. She looked at Tawade's bleeding arm once more and said, "Yes, it's in the bedroom. I'll go get it."

She began walking toward Suzy's bedroom. She took a couple of steps and heard Inspector Shinde's voice from behind, "Sorry, Miss Maya, that room is sealed. Do you have a medical kit at your apartment?"

Maya thought momentarily, nodded, and hurriedly headed toward the main door with taping foot. She felt her body temperature was raised.

While approaching the main door, her ears picked up the conversation,

"Tawade, first go and wash your wound...Uh...uh...aaa, not here. Go to Miss Maya's apartment. You can bandage it there as well."

Maya entered her apartment with constable Tawade. She heard the closing sound of the main door. After entering the hall, she headed to her bedroom when she heard the words from behind.

"Ma'am... where's the bathroom?" Tawade asked from behind. His voice was soft but painful.

Maya pointed toward the middle bathroom, "Further down, to the left."

"Thank you, Ma'am!" Tawade hurried to the bathroom. He was holding his left palm firmly on his upper right hand. The blood was dripping, forming a red dotted line on the floor behind him.

While looking at Tawade's trail of blood, Maya entered her bedroom and opened her wardrobe. She began looking in each and every shelf for the medical kit. While she was looking for a medical kit, she heard the sound from behind.

"Ma'am?"

'It sounded like Constable Tawade, but his voice was hoarser than earlier.' Maya thought for a second.

"Ma'am!" Tawade called again.

'What is he doing here?' Maya thought.

"Ma'aaaam!"

Maya sensed the eagerness in Tawade's tone. She turned slowly, and she missed the heartbeat. She got goosebumps all over her body.

She kept looking at Tawade with bulged eyes and a pondering heart. Tawade's clothes were full of blood. . His face was bloody as he had washed his face with blood, and he was in great pain. Maya was looking at him, and suddenly, Bhagat emerged from behind. Maya froze on the spot. Her eyes filled with fear. It sent a chill through her, and she felt a quick shiver.

"Heh... Heh... Heh... Maya. Why are you bringing more people here, Maya? I don't like it." Maya felt her heart beating faster. She saw Bhagat's ghost merge into Tawade, and his body shook violently as a bolt of lightning had struck him. Maya's face turned pale with fear.

"I told you I don't want anyone here. I don't like it. I hate it. Now I'll have to deal with these people as well. Ha, ha, ha! And it will all be your fault," Tawade said in a loud authoritative voice.

Momentarily, Bhagat's face emerged on Tawade's face.

'Oh...no! Bhagat's ghost has possessed the constable through his blood and wound.' Maya realized.

Maya saw, Tawade begin walking toward Maya menacingly, and he had a wicked smile on his face. Maya felt a shiver run up her spine. Maya accessed the recent calls list on her mobile screen and tried to press the row displaying 'Michael' with a shaky finger. But she could not. Tawade came close to her.

She mustered up all her courage, got out of her bedroom, and headed to the hall. She ran toward the main door. But fear had a firm grip on her movements, and it was not allowing her to move quickly.

Suddenly, she felt a strong hand grab her shoulder from behind. Maya looked back and saw Tawade's blood dripping front teeth. He had a scary grin on his face.

"Aaahhh!!!" Maya scrammed. Tawade pushed her with force, and she fell to the floor. She lost her grip on her phone, and it plunged, a couple of feet away, into the hall.

Tawade pinned Maya to the floor. He grabbed her neck and began squeezing. Maya's nostrils flared, and she felt choked instantly. She started convulsing and gasping for breath desperately.

Suddenly, Maya felt Tawade's grip loosen a bit. She pushed him and stood, coughing severely. She quickly gathered her wits and started running toward the main door. Tawade came fast from behind and got between her and the main door.

"He, he… he, he… he, he…." Bhagat's face again emerged in Tawade's face, with a poisonous smile.

Maya noticed a knife lying on the nearby teapoy. Suzy's words echoed in her mind. 'Somebody stabbed Bhagat with a long knife multiple times in his chest. He scares to a knife.'

Maya leaped toward the teapoy and grabbed the knife in her hand. Upon seeing the knife in Maya's hand, Tawade's face changed. His poisonous smile disappeared, and fear appeared on his face. Maya leaped toward Tawade and slashed him on his hand with bulging eyes. Blood oozed out from the fresh wound.

"Aaahhhhhh…" Tawade shouted while looking at the blood from his hand. Momentarily, Maya again saw Bhagat's painful face overlapping Tawade's face. Seeing Tawade's condition, Maya became confident. She raised her hand to stab him again… but before she could attack, Tawade ran toward the main door.

He darted out the main door and began descending the stairs. A trail of blood formed behind him on the staircase. Maya followed steadily with murderous intent in her eyes.

Tawade came out of the building entrance, through the lobby.

It was dark outside.

He ran through the compound toward the main gate. Occasionally, he looked back and found Maya close at his heels, the knife ready to strike.

"Sighhhh, sighhhh." He started panting.

Tawade tripped on a crack and fell on the way to the gate. Maya grinned her teeth and attacked him. Tawade rolled out quickly to avoid the knife's blade.

"Aahh... ahh... no, no...." Tawade cried out with fear. Bhagat's painful face flashed on Trade's face.

Tawade got off the ground and ran toward the main gate. Maya was undeterred and kept up close behind him.

"Ahh...ah...ah..ah...ah...ah...." Tawade was gasping for breath. He passed through the main gate.

He crossed over to the middle of the road and moved to his left.

Maya got to the road and angrily followed behind him and...

"Beeeeepppp!!"

The sound of the horn was followed by the ear-splitting sound of tires under stress,

"Screeeeeeeeech!"

Maya looked in the sound direction, and her eyes were filled with yellow light from the approaching car's headlights.

"Thud!!"

Maya flung and fell further on the ground. Her head struck severely on the road.

In her daze, Maya saw the smoky shape of Bhagat leaving Tawade's body; his smile was menacing as ever!

*****

4

Chapter 4

Maya opened her eyes and looked at the wall clock. It was showing 7 A.M.

While watching herself in the broad square mirror above the bathroom washbasin, she thought,

"Oh..how come I become so tall fast? ..and chubby too..." She touched her cheeks.

Her eyes were glued to the bathroom floor.

'After coming from the hospital, I am trying to remember what's changed on this floor?' Maya kept staring at the floor tiles in the mirror.

Suddenly, her face lights up.

'Oh yeah! These tiles seem to have changed. Earlier, the tiles were gray. When did these tiles change?' She kept staring at the floor tiles for some time.

Maya came out of her bedroom and sat at the dining table with a bemused look on her face.

"Good morning!" Rita kept a coffee mug before her and went back to the kitchen.

Maya looked at Rita for a few seconds.

"Mom, In recent days, I thought to ask you .." Maya began a conversation.

"What?"

"You look different.."

"What you mean, different ?" Rita asked in a plain tone while Her hands were chopping vegetables with the knife.

"Different means..aged ..old.."

"Really ?"

Maya took her first sip of coffee, and suddenly her face glowed,

"Mom, I figured out what changed in my bathroom."

"What is that?"

"It's the floor. The tiles were gray earlier, and now they are off-white. When did we change the flooring?"

Rita raised her head in surprise, but the knife was still cutting the spinach in her hand. She was about to ask something, but the pressure cooker on the gas burner whistled. Rita stopped the cutting and lifted the steamy cooker. She kept it on the kitchen platform and resumed her spinach cutting.

'There are other changes in this hall, kitchen as well.' Maya thought while looking around.

She finished her coffee and came into the kitchen.

"Where is Suman? I have not seen her since I got back from the hospital?" Maya began washing the cup under a steady stream of water. Rita gave a confused look at Maya with her brow furrowed. She was about to say something, but the doorbell rang.

"I'll get that." Raita hurried out of the kitchen.

She opened the main door. Michael and his mother, Hema, were at the door.

"Come in, please come in," Rita said with a smiling face.

Maya's head popped out from the kitchen for a moment.

"Please make yourself comfortable. I'll bring some water." Rita said courteously.

Hema and Michael sat down on the couch next to each other while Rita headed back to the kitchen.

In a few seconds, she came out with two glasses of water in a tray and kept them on the teapoy. She carefully handed a glass full of water to Hema and Michael and sat down on the chair in front of the couch.

"We are meeting after so many days, Hema. How are you? Recovered after your heart attack?" Rita asked.

Hema sipped some water and kept the glass back on the tray.

"I'm fine, thanks. I came specifically to see Maya. How is she now?" Hema asked.

"She's better now. " Rita answered, and she turned toward the kitchen and called.

"Maya...?! Look who's here to see you."

Maya came to the hall. Her face flushed a reluctant smile.

"There you are. Come, sit with us." Hema said enthusiastically. Maya stood clumsily. She was standing between the couch on one side, where Michael and Hema were seated, and Rita on the other.

"How are you feeling now, Maya?" Hema asked politely.

"I'm fine. Thanks." Maya said briefly and looked at Michael, whose eyes were asking,' How are you dear?'

"I was getting regular updates, from Michael, about your health. I had been to the hospital too, to visit you, but you were resting at the time, so I didn't want to disturb you. Since I had some free time today, I thought of coming to see you. Glad to see you are feeling better." Hema said.

Maya gave another reluctant smile. Her eyes darted between Rita, Hema, and Michael.

An awkward silence began to occupy the room.

"Come sit. Why are you standing there?" Rita's hand gestured to the chair next to her.

"Maybe later. I have some urgent work. I must go finish it." Maya said and quickly walked toward her bedroom. Hema gave a perplexed look to Michael and one to Rita.

"Maya... Maya...?" Rita got up quickly and followed Maya.

She could barely enter the bedroom before Maya shut the door.

"Maya, they have come here especially to see you. Why are you ignoring them?" Rita said. Maya laid down on her bed with her eyes closed.

"Maya, it does not look good. They are our guests." Rita urged.

In response, Maya turned over and lay on her chest.

"Maya! Please, come out for some time."

Rita waited for a few seconds, but Maya did not reply.

Rita returned to the hall and saw Hema and Michael were on their feet. Rita cleared her throat, "Sorry. Suddenly, Maya's not feeling well. Why are you guys standing? Please sit down; I'll make some tea or coffee quickly."

"No, it's alright, Rita. We just had tea earlier. It looks like Maya needs rest." Hema looked at Maya's closed bedroom door and gave a suggestive look to Michael.

"Yes, auntie. We are fine. Let Maya take some rest." Michael said. He and Hema moved toward the main door.

'It doesn't look good for guests to leave without being served anything.' Rita thought. She hurriedly got in their way and said anxiously,

"It won't take much time to prepare tea or coffee. I will have it ready quickly."

"It's really okay, Rita. Don't make anything of it. As I said, we just came over here to see Maya." Hema said.

Michael opened the main door and moved aside for Hema to step out first.

Hema got out and called the elevator. While Hema and Michael waited in the corridor for the elevator, Rita stood at the main door and said in an apologetic tone,

"Sorry for Maya's behavior. Normally, She is in a good mood in the mornings, but I'm not sure what happened today. Sometimes kids behave so weirdly that you feel you are dealing with a different person altogether."

"No worries, Rita. I understand. Why don't you two come over to our place when Maya feels better." Hema said happily and looked at Michael.

"Yes, that's a good idea." Michael nodded.

The elevator arrived, and Sarah came out from it.

"Hi, Michael!" She greeted enthusiastically,

"Hi, Sarah. How are you? Mom, this is Sarah, our office colleague."

"Not only an office colleague but Maya's friend since childhood," Sarah grinned pleasantly.

"Hello, Sarah," Hema said.

"Hello," Sarah replied with a pleasant smile, looked at Rita, and asked,

"Where's Maya, auntie?"

"She's in her bedroom."

"Okay, I'll go in. Bye..." Sarah waved to Michael and Hema while going inside.

Before getting into the elevator, Hema said,

"Bye, Rita... take care..."

*****

"Do you still see Bhagat's ghost, Maya?" Dr. DeSuza asked.

"Yes, Doctor."

"Do you see him every day?"

"Yes, Doctor. He calls out to me every day. Initially, I was scared, but now I feel..." The appearance on Maya's face changed, nostrils flared, and a wave of sudden anger rose on her face.

"feel...?"

"..."

"...go ahead, Maya. Now you feel what?"

"I feel angry about him now. I feel to stab him with a knife," Maya said.

"Then go ahead, Maya, stab him, kill him. Finish him!" Dr. DeSuza said encouragingly.

"..." Maya remained silent.

'Ask him... you must ask him.' Her inner voice whispered in her ear. 'No...this is not right the time to ask....' Maya murmured back.

'No... ask him...you must ask him.' Her inner voice insisted. She took a deep breath and closed her eyes for a few minutes.

"Doctor..." Maya asked after opening her eyes.

"Yes." Dr. DeSuza replied while writing on his prescription pad.

"...everything appears new to me. I feel like I have woken after a long time." Maya said with inevitable tiredness.

Dr. DeSuza suddenly stopped writing and raised his head. He stared at Maya for a few seconds and asked.

"Do you remember how you met with the accident?"

Maya sighed and said gloomily. "No, I don't recall."

"Really? You don't recall about your accident ?"

"No."

"You don't recall anything at all?" Dr. DeSuza repeated his question in a raised voice.

"No."

After looking at Maya for a few more seconds, Dr. DeSuza suddenly asked, "Don't you remember how you got down from your building? How you reached the road?"

Maya tried to think hard but could not recall anything.

"No doctor, nothing." Maya shook her head.

Dr. DeSuza's face changed. It became serious. He looked straight into Maya's eyes and asked sharply,

"What is the last thing you remember?

"aahh...I remember I woke in a hospital bed. Mom told me I met with a car accident."

"Not that...What do you remember before waking up in the hospital ?" Dr. DeSuza asked eagerly.

Maya stressed her memory again.

"All I remember is that I returned from school in the evening. I was exhausted, and so I straight went to bed."

Dr. DeSuza sighed.

'Why is the doctor looking at me in such a way?' Maya thought.

"Is Mrs. Gomes waiting outside?"

"Yes."

"You please wait outside and send her in."

Maya went out of the cabin.

In a few minutes, Rita came in and sat in front of Dr. DeSuza.

"How is Maya doing?" Rita asked with a concerned face.

"Ah... for her hallucinations, she needs to take her medicines regularly...and..."

"and?" Rita anxiously looked at Dr. DeSuza.

Dr. DeSuza thought for a moment.

"I think Maya has developed one more problem after the accident."

"What's that?" Rita froze in the chair.

"After her accident, she might have suffered memory loss. From what she said, I estimate, at least...her last seven to eight years of memory loss."

"Oh!" Rita's heart sank into her chest. She felt heaviness in the limbs. The shock of Maya's memory loss was evident on her face.

A few minutes went by in odd silence.

"She got the bathroom floor tiles changed last year. She chose the color and the design herself. However, yesterday morning she asked me when the tiles were replaced ? She doesn't remember any of that...." Rita said in a teary voice.

She again lost in her thoughts for a couple of minutes.

"... Maya's Father died three years ago. After her accident when she woke up for the first time in the hospital... ... ...ah!!!" Rita kept her right-hand palm on her mouth and repressed her emotional build-up.

"...after her accident, when she first woke up in the hospital, what she asked first was, where is Dad?" Rita's eager tears began flowing down her cheeks. The emotional upheaval in her heart emerged as pain on her face.

Dr. DeSuza let a few minutes pass in silence for Rita to gather her emotions.

"We will have to examine her in detail. I may have to refer her to another doctor." Dr. DeSuza said. Rita took a few more minutes to control herself.

"How much time it will take to regain her memory?" She asked while wiping her tears.

Dr. DeSuza took a breath and reclined back into his chair.

"In such cases, we can't say for sure when a patient will get memory back, in fact...."

"In fact?" Rita asked eagerly.

"...in fact, we are not sure even if she will ever regain her memory at all."

"Oh! Jesus Christ!!" Rita sat back and wept silently.

A few uncomfortable minutes passed by.

"Seven years of memory loss! You mean to say she will neither remember her college years nor her office period?" Rita asked in disbelief.

"Yes." The doctor nodded.

"Oh! No, nooo...!!" Rita moaned. Pain on her face was palpable. She remained seated silently with a grave face. Dr. DeSuza began scribbling on his prescription pad.

"There is a glimmer of hope, though." Dr. DeSuza said in a slightly reassuring tone while tearing out the prescription page. '

"What is that?" Rita asked eagerly. Twinkles of hope appeared in her sad eyes.

"Maya needs to talk to the people with whom she has spent time in the last few years. She needs to talk with them about her their gatherings, meetings, parties, and picnics in the past few years." Dr. DeSuza kept the prescription page in front of Rita. She was keenly listening to him. Dr. DeSuza continued,

"She must visit the same places she had been to, like, her college, restaurants, different locations in the city or even outside the city and that too with the same people. That might spark off memory recall."

*****

It had been raining since morning.

"Good morning Maya," Rita said from the kitchen as Maya walked into the dining area. Rita was making coffee on one stove and stirring gravy in a pot on another stove. The aroma of chicken masala had filled the kitchen and could be smelt till the dining area.

"Good morning," Maya said while yawning. She sat on one of the chairs at the dining table.

Rita poured hot coffee into a mug. She kept the mug in front of Maya and sat on the other chair.

Maya began drinking coffee. After a few sips, She noticed Rita was looking at Maya.

"What's the matter, Mom?"

"Nothing..."

"No... no... tell me..." Maya took another sip of coffee.

"You really don't remember what happened at the office on that day?" Rita stressed the word 'that' day.

"No. What happened on that day?" Maya asked innocently.

Rita sighed deeply.

"Maya, listen to me carefully... you have been accused of murder. "

"What?!" Maya was shocked. Her mouth fell open.

"You are out on bail," Rita said while coughing.

"Do you believe I have committed murder, Mom?"

"Of course not, Maya," Rita put her palm on Maya's palm and patted lightly.

"Michael and Sarah believe... believe someone has...has set you up." Rita coughed again. Maya poured a glass of water from a nearby jar and kept it in front of Rita.

"Who... who do they think set me up?"

"That's no one knows." Rita had a sip of water.

"So what are our next steps now?" Maya asked with a shaky voice. She felt a heavy feeling in her stomach.

"We need to collect evidence of your innocence."

"That's the police's job, isn't it?"

"They are conducting their investigation, but we also need to find any evidence of your innocence. Do You remember any unusual thing that happened to you in the office? Any odd behavior from your colleagues? "

"No, I don't remember anything?" Maya said with a straight face.

"Anything, Maya? Any small thing? If you could remember slightest of an odd incident, it may lead to something."

"No ...Mom...I do not remember anything." Maya murmured and nodded her head negatively.

She remained quiet for a few minutes. As she was lost in thoughts, Rita interrupted her,

"And Maya... your uncle helped us with some money before your accident. You were about to deposit that money in the bank, but you met with an accident before that. Can you could get that money now?"

"Which money?" Maya's posture turned stiff.

"Maya, please don't say you don't remember that as well. " Rita leaned forward on the table and asked in a worried tone.

Maya stressed her memory.

"No, Mom, I don't recall about any money." She sighed.

Rita's face turned pale.

"After your accident, we are in financial distress. We really need that money." Rita said anxiously. "You kept the money in a bag to deposit it in the bank." suddenly, her voice became teary.

"to deposit in the bank?" Maya's eyes grew wide open.

"Yes, you were about to deposit the money in the bank." Rita tried to speak speedily but again coughed.

"Mom, I told you. I don't remember anything." Maya irritated.

Rita sunk back into her chair hopelessly. An agony revealed on her face. Her eyes filled with tears, and in a few seconds, they rolled down her cheeks.

Maya felt terrible. She came to Rita and softly kept her hand on her shoulder.

"I'm sorry, Mom. But I really don't remember anything. Do you know how that bag looks? I will search it in my room."

Rita wiped her tears and sighed deeply. But the shock of losing money was still on her face.

"It was a medium-size blue plastic ba..bag, and you sa...said" She began coughing again.

"Mom, have a puff from your inhaler first, and then we will talk." Maya insisted. She gave the inhaler to Rita.

Rita brought the inhaler's mouth to her own and pressed the button.

"Fsssh... Fsssh!" A spray of liquid passed through Rita's throat. Her coughing stopped, and she felt better at once.

Rita shook the inhaler near her ear. "This inhaler is almost empty."

She kept the inhaler on the table and turned back to the kitchen.

Maya looked outside of the window. "Rain seems to be stopped. I will get you a new inhaler. " From the door of the kitchen, she asked, "Where should I purchase your medicines from?"

Rita gave a distressed look to Maya and turned to the mixer.

"The Pharmacy is around the corner. The person at the counter knows you very well."

*****

Maya got down from the building and came out of the main gate. She stood on the pavement, adjusting to the front road. She looked cluelessly to her left and right.

'Mom said it's around the corner, but on which side?...let me try this side.' ' She murmured and began walking to her left.

While walking, she watched the surrounding residential buildings. Each building had its name displayed on its main gate. Maya read the building names with furrowing eyebrows.

'Mom said we've been living in this area for a long time, but nothing looks familiar to me.' Maya thought.

"Hey, Maya!"

A loud female voice asked from behind. Maya stopped. She turned around and saw a short, plump, old lady standing a few feet away from her. The lady was wearing a colorful gown of a floral design that went between her knees and ankles. In one hand, she had a yellow umbrella over her head, and her other hand was busy clutching a brown plastic bag.

The bulge of the bag indicated it was packed with stuff.

The old lady came near Maya. She looked at Maya through her old-fashioned thick frame glasses and asked,

"Maya, how are you?"

"I am fine," Maya said in a low voice.

'Oh. God, please... please... please tell me this lady's name.' Maya silently prayed.

"Where are you off to?"

"To the pharmacy shop."

"The Pharmacy shop? There is no pharmacy shop in this direction. The one you want is in the opposite direction." The old lady raised her hand in the other direction.

"Oh!" Maya confused. She touched her palm to forehead and quickly turned around. She could see the moving vehicles on the road at a distance.

"How is your mom?"

"She is fine," Maya said briefly and stepped forward in the other direction.

After a few steps, she heard the lady call out from behind.

"Tell your Mom, Rosie asked, when is she going to start coming to Church?"

"Yes, Rosie auntie, I will tell Mom. Bye." Maya shouted without looking back.

Maya walked quickly and reached the corner of the road within a couple of minutes.

"Where to go now ?" Maya looked at her left and right.

"Is there a pharmacy nearby?" She asked a passerby, and he pointed his hand toward the pharmacy shop at the right.

Maya began walking toward the Pharmacy. The road and pavement were full of people, as though ants had swarmed out from their anthills. Maya became part of the vibrant crowd. She, too, got forced and shoved many times, although gently, in both directions.

Maya entered the Pharmacy and was instantly greeted by the typical mild smell of medicines and tonics.

"Good morning, Maya madam. How are you?" A middle-aged person from the counter welcomed Maya with a smiling face.

"I am fine."

"How can I help you?"

"Can you give me these medicines?" Maya took out Rita's prescription from her bag.

"Sure." The counter person took the prescription and went inside the shop.

Maya started looking around the Pharmacy. The various sizes and colors of the medicine bottles and boxes were arranged neatly on the shelves. The shelves were stacked up till the ceiling. Pharmacy guys were busy reading prescriptions of customers and providing them their medicines.

"Here are your medicines." The person across the counter brought Maya's medicines and began preparing the bill.

After payment, Maya came out of the Pharmacy and started walking.

She walked in the same chaos for a few minutes but could not see the corner from where she had turned. She suddenly halted in the middle of the road, full of people, and began looking around for the corner. Her eyes darted everywhere, but she could only see people, shops, hawkers, cabs, bikes, and unfamiliar hoardings.

'I think I'm lost.' Maya thought while repeatedly looking at all the directions. A sudden fear gripped her mind, and she felt a sense of panic. Her heartbeat raised. Her hand frequently touched her sweaty face. Her throat went dry, and her eyes kept desperately looking in all directions for a way out...... While breathing heavily, she fumbled and took the support of the nearby parked car.

*****

"Doctor, it's tough for me to continue without the memories of the last few years. The weight of that dark void in my mind is unbearable." Maya said in a melancholy tone. Her throat narrowed, and her eyes went moist.

She lowered her head. Dr. DeSuza was listening patiently.

"Well, Maya, to be honest, there is no fix solution for your problem. Every person responds differently. As I mentioned earlier to Mrs. Gomes, the best thing for you is to visit those places where you have been in the last seven-eight years. Spend time with the same people who had accompanied you in those places."

Maya's eyes had unfallen tears.

"Don't lose heart, Maya." Dr. DeSuza said in an assuring tone.

"...and Maya, what if you don't have a few years of memories? Life is long. Have a good time with family and friends. Create new memories. "

"Doctor...During the last few years, I formed my identity. Now, I can't remember my friends, education, job, or any of that. I feel my past is empty. Most of all, I don't have any last memories of my Father." Maya's frustration started flowing out through her tears.

Dr. DeSuza offered Maya a glass of water. He waited for a few Maya to let out her emotions.

"Maya..." Dr. DeSuza leaned forward on the table and said softly, "I know this is difficult. Unfortunately, it is what it is. But there is no shortcut for your situation."

Maya got a grip on herself. She reached for a box of paper napkins on the table. She pulled one out and wiped her face, and took a deep breath.

She was again lost in her thoughts for a few minutes. She scratched her throat and began in a dull voice,

"Doctor, getting my memory back is essential to me... not only to provide my innocence against the murder charges but also from a financial one. Mom does not keep well nowadays... she suffers from bronchitis. I am the only breadwinner in my house. I have to do the job. The emptiness of my past is eclipsing me and my family's future."

*****

It was 11 A.M. The sky was covered with dark clouds. Maya was standing in front of Ruby Park's main gate with her brown leather bag pack at her shoulder. She had worn a black skirt and white top. Her hair was tightly tied, in a ponytail, at the back of her head. She was looking at her right for Michael's car to show up.

A couple of hours ago, she had received a phone call from Michael.

"Hello."

"Good morning, Maya...Wow, I can't believe you answered my call. I thought, as usual, you won't pick up." Michael said in an energetic voice.

"Can we meet?" Maya asked in a plain tone.

"Okay."

"Where?"

"We'll decide that later... where and when do you want me to pick you up?"

"11 A.M, I will be standing outside my building's main gate," Maya replied.

The rain began drizzling. Maya holds a red umbrella over her head.

'The best thing for you to visit those places where you had been in the last seven-eight years. Spend time with the same people who had accompanied you in those places' Dr. DeSuza's words were echoing in her mind.

"Beep...! Beeeeep!!"

A car horn came from the left. Maya quickly turned around and saw a white sedan was waiting a few feet away from her. Its wipers were on, so Maya couldn't see the driver's face through the windshield.

Maya came to the car at the passenger-side door and lowered her head. She looked inside through the closed glass window. Michael was in the driver's seat. When Michael saw Maya, he stretched to his left and opened the door from inside.

"Come on... get in." Michael hurried.

Maya closed the umbrella, took her bag off her shoulder, and was about to slip into the car's passenger seat. Suddenly, the rain became heavier. It took her a few seconds to get into the car, but it was enough for the rain to drench her top.

"Where would you like to go, Ma'am?" Michael asked energetically while keeping both his hands on the steering wheel.

Maya thought for a few seconds and said in a low tone, "To our regular eating place?"

"Okay... let's go to Roman's at Bandra Bandstand." Michael put the car in gear and pressed the accelerator.

Michael's car began moving toward Bandra Bandstand on the wet road. Water had collected in countless potholes on the road. When the car happened to go over a series of potholes, it was giving the experience of riding a roller coaster. The car's windshield wipers were oscillating at their maximum speed, but still, the water from heavy rain's splash on the windshield was momentarily blocking the front view. All vehicles were moving slower than their usual speed.

Maya remained quiet during the ride. She folded her hands across her chest and kept looking at the wet outside world with a straight face. She keenly watched the damp buildings, slums, houses, shops, and newly created puddles of muddy ponds pass by.

Michael observed that Maya's top was still wet.

"Shall I turn off the AC?"

"No."

" "
...

"Aren't you feeling cold?"

"No, not really."

"Usually, You feel cold as soon as you get wet."

Maya did not reply. She continued to look outside with a zero expression on her face for a couple of minutes.

"No, I'm not feeling cold at all. Actually, can you please turn up the AC?"

"Turn up? "Michael looked at Maya in surprise.

"It's raining heavily outside, and inside temperature is cool. You may catch a cold." He said.

"Please turn up the AC," Maya said while continuing to look outside.

Michael turned up the AC a bit.

"Did you sleep well last night?" Michael asked.

"Yeah, I slept for some time," Maya said with her eyes glued to the windshield.

"Do you take your medications on time?"

"Yes," Maya's reply was as cold as the car's temperature.

"And..." Michael was about to ask her another question, but Maya hurriedly said,

"Can you please switch on the radio?"

"Sure." Michael pressed the radio's turn-on switch.

Instantly, the car's speakers began emitting a Radio Jockey's enthusiastic and energetic voice. In a few seconds, a famous Bollywood Hindi song started playing. On listening to the initial tune of the song, Michael turned to Maya with a sweet smile on his face.

"This is your favorite song, Maya."

"Can you please turn up the AC more!!" Maya said in an irritated tone.

"Turn it up even further?" Michael asked in an elevated voice.

"I'm burning up inside. Please turn it up." Maya said softly. Michael unwillingly turned up the AC.

' He says this is my favorite song but... but... the tune does not seem to be familiar! Shit! I can't remember a single word of the song. ' Maya irritated.

Maya suddenly leaned forward and turned off the radio. Michael gave her a startled look.

Maya ignored Michael's look. She lowered herself on the seat and closed her eyes.

*****

"Ready to order, Sir?" The waiter politely asked Michael who was going through the laminated pages of the blue-covered menu booklet repeatedly.

"Give us a minute?" Michael said while looking at Maya.

Maya flipped through her copy of the menu booklet and kept it on the table.

"What you would like to eat, Maya?"

"What's the specialty of this restaurant?"

"..." Michael looked at Maya.

"What's the special food of this restaurant?" Maya asked again.

Michael's mind drifted into the past. The romantic, magical moments of their first dinner date flashed in his mind.

"What's the specialty food of this restaurant?" He heard his voice in his ear asking the same question.

'All Italian dishes.' Maya replied without even looking at the menu card.

"Sir, your order, please?" The waiter again asked politely. Michael snapped back to the present.

"Yes...What would you like to have?" Michael asked.

"Anything is fine for me. " Maya said casually. She was observing the hotel's interiors with kids' curiosity. Michael went through the menu book and gave the food order.

"We used to come here regularly, Maya," Michael said gently.

"Can you tell me something more?"

"About what?"

"About the fun we had, about our college days, the picnics, any interesting incidents...." Maya asked in a faint voice while looking straight into Michael's eyes.

Michael smiled. His mind instantly drifted into the past. He started talking passionately about their college days. Maya bent forward, kept both her hands on the table, and listened to him keenly with a blank face.

Michael spoke non-stop. On many occasions, he said, "... then you said..., then you did...then you laughed like..." and followed it up with a small laugh. Maya was tight-lipped, except sometimes she answered with 'Yes' or 'No.'

'Michael is talking continuously about our past incidents, but I'm not able to recollect them.' A thought came into Maya's mind. She suddenly felt nervous. She winched in her chair and continued listening to Michael with a straight face.

*****

The rain had stopped.

Maya and Michael sat on one of the rocks of the Bandra bandstand.

Michael was looking at the seafront. An army of waves continuously crashed on the shore rocks with a thunderous roar.

They sat silently for some time while enjoying the view.

'...the best thing for you is to visit those places where you had been in the last seven-eight years. Spend time with the same people who had accompanied you in those places.' Dr. DeSuza's words were continuously echoing in Maya's mind.

Michael spoke about all the amusing incidents they had shared. He talked about their first meeting, their first date.

"You know, Maya, I remember, when we met for the first time, the weather was exactly like this. The rain had stopped, and a cool fresh breeze was flowing. We were sitting right there." He pointed at one rock to his right. He slowly kept his palm on Maya's palm. Maya instantly felt a flutter in her heart, and it began pounding heavily.

"And this is the same place where we first..." Michael slowly leaned across and brought his face closer to Maya's face. Maya's breathing became heavy. Her face turned ashen. She moved back strongly with tight shoulders. An uneasiness emerged on her face.

"I have to go, Michael." She said in between heavy breaths. She suddenly stood and started walking hurriedly. While walking, she realized that her leg muscles were tightened.

"Maya!" Michael shouted from behind.

A bolt of lightning illuminated the entire surroundings, followed by a loud crack of thunder. Michael looked toward the sky and saw dark clouds had appeared, blown in from the sea.

"Wait, it's going to rain," Michael shouted and followed Maya.

Maya waved hastily to an approaching cab.

"Maya! Maya!" Michael shouted from behind.

Cab stopped.

"Maya! Maya!" Michael called.

Maya did not look at Michel and quickly got in the cab.

"Maya!" Michael again called from behind. He tried to reach the cab, but it drove off speedily. His sad eyes were looking at the Maya's speedily going cab.

*****

Michael came home with dripping wet clothes.

"You are so wet !" Hema exclaimed from the door.

Michael did not reply. He slowly entered the hall and took off his wet shoes and socks.

"You had an umbrella, didn't you?"

"It's okay, Mom," Michael murmured under his breath. With dropped shoulders, he headed toward the bathroom.

"Come to the table. I am waiting for you to have dinner."

Michael turned around in a daze.

"I am not hungry, Mom. Please go ahead and have your dinner." Michael said in a low voice and opened the bathroom door.

"Not hungry?! "Hema turned around in surprise. She sensed the lack of energy in Michael's movements and voice.

"But Michael today..." She began her sentence, and Michael closed the bathroom door.

Hema went into the kitchen, picked up two plates, and arranged them oppositely on the dining table. She kept two half-filled glasses next to each plate.

After a while, Michael came to the kitchen in his pajamas and a t-shirt. He opened the refrigerator and took out a bottle of cold water. While opening the bottle cap, he spotted Hema sitting at the dining table.

"Sit, Michael, eat some food." Hema insisted.

"No, Mom. I am not hungry." Michael said in a sad tone.

"Nothing doing, sit down. Today is your special day." Hema stood and walked toward the kitchen platform.

"Mom. I am really not hungry." Michael urged.

"No... no...sit." Hema insisted again.

Michael sighed deeply. He shook his head, pulled the dining chair, and sat down. Hema lit the stove and put a pot of chicken curry on it.

Soon, the spicy aroma of chicken curry spread all over the kitchen and dining area. Michael dialed Maya's number. He held the mobile to his ear for multiple rings and then disconnected.

Hema served some rice and a bowl of chicken curry on both plates with some salad and pickle. They both ate quietly.

Michael drank some water and was about to stand when Hema stopped him,

"Wait, don't get up... your dinner is not finished yet. Just give me two more minutes." Rita said, and she moved the kitchen platform.

"What now, Mom? I ate, forcefully, because of you." Michael irritated. He sighed and walked toward the window.

Michael slid open the sliding window. A sea breeze blew across his face. He felt slightly better.

He looked toward the horizon. At the horizon, the arabian sea was hiding behind the curtain of darkness.

Captivated by his chain of thoughts, Michael tilted slightly. His eyes caught a glimpse of a yellow dotted line. It was pole lights on the magnificent Bandra-Worli sea-link bridge.

"Michael, come inside," Hema called.

In the hall, Hema was standing behind a small glass-covered teapoy. A round chocolate cake was on the table. Michael read the letters, written in icing, on the cake, and he froze on the spot. A chill traveled through his body.

' Happy Birthday, Michael!' Hema said cheerfully.

"Oh! I forgot my birthday." He murmured and looked at Hema in disbelief.

"In the morning, I didn't even realize when you left. I tried to call you, but you did not answer any of my calls." Hema complained sweetly; a broad happy smile was on her lips.

"Oh... Mom." Michael came to Hema and gave her a hug.

Michael cut the cake. Hema fed him a small piece of it.

Michael again went back to the window. While eating the cake, he took a deep breath and kept looking at the dark horizon.

*****

5
Chapter 5

Mrs. Pinto's murder case befell Judge Mathew's courtroom for the hearing.

"Your Honor, the deceased victim, Mrs. Jean Pinto, is a 55-year-old female . " the public prosecutor, Advocate Patil, started his opening statement in the courtroom. He was a half-bald fat man of medium height and dark complexion, in his early fifties.

On his right table, Maya's lawyer, Advocate Deshpande, was sitting in his black robe. He was a fair, tall, and slim man in his early forties. He was wearing thin frame spectacles on his bright eyes.

Judge Mathew was seated in his judge chair in a black robe. He had thick-framed glasses on his eyes. His old expressionless face was a mixture of seriousness and strictness.

"Your honor, the accused, Miss Maya Gomes, did not have good relations with Mrs. Pinto, her boss. Mrs. Pinto's dead body was found in Miss Maya's cubicle." public prosecutor passed the photographs of Mrs. Pinto's dead body to Judge Mathew, who glanced at it with an impassive face.

"These are the log records of the swapping system from Miss Maya's office system." The public prosecutor passed the log records to Judge Mathew.

"It clearly shows that on June 15th this year, Miss Maya was the last person to leave the office...We have also found a bracelet near Mrs. Pinto's body. Your Honor, Miss Maya has already acknowledged that the bracelet was hers." Two photographs, one with extreme close-ups of the bracelet and the other showing Mrs. Pinto's body's along with the bracelet , were forwarded to Judge Mathew.

Judge Mathew carefully examined the photographs and log records.

"With your permission, your Honor, I would like to cross-examine Miss Maya." Advocate Patil pointed at Maya, who was sitting with Michael and Rita in the courtroom. Inspector Jadhav, in his uniform, was also present in the courtroom.

Judge Mathew looked at Maya for a moment. Maya looked at Judge momentarily and instantly crossed and uncrossed her legs.

"Your Honor, before you permit for Miss Maya's cross-examination, Please take a look at Miss Maya's medical reports from court-appointed Doctors." Advocate Deshpande passed a large brown colored envelope to Judge Mathew.

"Miss Maya had met with a road accident, and now she is suffering from memory loss. She also suffers from hallucinations from time to time. So at present, she is not in good mental state for any cross-examination." Advocate Deshpande made his point.

After reading the report carefully, Judge Mathew looked at Advocate Deshpande. and said in his authoritative voice,

"It seems Miss Maya is not in a mental state for cross-examination. If Miss Maya can't go through the cross-examination, you have to prove her innocence. You need to present the evidence of her innocence in this court."

"Yes, your Honor, if you give us some time, We will certainly produce evidence of Miss Maya's innocence in this court."

"You have four weeks to provide the evidence to the court. During these four weeks, Miss Maya may not leave the city without permission." Judge Mathew struck his gavel on the sound block and stood to leave.

The entire courtroom stood as respect for Judge Mathew.

*****

"We are lucky. Judge Mathew has given us four weeks. " Advocate Deshpande said pleasantly to Michael. Rita and Maya were following Advocate Deshpande and Michael. Maya was wiping her forehead sweat from her little handkerchief. Her mouth was dry, and she was feeling empty in the pit of her stomach.

"At present, all the evidences are against you. But we must acquire and submit the evidence of Maya's innocence to the court. " Advocate Deshpande said excitedly.

"Evidence can lead to illusionary reality. Actual facts could be different." Michael said.

"Maya has not done anything wrong." Rita's anxious voice came from behind. Advocate Deshpande stopped for a moment. All halted with him.

"That's what we all know, but the court needs evidence of Maya's innocence." Advocate Deshpande said and resumed his walk.

"But how to get the evidence ?" Michael asked.

They all came out of the court building and began walking toward the court's main gate through the court premises.

"Bring the car. I am outside the main gate." Advocate Deshpande ordered on the phone.

While keeping mobile back into his coat's pocket, he said with a serious face,

"Get me something; otherwise, the verdict will definitely go against Maya. She will be sent to jail for a long time." Rita and Michael looked at each other with stunned faces. Maya did not react. Her blank eyes were taking a long gaze at the down of the road.

Suddenly, a posh car arrived and stopped in front of advocate Deshpande. The driver came out hurriedly and opened the passenger door for the advocate.

"I have to go now." Advocate Deshpande said, and he got in the car. The driver closed the door and hurriedly walked toward the driver door. The black glasses of the passenger seat window rolled down.

"Call me if you find something." Advocate Deshpande said through the window.

"Yes, Sir!" Michael and Rita nodded. Maya's eyes were still gazing toward the end of the road.

The window's black glasses rolled up, and the car sped off.

A small wave of dust passed through the gloomy faces of Rita and Michael.

*****

Maya took out her university books from her wardrobe and spread them all over the bed. The books were of different shapes and sizes.

While sipping her morning coffee, She picked one book and turned to its first page.

Letters, 'Maya Gomes, First Year.' were written in blue ink on the upper right corner of the page in neat handwriting.

She began flipping through the pages. She occasionally stopped to look at pictures and diagrams from the pages. It took her a few minutes to go through the entire book.

Maya picked up another book and read its title. She turned to the first page, and here too, she saw her name was written neatly in blue ink on the upper right corner of the page. Maya went through the entire book and kept it aside.

She repeated the same for a few more books.

'Oh! Nothing looks familiar.' She murmured in a broken voice with a lost stare at the books. A mixed feeling of sorrow and annoyance emerged on her face.

'I have studied these books! But now, I don't remember anything. Not a single title, not a single book, not a single page.' She felt the hollowness in her heavy chest. Her eyes welled up, and tears trickled out.

A few moments passed, and her mobile rang. She sighed. She wiped the wet tear line from her face and answered the phone.

"Hey, What's up?"

"Nothing. Sarah, Do you really think I have been involved in Mrs. Pinto's murder?"

"Of course not, Maya!" Sarah almost shouted.

"But mom was saying all the evidences are against me."

"Yeah, I know. I am sure somebody has framed you."

"Who, Sarah? Who? Who framed me?" Maya asked in a severe tone.

"I don't know, Maya...Before your accident, you received calls from one mysterious caller?"

"Mysterious caller?" Maya's voice raised.

"Yeah, Michael told me that one mysterious caller called you twice and claimed he had evidence of your innocence."

"Really? " Maya startled.

"Yes !"

"Then where are the evidence ?"

"Michael said both the times you got the evidence, but you could not hold it."

"Oh! but why ? why I could hold on to such important evidence? What happened?" Maya asked in disbelief.

"Not sure, Maya. But did that Mysterious caller call you again after your accident?" Sarah asked.

"No. But who was that Mysterious caller ?" Maya asked in an urgent tone.

"No Idea, Maya,"

Maya suddenly disconnected the call.

"Think...think ..who called? ..think..think..think.." Maya held both the palms tightly on her head and tried to remember. But she couldn't.

"Shit.Shit...I don't remember about that mysterious caller as well. " She irritated. She jumped multiple times on the spot and moved desperately throughout the room. She was breathing heavily.

After a few minutes, She took a deep breath and sat down on the bed, still steaming inside. While thinking, she desperately bit her fingernails.

"How can I don't remember anything? I desperately need evidence to prove my innocence...But bloody my dam memory. It's not giving me any answer." She shouted angrily at herself. She kicked the wardrobe door intensely. In the rage, she picked one thick book from the bed and threw it at her dressing table mirror.

Mirror shattered.

Breathing heavily, she kept looking at her multiple images in the cracked mirror.

*****

"Hello, Michael ?" Sarah called Michael.

"Yeah, Sarah," Michael answered.

"Remember, You were telling about a caller who had called Maya."

"Yes, He mentioned that he has evidence of Maya's innocence, and he wanted it to give Maya."

"I checked with Maya, and that caller has not called her after her accident. Why did he suddenly stop calling Maya?" Sarah wondered.

"Not sure...and since he delivered the package, he knew Maya's home address too," Michael said thoughtfully.

"Yeah, so who could he or she be? a school, college, or neighborhood friend?" Sarah asked.

"Or maybe a colleague from the office?"

"Yes, could be." Sarah nodded.

A few thoughtful seconds passed, and Michael said in a conclusive tone,

"Okay, I will check with her friends, and you check with our office colleagues."

*****

Maya... Maya... Maya." Maya heard the voice in her sleep. She partially opened her eyes but could not see anything.

Her eyes remained open for a few seconds but slowly closed again.

*****

"Maya... Maya... Maya." Maya heard the voices again in her sleep. She opened her eyes. This time she saw a faint figure sitting on the chair in front of her bed.

"Oh... it's Bhagat's ghost again..." Shiver went through Maya's spine. Sleep in her eyes vanished instantly.

"Maya... you must leave my land," Bhagat said furiously. Maya missed the heartbeat. She tried to get up from bed, but she felt her legs were deadened.

"Maya... you must leave my land. I am not going to spare you. "Bhagat glowered with bulged eyes. Maya could sense the rage in his tone. He was furious.

Maya tried to get up from her bed, but she realized she couldn't. The fear had taken control of her body.

"You are going to die painfully, like me, Maya, and I will enjoy you seeing dying. Ha..Ha..Ha...Ha," Bhagat grinned viciously and stood from his chair.

"aaaahh..aaahhhh." Maya used all her strength to stand from the bed, but she tripped and fell on the floor.

"Ha... Ha... Ha..." Bhagat laughed again and advanced toward Maya.

"No .. Don't come close to me," Maya yelled. With a wicked smile on his face, Bhagat inched toward Maya and raised his bloody hand.

"Nooooo..No...go away," Maya screamed. Her shouting gave her energy, and she stood on her feet. Her body was still shivering and sweating in fear.

Bhagat raised his hand again and was about to touch Maya when she again groaned in fear,

"No...No...No.." and ran out of the room.

*****

At 2 PM, the sky was still wearing a blanket of black clouds. In the drizzling rain, Maya was standing at Ruby Park's main gate with an umbrella overhead.

Soon, Michael's car arrived and stopped in front of Maya. Sarah was sitting in the passenger seat.

Sarah rolled down the windows and said,

"Maya, get in."

Maya got into the back seat. Michael started the car.

"Where are we going, Sarah?"

"To one of your co-worker's house. He is having good working relations with you." Sarah answered while looking through the windshield.

"Co-worker's house? Who is it?" Maya looked forward and asked curiously.

"Sam! Do you remember him?" Sarah asked.

"No!"

A few minutes passed in silence.

"Why are we going to Sam's place?" Maya suddenly asked.

Sarah and Michael looked at each other.

"Sarah? Why are we going to Sam's place?" Maya asked again. Wrinkles formed on her forehead.

"Sam resigned from the company, all of a sudden, and left a note on my desk." Sarah momentarily looked back at Maya.

"Note? What note?" Maya became curious.

"The note said...Come to my house this afternoon to learn about Maya's innocence. I will be leaving the city this evening...and one address was written on the bottom."

"Okay, but why did he leave the note on your desk?" Maya was confused.

"That's exactly what I am thinking, too. He works in a different department. I don't know him that well." Sarah said with a thoughtful face.

Michael turned around for a moment and said, "So, we think... he may be your mystery caller."

'Mystery caller?' Maya thought. "You mean, it was Sam who called me twice to give the evidence of my innocence?"

"Uhhh...Maybe .." Sarah and Michael nodded at the same time.

After a ten-minute drive, the car stopped near an old, two-story building in a quiet locality of Worli.

The sky grew darker. It turned the afternoon into the evening. The rain had raised its speed.

"This building looks old...very old. Are you sure Sam lives here?" Maya asked while looking skeptically at the building.

"This is the address mentioned in his note," Sarah said while getting down from the car. Maya, too, came out of the car.

Michael had already started walking toward the buildings' main gate. Both the girls followed Michael with umbrellas on their heads.

They walked a few steps into the building premises and entered the building.

All three began climbing staircases carefully in the dusk.

"It's too dark here, Sarah. I can' see clearly. Can you stroll? "Maya said tensely.

"Sure..." Sarah slowed down.

They climbed the staircase and reached the 2nd floor. There were four main doors on the floor. Sarah looked at her paper note and pointed toward one of the doors.

Michael rang the doorbell.

Sam, an average height and body man in his late twenties, opened the door. His right hand was in a cast. He was wearing pajamas, a sleeveless t-shirt, and a white, cotton, half-shirt through which his cast hand was sticking out.

"Come in." Sam looked at them, one at a time, and went inside.

All the three followed him into his apartment. They entered the dimly lit hall. There were clothes, books, shoes, and other items scattered everywhere on the floor. Maya noticed a small chessboard with all its pieces neatly arranged at both ends on the small table at the corner.

"Sit," Sam said.

Maya and Sarah sat on a couch while Michael took a chair. Sarah noticed a big travel suitcase lying open at another corner of the floor. It was partially filled with stuff.

"Sorry for the mess." Sam apologized. He picked up one shirt from the floor, rolled it up, and dumped it in the suitcase.

"Do you want anything? Water?" Sam asked Sarah while picking up another shirt from the floor.

"No, thanks. We are good." Sarah said.

"How are you Maya?" Sam asked politely to Maya. First, Maya did not reply. She was lost in her thoughts.

"May ?! "Sam asked again.
Maya looked at him with an unknown face.

"I asked How are you?

"I am Okay.." Maya murmured.

"Okay..." Sam sighed. He continued with the packing of his stuff.

A couple of minutes passed by in awkward silence.

"Sam, You mentioned in your note that you know what we are looking for?" Sarah asked while leaning forward. Maya's eyes were continuously staring at Sam's face.

Sam took a deep breath and said, "Yeah...I know everything." He continued dumping clothes into the suitcase more intensely.

"Sam, can you switch on the tube light, please?" Michael asked.

"Sure.." Sam switched on the light. The room bathed in white light.

"What happened to your face, Sam?" Michael asked while looking at a reddish swelling on his face.

"Don't worry about it." Sam sighed sadly and let out a half-sad laugh.

"Tell us, Sam, what do you know?" Sarah asked again.

Sam stopped throwing clothes into his suitcase and sat on the floor. Sudden anguish appeared all over his face.

"I sent her the evidence of her innocence, twice." Sam pointed toward Maya. "But this she could not collect it in time on both occasions." He sighed deeply.
Maya was looking at him with a void face.

"I was with her during the first incident," Michael said.

"We saw the brown envelope in the letterbox, but before we could get it out, Maya went into hallucination mode. Later in the evening, we returned to the letterbox, but that envelope was gone."

"Yeah, that's bad luck," Sam said sadly.

"What was in that envelop?" Sarah asked.

"A photo of Mrs. Pinto's murder in a pen drive," Sam said in a plain tone.

"Oh no! We missed a critical piece of evidence." Michael said excitingly while looking at Sarah and Maya.

"Yeah." Sam picked up one of his shoes, lying nearby, and flung it to the other side of the room.

"I gave her required evidence by risking my life. The only thing she had to do was to collect it and give it to the Police, but she couldn't even do that." Sam threw the other shoe.

The room slipped into an uneasy silence.

"Sorry, Sam. We really appreciate your help, but we don't know what happened to me because of which I could not get hold of that evidence." Maya lowered her head and said in a sad tone.

"Maya had met with an accident some time ago. She is currently under treatment to recover from her memory loss." Sarah said.

"Yeah, I know that, and I realized she hasn't got the second packet," Sam said.

"Then why did you not deliver another packet?" Michael asked.

Sam stared at Michael's face for a few seconds.

"Before I could deliver another packet, my originals were gone. "

"Originals were gone?"

"Yes."

"Who took them ?"

"Same guy who murdered Mrs. Pinto. I shouldn't have helped you. Now my life is in danger." Sam continued to glower.

"Who is after your life?" Michael asked. Suddenly, Sam's confident posture melted. A fear emerged in his eyes. While wiping his forehead's sweat through this palm, he said,

"The same guy who murdered Mrs. Pinto."

"Who murdered Mrs. Pinto?" Sarah asked intently.

"You know him,"

"We know him? Who is it?" Sarah asked eagerly. Maya was continuously observing Sam with a blank face.

Sam did not reply. He took a deep breath and was lost in thoughts for a few moments.

"What is the name of that guy, Sam?" Sarah asked again.

Sarah's words did not stop Sam's thought machine. He remained seated quietly.

"Tell us, Sam, who is that person?" Michael asked eagerly.

Sam took a deep breath and said in an elevated tone,

"His name is Roy,"

"Roy? Roy smith from our company?"

"Yes!" Sam replied confidently.

"Yeah? But why would he kill Mrs. Pinto? "Sarah asked.

"That I don't know. But I had his photos murdering Mrs. Pinto. It's clear, Roy did it!" Sam said confidentially. He stood up and continued packing his suitcase with one hand.

"But why you did not reveal his name to the Police?" Michael asked.

"I don't want to get involved with the Police," Sam replied in a plain tone.

"But you still revealed Roy's name to us? Why?" Sarah asked after a thoughtful pause.

"Because..." Sam stopped packing for a moment and sat down on a chair.

"Because... he cheated with me."

"Cheated with you?! How?" Sarah asked.

"He and I were working on one software idea. Our agreement was that I would develop the prototype software, and he would find clients to sell."

"Then?"

"I worked day and night for six months and created a nice working software...I did my job...but" Sam stood from his chair and poured some water in a glass.

"...but what?" Maya asked.

"...but without informing me, that bastard Roy secretly sold the idea to another company and pocketed all the money." Sam threw the glass of water against the wall. His body was shaking with anger. He was furious.

"What you did then?" Sarah asked.

"I did not say anything to him or show my anger to him. I just waited for the right moment to hit him back, and that moment came soon when he called me one day. He was outraged at Mrs. Pinto. She was stopping his promotion for the last three years. Roy is a very ambitious and, at the same time, extremely hot-tempered and greedy guy. He will go to any extent to get his goal. I knew Roy was up to something against Mrs. Pinto. So I was keeping an eye on him and Mrs. Pinto. That night when he murdered Mrs. Pinto, I took its photos while I was hiding."

"So, to take revenge on him, you took the photos and sent them to Maya so she would give them to the police?" Michael connected the dots.

"Yes." Sam nodded.

"Do you have another copy of the photos ?" Sarah asked. Sam looked at her and smiled sadly.

"I wish I did. As I told you, Roy took my originals."

"How did Roy come to know about originals?" Sarah asked.

"Roy is a cunning fox. He has contacts with goons. I don't know how, but he came to know that I had photos of him murdering Mrs. Pinto. Two days ago, four goons came here and beat me and fractured on my hand. They took the original photos at gunpoint. They destroyed my laptop and my phone." Sam showed wounds on his face and his hand in a cast.

"Oh no!" All were stunned.

After a couple of minutes, Sam sighed and said,

"I am not safe here. I have decided to leave this city." He walked to his bedroom with drooped shoulders. While closing the bedroom door, he said,

"You guys can leave, now., You, too, are not safe here. Good luck with everything."

*****

Michael, Sarah, and Maya returned to the car. All three were in their own web of thoughts.

The rain had intensified into a deluge. The car's windshield and windows glasses lost their visibility.

Finally, Michael broke the silence.

"I came to know Roy quit his job just after the incident at the office." He said thoughtfully.

"So, Is it Roy who is behind the murder of Mrs. Pinto?" Sarah asked eagerly.

"..." Michael did not reply. He was deep in his thoughts.

"Maya, Do you remember any suspicious or odd activity from Roy or anyone else from our office?" Sarah asked.

"No, I don't remember anything." Maya shook her head.

A few more seconds passed pensively.

"But we even don't know Roy's whereabouts," Michael said.

"I know. Roy is in Mumbai only. Now, take a wild guess which company he works for?" Sarah asked.

"Not sure..." Michael thought for a few seconds and said with a lost face.

"Our competitor, HSDTecSoft !"

"What? HSDTecSoft?" Michael was shocked. "..hmmm.. isn't it too much of a coincidence?" He wondered.

"Ohhh, yeah!" Sarah said, and she quickly dialed Kapoor's number,

"Sir, we just found out from Sam that Roy was the one who murdered Mrs. Pinto."

"Who? Roy Smith ?!" Kapoor's voice was full of surprise.

"Yes!"

"He had the photos of Roy murdering Mrs. Pinto as evidence."

"Where are those photographs now?" Kapoor asked eagerly.

"Unfortunately, it's all gone, Sir."

"What you mean gone?"

"Before Maya could get it, they were lost."

"Do we have copies of those photographs?"

"No, Sir..."

"Do we have any other evidence?"

"After resigning from our company , he immediately joined our competitor HSDTecSoft."

"But that's not the evidence. Do we have any other evidence?"

"..."

"Sarah?"

"No, Sir, but we are sure it's Roy who did all this."

"Maybe, but without any evidence, we can't do anything here." Kapoor disconnected the call. While keeping her phone in her bag, Sarah said drily,

"Kapoor Sir won't agree. Like the Police, he needs the evidence."

"Then, the only option is to find evidence against Roy," Michael concluded.

"Yeah." Sarah agreed.

"Let's find the evidence then." He said in an elevated tone and started the car.

*****

Maya and Sarah took a Mumbai suburban railway train and got off at Charni Road station around 10 A.M.

After walking for about fifteen minutes from the station, they reached a lime-colored stony building.

" Any clue about this building ?" Sarah asked while looking at the building.

Maya looked at the building with a slack face. Her eyes slowly scanned the building from the bottom to the top. She read the words carved on the stone arch above the gate.

'Looks like some college.' She realized.

"Ringing any bells?" Sarah looked at Maya in anticipation.

Maya shook her head.

"This is our college. We studied here. Come on, let's go in." Sarah said excitingly and headed toward the gate.

Maya surprised. She hurriedly followed Sarah through the gate and asked,

"But why are we here?"

"Today is our batch's alumni function. We will meet our batch mates." Sarah continued walking in excitement.

"Oh!" Maya said in a low voice and bit her lower lip. She halted and stood like a statue. She thought for a few seconds and again caught up Sarah from her back and stopped her.

"Sarah, I don't think I should be here," Maya said in a low voice.

"Why not?" Sarah halted and turned to Maya. A mixture of surprise and confusion was on her face.

"Sarah, I'll not be able to recognize our friends," Maya said anxiously with a sad face.

"Don't worry. Just Keep smiling." Sarah answered and resumed her walking.

They both went inside and came to a big central square surrounded by three-story buildings. Maya turned around slowly, in a circle, and saw long balconies on each floor. Maya felt like she was at the bottom of a big, square-shaped well.

Suddenly, a loud sound came through speaker. Maya looked in the sound direction and saw a temporary stage at one end of the central square. Lots of chairs were arranged in front of it. All the chairs were occupied by alumni students. The speaker was delivering a speech on a microphone, but all were looking, finding, and greeting their old friends. There were cheers of surprise, shouting, laughter and hugs all around. Many were busy with their selfie photo sessions. The atmosphere was energetic and full of joy and pleasure.

Maya sat in the crowd along with Sarah. Occasionally she was scrapping her hand through her hair. She smiled and waved back, who called her. Many of them came and spoke to her in person. She kept smiling but did not maintain eye contact.

Soon, Maya became bored. She saw Sarah was busy with other friends. She looked for the exit and came out of function. While walking toward the staircases, she glanced above at the balconies.

"These long balconies look strange." She murmured.

Maya began roaming everywhere in the college with the curiosity of a child. She went into many empty classrooms. She visited the computer labs, the physics, chemistry labs, the library, and finally, the cafeteria.

'Ahh..nothing looks familiar !' Maya descended the staircases with a broken heart. Her shoulders were dropped. She took a deep breath and sat down on the staircases with the lost face. Her ears could hear the noise, shouting, cheers, and clappings from alumni function, but she did not raise her head. She remained seated with her head down.

*****

After the function, Maya and Sarah headed to Girgaon Chowpatty. A 'Chowpatty' is a local word, means a beach.

They walked for fifteen minutes. As they came near the beach, Maya smelt the salty air.

'Oh. This smell seems familiar.' Maya's nose took in some whiffs of the familiar air.

'When have I smelt this before?' Maya thought hard but could not recollect it.

'Hmm... just another thing that I cannot remember.' She sighed deeply.

In a few minutes, they reached the beach.

The magnificent Arabian sea was spread in front of them in its glory. A wind was blowing from the sea inland. The high tide had rolled in, and the waves were close to the shore.

Maya and Sarah took off their sandals and carried them in their hands. They began walking on the beach's warm sand parallel to the waves. Waves were close enough to caress their feet. Their hair was blowing in the wind and invariably kissing their faces.

Sarah was constantly talking, and Maya was walking beside her with a blank face. She was continuously biting her fingernails. A part of Maya's mind was listening to Sarah, and another part was busy in her webs of thoughts.

After some time, tired, Maya and Sarah walked to the food court. They cleaned the stuck sand particles from their wet feet and sat down in front of a food stall.

"Two pani-puris," Sarah ordered.

Puri was a lemon-sized, deep-fried bread, hollow on the inside and crisp outside. The vendor stuffed it with a mixture of chili, spiced mashed potato, and onions. He then added some tamarind and mint flavored water and served them one puri each in a bowl.

After eating the pani-puri, Sarah did some clicking on her mobile phone's screen and showed it to Maya. Maya looked at the phone carefully and shouted in surprise,

"Oh! It seems these photos were taken on this same beach."

Sarah nodded with a broad smile on her face. The photos had been taken during their college days on the same beach.

Suddenly, Maya's face dropped.

"It is the same beach, but I don't remember it," Maya murmured. She kept looking at the photo carefully and at her surroundings, again and again.

*****

The Sun had begun inching toward the horizon in preparation for its immersion into the sea. A glorious mixture of bright yellow, red, orange, and gold colors filled the sky, marking the advent of a remarkable sunset.

Maya looked to her left at Marine Drive. The drive is around two and a half miles long, a multi-lane bidirectional road shaped like two-thirds of an oval. Its broad pavement runs parallel to the sea with a small platform at its edge to sit and enjoy the seafront view. In bright yellow streetlights in the night, Marine Drive resembles a string of pearls like a necklace.

"Do you think Roy has murdered Mrs. Pinto ?" Maya abruptly asked Sarah while staring at the golden horizon.

"Yes, Sam had the hard evidence against Roy," Sarah said confidently.

"But we do not have the evidence now. Shall I ever able to get new evidence against Roy and prove my innocence?" Maya asked in a low tone.

"Of course, Maya, You will."

"If I can't produce the evidence, the judge will rule decision against me." Deep concern emerged on Maya's face.

"Don't worry, we will find evidence of your innocence," Sarah said encouragingly.

A few more minutes passed in silence.

"Thanks for everything, Sarah. " Maya said in a soft tone.

"What for Maya?" Sarah shrugged her shoulder.

Maya smiled sadly at Sarah and again lost in thoughts. She looked with a straight face at sea. Her mind was occupied with more shaded thoughts than the different color shades at the horizon.

The Sun's daily journey across the sky finally came to an end.

Maya was still lost in her mesh of thoughts while staring at the golden horizon.

She took a calming breath. Her pupils were dilated. Her mind's horizon of thoughts was becoming darker and darker.

"I have...I have...another problem.....M..my..last few years...mem..memory is lost. I'm not sure if I'll ever get my memory ba.. back," Maya stammered. Her eyes were still focused on the horizon.

Sarah's eyes were glued at the waves. While watching the golden water, she said,

"Our mind too is like the sea, Maya. It takes in whatever stimuli our senses provide it with and preserves them in the form of memories. I am sure you will get your memories back." Sarah said in an optimistic tone.

Sarah's encoring words did not have much effect on Maya. She continued staring at the horizon with a sad face.

*****

The darkness of midnight had engulfed the forest. Every barren tree's skeletal silhouettes appeared monstrous and scary. Wolves were howling in the distance, and a dense fog played around with the night darkness.

Maya was running in the dense dark forest. She was breathing heavily. A white mist was leaving her mouth with every breath, as though the life force was leaving her body. The frightening blend of all-enveloping darkness, mysterious fog, and the blood-curdling howls of wolves were sending shivers down in her spine. While running, Maya continuously looked behind to ensure she wasn't being followed.

While looking back, she spotted a faint figure in the darkened void on one occasion. She stopped momentarily to have a better look at the figure.

As the figure grew more apparent, Maya's heart began racing at a frenetic pace. With each passing second, the figure gained ground.

Maya saw a man dressed in a blood-stained white shirt and white pants.

'White shirt, white pants, bloodstains.... Oh...my God. It's Bhagat's ghost!'

Maya's body began shivering. Her heartbeat went off the charts. Fear began crushing her from all sides. She mustered all her strength and took off with full speed. She resumed her desperate run in the darkness.

At one point, she hurdled, tripped on a stone, and went tumbling to the ground.

"Ah... a... AAAA!!!" Maya's scream cut through the night. With closed eyes, she took a few quick breaths.

She slowly opened her eyes and...

"..." The scream was stuck in her throat.

Bhagat was standing a few feet away.

"Hee, Hee...Hee..." Bhagat laughed. Maya's entire body was paralyzed with fear. She tried to stand up, but her legs were shaking.

"Where will you go now, Maya? I already told you to leave my land, but you did not pay heed to my warning." Maya saw the anger on Bhagat's black face. While he was speaking, she could see his red tongue in his bloody red mouth.

"Go away! Go away!!" Maya shouted. She tried to run with her shaky legs but could not move further. Bhagat overtook her and came in front with his arms spread wide. Maya halted in her tracks.

"GO AWAY, LEAVE ME ALONE!!" Maya yelled. Bhagat slowly began inching toward her.

Maya turned around and ran in the reverse direction as fast as possible. She was running through without looking back.

After running desperately for a while, Maya stopped. There was an old stone wall in front of her. While breathing heavily, Maya scanned the wall from the bottom to the top.

'This wall is too tall... I can't climb over it.' Maya thought while gasping for breath. Her eyes were full of fear. She turned back and saw Bhagat at a distance.

'Oh, No! Bhagat will corner me here.' Maya realized.

The breathlessness, along with a racing heart, were keeping Maya away from acting. She just stood there in shock and kept watching Bhagat.

When Bhagat came near, Suddenly, Maya grew furious. She picked up a stone from the ground and strongly flung it at him.

The stone found its mark. It hit Bhagat's forehead, and he stopped for a moment. Maya felt confident. She threw more stones at him.

"Ahhh... ahhh..." Bhagat moaned in pain and sat down on the ground. Maya runs past him. While running, she gave him a look and found him on the ground wincing in pain.

As she got further away, Bhagat's moaning turned fainter and fainter.

Maya continued to run while panting without looking back.

Suddenly, she heard her name.

"Maya... Maya...!"

The sound was coming from all directions through the surrounding darkness.

"Maya... Maya...!"

She saw a door in front of her.

"Maya... Maya...!" She again heard the voice

'Let me get in there.' She thought. She pushed the door inward and dashed in.

*****

Rita was in the kitchen near the burner. As she heard a loud sound from Maya's room, she rushed to Maya's room. She saw Maya was in one corner of the room & throwing books and other items everywhere.

"Maya... Maya..." Rita ran inside and tried to control Maya, but her feet scraped against the broken pieces of a coffee mug.

"Maya... Maya..." Rita shouted at Maya, but she was not in a state to listen. She rushed toward the bathroom and stopped in front of its door.

Maya stared at the door with a dazed look on her face for a few seconds. She pushed the door inward and dashed in. Rita ran toward the bathroom, but Maya closed the door on her face.

"Maya... Maya..." Rita kept banging on the door hard.
*****

Maya wondered the whole day in the city. She caught the suburban train from 'Mumbai Central' station and got down at 'Dadar' station. She changed the lines and caught another train for 'Ghatkopar.' She changed the platforms and came on the Metro train platform.

She waited for the train for a few minutes on the elevated platform of the metro train.

The train came at high speed. Automated doors opened obediently. Maya got into one of the narrow compartments and preferred to stand near the door. The automated doors closed.

The train started.

Maya began watching Mumbai's suburban life from elevation with a straight face. The train passed in front of residential buildings, commercial complexes, over the slums, shops, roads, and other establishments.

After some time, Maya's train ride ended at the train's last stop, 'Versova.'

Maya descended the platform staircases and arrived at an open space where autos were lined in the queue.

Auto Rickshaws are the small public transport vehicle, shortly known as 'autos' in Mumbai. It is a three-wheeled scooter with a metal body covered with a canvas roof. It has slide curtains and has a small driver cabin with handlebar control. At the back of the driver's cabin, there is a passenger seat that can accommodate three passengers.

"Romans, Bandra Bandstand" Maya sat on the passenger seat of the first auto in the queue and instructed the driver. The driver turned on the fare meter. The meter displayed the minimum fair in bright red digital numbers.

As the meter displayed the fare, the driver changed the hand gear located at the left of the handlebar. Then he raised the accelerator from the right of the handlebar.

The auto engine made its typical "Groom..Groom" sound, and the auto was on its way to Bandra Bandstand.

*****

After around an hour's drive in the traffic, Maya's auto stopped in front of 'Romans' at the Bandra bandstand.

"How many people, Ma'am?" As Maya walked in, a well-dressed waiter came forward and asked politely.

"One."

"Just one?"

"Yes."

"Please follow me."

The waiter took Maya to a corner table for two.

'This is the same table where Michael and I were dinned last time.' Maya recalled.

She hung her bag on the side of the chair's backrest and sat down on the chair.

"Ma'am, mineral water or regular?"

"Mineral, thanks." Maya dabbed the sweat on her forehead from tissue. She looked around for the AC vent and found it was just behind her.

The tables were empty. Waiters were waiting on the floor to receive the guests. Many of them were talking with each other in low voices. The light music in the background, along with pleasant yellow lighting were, enhancing the ambiance of the floor.

The waiter returned with a glass of water in one hand and a menu card in the other. Maya immediately picked the glass of water and gulped down the aqua.

The waiter stood patiently with the menu in his hand. After Maya had put the glass back down on the table, he offered her the menu card. Maya began flipping its pages.

'Everything is so expensive here.' Maya thought and kept the menu card back on the table.

The waiter looked at Maya in anticipation.

"One black coffee, please."

"Okay, and anything to eat?"

"That'll be all."

"Only coffee?" The waiter asked again.

"Yes."

"Okay." He shrugged his shoulders, picked up the menu, and went toward the kitchen.

'Michael said we used to often come here to eat... hmmm. If we came that regularly, I should have some sort of recollection.... But it all looks new to me.' Maya began observing the hotel carefully with a blank face.

She closely watched the interior of the hotel for a few minutes.

"Ma'am, your coffee." The waiter put the cup of coffee on the table.

While lost in her web of thoughts, Maya relished the coffee, sip after sip.

"Anything else, Ma'am?" Waiter asked politely.

"Not for the moment. I will let you know." Maya replied.

She took out her mobile and checked her's and Michael's photos of their earlier dates at Roman's.

Maya looked at every photo and looked keenly around the hotel's interior.

'The interior looks to be the same. It doesn't changed much in all these years, yet these photos look unfamiliar.' Maya murmured.

The tables at Roman's began filling up.

In the two hours, the waiter returned multiple times from Maya's table, and each time got an order for another coffee.

Maya looked at the photo repeatedly. She could sense the din of conversation around her, but she kept looking at the photos again and again.

'Damn, I can't remember anything. I came here and spent hours in the hope that something might trigger... but all I have now is a coffee high.' Maya irritated herself.

The waiter came again. He stood in front of her table and looked nervously at the empty cup of coffee.

"Ma'am, it's been almost three hours since you are here. Would you like to order something to eat?" He asked politely.

"No, thank you," Maya replied and her mobile rang. It rang multiple times, but Maya did not realize it.

"Ma'am, your mobile is ringing," the waiter returned and pointed to her bag.

"Oh, yeah..." Maya snapped out of her thoughts and replied guiltily.

"Hi, Sarah...Sarah?...Sarah?...Hello...Hello?"

Maya stood and moved around to find a robust network.

"Hello, hello, Sarah? Can you hear me now?... Okay. Good. Tell me... I'm at Roman's... I came here in...." Maya began talking.

"Is that lady ready to be billed?" The hotel's manager looked at Maya strangely and asked the waiter.

"No, sir." The waiter murmured.

"What she had so far? "The manager looked at the empty coffee cup and Maya's table.

"Five cups of coffee."

"Only coffee?"

"Yes, Sir, so far, She has ordered only five cups of coffee."

The manager glared at Maya from head to toe. He observed Maya had worn a red shoe on one foot and dark green on the other.

"She seems to have her screws loose. Give her the bill and get rid of her." The manager instructed the waiter.

After a few minutes, Maya finished her call. While walking toward her table, she saw one couple seated at her table. Her eyes began looking for the waiter.

"Ma'am, your bag and your bill." The waiter came from behind and handed over her bag and bill.

"Please pay the bill at the counter." The waiter said and left in a hurry.

Maya looked all over the floor. Waiters were buzzing hurriedly between tables, taking orders and serving food. There were frequent peals of laughter originating from multiple tables.

Maya glanced at all the people. She suddenly felt lonely in that noisy and enthusiastic atmosphere. She began turning all around herself, slowly, while observing the noisy world around her, lost within herself.

*****

"Miss Maya, We need to find evidence of your innocence. Three weeks have gone by, and only one week remains for the hearing. We need the evidence at any cost. "advocate Deshpande said in a severe tone. Maya and Sarah were in his office one afternoon.

Advocate Deshpande's office was in the Fort area. CST Railway Station's horizontal, C-shaped, multi-story, Gothic architecture style magnificent building was clearly visible from his cabin's window.

"Yeah, understand, but we haven't got any evidence yet," Maya said in an apologetic tone.

"I don't know what to say, but I repeat, we must find the evidence to prove your innocence in court," Deshpande said in a seriously raised voice.

Maya sighed and softly said, "I get it."
*****

Maya and Sarah exited advocate Deshpande's office building and began walking on the pavement full of people.

"Where are we going?" Maya asked.

"I have given my dad's camera for repair to a shop in the fort area, near the Gateway of India. I need to collect it. "Sarah said.

"Okay, but before that, let's eat something." Maya was famished. " I am starving."

They left the CST Station's premises and began walking toward The Gateway of India.

The Gateway of India is a tall arch- monument built during British rule in India in the early 20th century. The structure is a blend of Indian and Islamic architecture. It has three arched gates built from yellow basalt stone.

After about a ten-minute walk, they came to a fast food place called 'TastyVadas.' Maya saw the massive arched structure of the Gateway of India at a distance.

As they reached 'TastyVadas', they were instantly greeted by warm sea wind from Gateway of India's direction. Their hair started flowing in the wind. Some of them were covered on their faces. While removing the curtain of hairs from her face, Maya glanced at Gateway of India and the sea behind it.

'TastyVadas' was famous not only in Mumbai but all over the country for its delicious food, called Vada-Pav. Vada is a round ball of spicy mashed potatoes coated in an aromatic batter and then deep-fried in cooking oil. The deep-fried ball is sandwiched between a soft and fluffy bun called Pav. The mashed potatoes are perfectly spiced with ground green chills, garlic, and onions.

"Two Vada Pavs," Sarah ordered.

In a few minutes, they were served their 'Vada Pavs.' They had their 'Vada-pav' keeping Gateway of India at their background.

Sarah showed Maya a picture of their college friends at the exact same location with the Gateway of India in the background. In the picture, Maya was standing in the middle of the group. Maya gazed at the photo but could not remember it.

'Oh! I can see myself in this photo, but I don't remember it at all.' Maya thought in irritation.

She hastily took Sarah's mobile in her hand and repeated looked at the picture and at the Gateway of India and its surroundings to jog her memory.

"No, Sarah, I don't remember anything about this photo." Maya returned Sarah's mobile and said in a heavy tone.

"Okay, don't be sad. Keep trying; I am sure your memory will trigger." Sarah said encouragingly and turned to the billing counter.

While Sarah was paying the bill, Maya looked at the Gateway of India building and its adjoining gray and white-colored, centrally domed old horizontal building of a hotel.

Suddenly, an image flashed through her mind. She closed her eyes and saw, at the seafront, she was cheering with friends; in the background of a prominent stony structure with a massive arched gate, an old gray horizontal building stood beside it.

She promptly opened her eyes and looked ahead. At the seafront, she saw the Gateway of India's stony façade with its arched gates, and behind it was the hotel's old grey-white horizontal building.

'That's the same view that flashed through my memory.' Maya thought. Her heart began racing and emotion-filled her.

'I may be recalling bits and pieces. It's coming back!' Maya thrilled.

She closed her eyes again, but she could only see the dark void. She repeatedly tried to recall the scene from her memory, but it only got fainter and fainter.

'Damn it! I can't recollect now what I just saw.' Maya's face turned sad. She kept looking at the arcs of Gateway with teary eyes.

*****

Sarah collected her father's camera from the shop near Gateway of India.

After wandering in Fort Area for the entire afternoon, Sarah took Maya to an Irani restaurant, 'Café Tehran.'

'Café Tehran' was a typical Irani restaurant with high ceilings, black curved wooden chairs, and round wooden tables with marble tops. It had two arched entrances to both sides of the billing counter in the usual fashion.

While walking through the entrance, Maya halted in her tracks. Again an image flashed through her mind. In the image, she was following a man through the arched gates of the Café. It was evening time, and yellow lights were on the inside. The round tables were not fully occupied. The walls were adorned with big posters showing black and white images.

"Maya, come here." The sudden sound of Sarah's voice disrupted Maya, and her eyes opened in the present. Sarah was standing beside a table and waving to Maya.

"Maya...Come here." Sarah called from across the floor. Her voice echoed in Maya's mind. Maya closed her eyes again and tried to recollect the image she had just seen, but she could only see the darkness.

"Maya! Come over here." Sarah called again.

Maya opened her eyes and walked over to the table.

"What's the matter?" Sarah asked while sitting on the chair. Maya was still trying to recollect the image.

"I think... I think..." Maya looked around with eyes full of search. She saw a bright yellow glow from the antique lamps, the big black and white posters of Bollywood heroines from a bygone era.

"I think I've been here before," Maya said excitedly. She sat on the wooden chair in front of Sarah.

"Really? Is it coming back?"

"Yes..slowly..."

"This is excellent news! It seems you are slowly recalling your lost memory." Sarah's face lightened with joy.

The waiter put two tall glasses full of water.

"Two Bhurgi-Pav" Sarah gave the order, and her mobile rang.

"Hello...Hello...Your voice is breaking. Let me go outside." Sarah got up and hurriedly walked out of the Cafe.

Maya began going through the big black and white posters of Bollywood heroines from the wall. She liked one posture in particular. She quickly grabbed her phone, positioned herself in front of the posture, and clicked a photo.

While clicking the photo, again, a scene flashed in her mind. She closed her eyes, and her breathing got heavy.

She saw herself was about to click a photo of a black and white poster, and in the background, there was a red car across the street, visible through the entrance of the Cafe. She saw two men in front of the red car. They talked briefly, and one gave the packet to the other.

Maya opened her eyes. She saw the same spot through the entrance, where the two men from her memory had been standing. She closed her eyes again, but the scene became blurry.

Maya ran to her table, took a pen from her bag, and wrote it down on a paper napkin. A red car...two men met...one gave the packet to the other.

Maya was excited, and her heart started racing. She drank the whole glass of water rapidly.

Sarah came back to the table and saw Maya was panting.

"Maya? What happened? Why are you panting?" Sarah asked worriedly while sitting down. Maya did not reply. She gave the paper napkin to Sarah, who read the text loudly,

"A red car... two men met...one gave the packet to the other."

Sarah gave a surprised look to Maya and asked,

"Do you remember more?"

Maya nodded as she dabbed the sweat from her forehead.

"Yes. An image just flashed through my mind while I clicked a photo of that poster near the entrance. " Maya pointed at the poster near the entrance.

"The image was clear the first time, but slowly, it was getting hazier. Hence I wrote down the details on this napkin." Maya looked at her writing on a paper napkin.

"That's great, Maya! That's great! I am so happy !" Sarah responded cheerfully.

Maya thought and suddenly stood from her chair. She felt tightness in her chest. Her eyes sparkle and gleam. She came close to Sarah.

"Sarah, let's go to my house. If I had clicked a photo that day, it must be on my old phone. It may lead to something. Come on... let's go... quickly." Maya began pulling Sarah's arm to get her up from the chair.

"Wait. Wait...What's so hurry? and What about the food we've ordered? " Sarah tried to resist.

The waiter put the two plates of bhurji-pav on their table. Sarah looked at that oily, spicy, delicious, scrambled egg dish.

"See ?! our food has been served. Let's eat first. We'll leave after that." Sarah pulled one bhurji-pav plat in front of her.

"No, no! We must go now." Maya pulled up Sarah from the chair.

Within a few seconds, they were out of 'Cafe Tehran.' While exiting the restaurant, Sarah quickly kept some currency notes on the billing counter.

*****

Sarah and Maya rushed back to Maya's house.

Without taking off her shoes, Maya ran straight to her room. She quickly went to her writing table and took out her old mobile from its drawer. She tried to turn it on, but its screen was dead.

"Oh! No!" Maya exclaimed.

"What happened?" Sarah asked while entering the room.

"The phone is out of battery. Let me recharge it." Maya inserted the charger's pin into the mobile's port in one quick move. The mobile beeped and began charging.

"It will take some time for the phone to charge partially." Maya sighed. Sarah relaxed on the chair. Maya sat on the bed.

Rita entered the room with a water bottle and two glasses.

"Why did you girls hurry back?" Sarah and Maya did not reply.

"Are you looking for something?" Rita asked curiously while handing over the glass to each of them.

"Nothing specific, Mom, just charging my old mobile," Maya said after two sips of water.

Rita glanced at the phone kept for charging and put the water bottle on the table. While leaving the room, she turned to Sarah,

"Sarah, I've prepared Biryani today. Why don't you have dinner with us ?"

"Okay, auntie."

Maya began pacing restlessly back and forth in the room.

"Come on... charge, damn it!" Maya said excitedly while looking at the charging status of the phone.

"Relax, Maya. The phone will take its own time to charge." Sarah said. Maya ignored Sarah's words and kept watching at the phone.

After an anxious wait, Maya quickly switched on the phone. It was partially charged. The battery icon appeared on the screen, and the mobile began switching on.

"I'm sure I have clicked a photo, and it may give us some clue," Maya was happy and nervous at the same time.

The mobile switched on completely, and Maya's face turned gloomy.

"What's wrong now?" Sarah noticed the change on Maya's face.

"It's asking for a pin and...." Maya said sadly while looking at the 'Enter Password' screen.

"So ? enter the pin. Oh! You don't remember the pin?!" Sarah quickly stood from her chair.

Maya sat down on the bed hopelessly.

Sarah came close to Maya and took the mobile from her hand.

"Oh!" Sarah looked at the phone's screen. While looking at it, she said,

"Try to remember, Maya. You must figure out your password. is it your date of birth? Auntie's date of birth? maybe something about your dad?"

Maya typed her date of birth.

'Invalid password!' words flashed on the mobile screen.

"Is it your name with something else?" Maya typed on the mobile screen.

'Invalid password!' words again flashed on the mobile screen.

"Favourite Movie or TV star?"

Invalid password again.

A few suggestions later, they still didn't make any progress.

"What else could it be? What else?" Maya grew hyper.

She tried one more option, but that too turned out to be a dud. She became impatient. "Come on... come on..." Maya irritated and anxiously typed one more password.

This time the screen got locked temporarily.

"Shit! Shiiiit!! Maya got angry and threw the phone on the bed.

"Dinner's ready!" Rita said from the door.

"Let's take a dinner break, Maya," Sarah said.

"No, You have it. I will try to unlock this." Maya said while continuing to touch the buttons on the mobile screen.

Sarah walked to the door and gave a nervous look at Rita.

"Maya, Come for dinner," she said.

"No, I am not hungry," Maya said without raising her head.

"Maya, Have some food. You have already loose lots of weight. You become so thin." Rita said worriedly.

"Leave me alone. " Maya said without taking her eyes off the screen.

*****

The bedroom clock showed 2 A.M. Maya's face was lit up from the illumination of the mobile's screen. She entered another password.

'Incorrect password.' and the screen got locked again.

Maya sighed deeply in sadness and remained on the bed.

*****

The following day, Maya woke up and promptly resumed her attempts to unlock the phone. Rita and Sarah had already lost the hope that Maya would open it, but Maya tried tirelessly with different passwords.

However, on the umpteenth attempt, the phone got unlocked.

"WOW!" Maya exclaimed with joy.

"Mom... Mmmmm!" She came running out of her bedroom into the kitchen.

"Mom, I just recalled the password, and the phone got unlocked.
"

"Oh, great!" Rita replied while stirring the curry in the pot on the gas burner.

Maya began scanning through the photos on the phone.

"How were you able to unlock it?"

" "
...

"Maya?" Rita looked at Maya, who was busy staring at her phone screen.

"Maya??"

Maya did not reply but hurried back to her bedroom. She dialed Sarah,

"Sarah, I have unlocked the phone."

"That's great! What did you find?"

"I found one photo. Let me forward it to you."

Maya sent the photo. There was silence for a few seconds

"Yes... you are right; there is a red car in the photo. Who are these men?" Sarah asked.

"Not sure...I am not recollecting anything." Maya said thoughtfully.

"Hmm...So this photo is not of any use. "Sarah said.

There was a silence of a few moments.

"Sarah! you know what...?" Maya said energetically.

"Yeah, tell me."

"I just forwarded one more photo. Take a look."

Maya forwarded the photo.

There was again silence for a few seconds.

"What is this, Maya?" Sarah's thoughtful voice came through the speaker.

"It seems it's the photo I took outside of our office. Do you know the other person in the photo? "

"Yes. Its Rachel. She was working in our company. It seems you two meet outside of our office." Sarah said.

"Oh !" Maya said.

"What happened?"

"See who is in the background."

"Oh! It's Michael!" Sarah exclaimed.

"Yes, It seems it's Michael!" Maya was surprised.

"Maya, check the date and time of the photo."

Maya quickly checked the date and time of the photo and said,

"It's 15th June this year, 10 PM."

"Oh my God! It's the same night when Mrs. Pinto was murdered. It looks like Michael went inside the office after you left. So, it's not you, but Michael was the last person to leave the office that day."

"Yes !" Maya was stunned.

"What was Michael doing that night at the office? "Sarah asked thoughtfully.

"How was Michael and Mrs. Pinto's relation?" Maya asked.

"Not good. She used to criticize Michael's work unnecessarily. Michael hated her." Sarah provided the information.

"So Michael is involved in this? Maybe Mrs. Pinto caught him in the act of doing something wrong." Maya's thought machine began running.

"Not sure, Maya, everything is so confused. Not sure whom to trust." Sarah said.

"Sam is pointing finger to Roy. But Michael was also in the office that night which he never told us. "Maya concluded.

" I will run this with Kapoor sir tomorrow. Let's see what he has to say." Sarah said excitingly.

"Okay..and also try to find Roy's whereabouts, and I will check with Michael. "

"but Maya ..be careful..at present, we can not trust anyone."

"Agree...Michael should have told me about his presence in the office at murder night. This was not expected from him." Maya said nervously.

*****

It was late in the night. Lights from the KKSwTech office floor were off, but Kapoor's cabin lights were on. He was tirelessly working on his computer.

"Tak...Tak...Tak...Tak.." The sound of Kapoor's keyboard typing was audible outside his cabin.

At around 11 P.M., Kapoor finished his work and began shutting down his computer. While his computer was shutting down, his mobile rang. The text 'Wife' appeared on the mobile screen.

"Yeah, tell me?" Kapoor answered the call.

"Are you still at the office?" Mrs. Kapoor's surprised tone came through the speaker.

"Yeah, leaving now." Kapoor started putting papers in his briefcase.

"Hope You remember, you need to take a cab today."

"Cab?" Kapoor's hand paused while putting papers in the briefcase. He was surprised.

"I knew you would forget. The driver is on leave today."

"Oh, yeah, yeah. I forgot. Thanks for reminding me. I will take a cab." Kapoor nodded.

"Okay. Bye." Mrs. Kapoor disconnected the call.

Kapoor put the remaining papers in the briefcase. He closed the briefcase and walked out of his cabin.

At 11:15 P.M. Kapoor reached the main road in front of the office building. He was still wearing a lanyard around his neck, holding his office Photo ID card.

He waived at a cab standing at a distance in the dark. Cab's headlight blinked, and it started.

In a few seconds, the cab stopped in front of Kapoor.

"Nepean Sea Road." He bent and asked the Cab driver through the window.

"Yes, Sir." The driver confirmed the ride. Kapoor opened the back door and got in the cab. The driver turned on the meter and started the cab.

Kapoor relaxed in the backseat and began looking outside at the moving cityscape. Mumbai city was illuminated by yellow streetlights. Most shops were closed, but the street food vendors had their businesses in the motion.

On one occasion, Kapoor noticed the driver was looking at him through the rear-view mirror. Kapoor ignored it. He continued looking outside at the nightly sights of shining Mumbai.

After a few minutes, he looked at the driver again. The driver was still looking at him through the rear-view mirror.

Kapoor propped his head with a fist and asked the driver through the rear-view mirror,

"Anything wrong?"

"Uhh... Sir, the ID card you are wearing looks familiar to me." The driver replied promptly. Kapoor realized the driver was staring at his ID card through the rare-view mirror.

"What do you mean?" wrinkles were formed on Kapoor's forehead.

"Many days ago, around midnight, I gave a ride to a person wearing the same type of ID card. I dropped him at Churchgate station."

"Okay." Kapoor gave a dry reply and again relaxed at the seat.

"...and Sir..." The driver continued, "He was in a hurry and tensed."

'hmm...who was that person from our office who traveled late that night?' Kapoor grew curious.

"Where did you pick him up?" Kapoor asked after a few thoughtful seconds.

"From the same spot where I picked you today. I dropped him at Churchgate station. The fare came to Rs. 345, but he gave me an Rs. 2000 note. I tried to give him change, but he did not wait and hurriedly walked toward the station. I even called him to give his change, but he did not look back."

'Sir, we just found out from Sam that it was Roy who murdered Mrs. Pinto...It was Roy who came to the office on that evening after Maya left.' Sarah's words echoed in Kapoor's mind. He began connecting the dots.

"Do you remember how he looked?" Kapoor asked.

"He was fair, average height and build. Nothing extraordinary." The driver said without taking eyes off from the front road.

"Did you talk with him?"

"No..he was quiet..and tense..he also did not talk much on the phone."

"He got the call during the ride?"

"Yes...He talked very briefly in a low voice and disconnected the call. "

"Anything odd you noticed?"

"Yes! He had a bizarre caller tune on his mobile."

"Bizarre tune? What do you mean?"

"It was a tune like a man laughing in loud."

Kapoor recalled Roy had a similar caller tune. He took his mobile from his pants pocket and opened one photo. It was a photo of one of the office functions. He slightly zoomed in on Roy.

"Was this that guy in the red shirt?" Kapoor leaned forward and showed his mobile to the driver.

The driver turned around to have a quick glance at the mobile screen.

"No, Sir. That's not the guy. But the one next to him, in the blue shirt."

"Are you sure? Look carefully."

"A hundred percent sure, Sir. He was wearing the same shirt as he is in this photo."

'Hmmm..It's Michael...what Michael was doing late at night in the office?' Kapoor wondered.

Kapoor kept thinking, "Do you remember what day it was?"

"Yes, Sir, it was the 15th of June."

"Really? How can you be so sure about the date?" Kapoor asked skeptically.

"The 16th of June is my son's birthday. So, I was doing overtime on the night of 15th, so I could take a day off on the 16th."

'hmmm... The date Mrs. Pinto was murdered was the 15th of June.' Kapoor grumbled. He relays back into his seat. He rubbed his forehead and kept looking outside the window with a thoughtful face.

*****

The next day morning, Sarah went to Kapoor's cabin. He was busy on his phone.

"May I come in, Sir?" Sarah asked from the door.

Kapoor waved her to come in and pointed to an empty chair opposite his. Sarah sat down while Kapoor continued speaking. He occasionally looked at his computer screen.

Sarah waited patiently for Kapoor to finish. After around five minutes, Kapoor hung up the phone.

"Yes, Sarah. Tell me..." He said while operating the computer mouse.

"Look at this photo, Sir. This was taken on the evening when Mrs. Pinto was murdered." Sarah gave her mobile to him and showed him the photo of Rachel and Maya. He glanced at the photo and said, "What's so special about it?"

"Sir, look carefully. A person in the background can be seen entering the office building. He is Michael." Sarah paused for a second to let Kapoor react.

Kapoor stopped typing and keenly looked at Sarah's mobile screen.

"So?" Kapoor said nonchalantly and resumed his typing. Sarah was surprised by Kapoor's cold reaction. She took a few moments to gather her thoughts to strengthen her argument.

"Sir, this means Maya was not the last person to leave the office on that day. It was Michel who left after her."

"Sarah! I met on Cab driver yesterday. He was calming that Michael took his cab for Churchgate station from our office on the same night when Mrs. Pinto was murdered. The cab driver said Michael was tense, and he even did not take the change after giving the fare. He was in a hurry."

"Yeah! That's what we are thinking, Sir. Michael's presence on the night of murder does not sound you fishy ?" Sarah asked.

"I thought about. I know Michael he will not do anything like this. And In this photo...He is just entering the building. That does not mean he went to the office. He could have gone to the restaurant on the first floor. Our swipe records do not show anyone enters or exits after Maya on that day." Kapoor said casually without taking his eyes off from computer screen.

Sarah controlled her instant reaction. She took a few thoughtful, deep breaths.

"Sarah?" Kapoor paused his typing, looked at Sarah, and reclined into his chair.

"I know you are trying to help Maya. First, you said it's Roy now your suspension is toward Michael. you simply can't accuse anyone on some photo and on your guesswork."

"My suspicion is not baseless, Sir," Sarah said in a sharp tone.

"Do you have any other sound evidence that Roy or Michael had done this? "Kapoor asked in a firm voice. He leaned forward and looked straight into Sarah's eyes and asked,

"Do you?"

Sarah took a step back. The intensity in Sarah's eyes reduced. She looked down.

"No, Sir, we do not have strong evidence against Roy or Michael at present. "Sarah said in a low voice.

"That's it then !" Kapoor said conclusively and turned toward his computer screen.

*****

Sarah left Kapoor's cabin, went to the cafeteria, put an empty cup into the coffee machine, and pressed the button on it. After a few seconds, dark brown coffee poured out from the nozzle into her cup. While the cup was filling up, her phone rang.

"Hi Maya, I was about to call you only," Sarah answered.

"Why?"

"I am sorry, Maya, but Kapoor sir did not get convenience about any foul play or any suspicious activity."

"What ?! Did you show him the photo I sent?"

"Yes."

"Did you tell him that Michael went to the office after I left ?" Maya asked in an elevated voice.

"Yes. It seems Kapoor Sir already knew that?"

"Really? How ?"

"He said he met one Cab driver yesterday who gave a ride to Michael from our office to Churchgate station. The Cab driver mentioned that Michael was looking tense, and after paying for the fare, Michael even did not collect the change. "

"When did that cab driver see Michael?"

"On the same night when Mrs. Pinto was murdered. "

"Oh !" Maya shocked. She was lost in her thoughts for a few seconds.

"Maya?"

"..."

"Maya?"

"..."

"Maya?"

"Yeah."

"What are we going to do next?" Sarah picked up her freshly filled cup of coffee and started walking toward her cubicle. On the way, she sipped her coffee slowly.

"..."

"Maya?"

"Can you give Roy's contact details?" Sarah sensed a heaviness in Maya's voice.

"Do you think he will answer your call?"

"Can you find out where he lives and hangs out?"

"Okay, I will try to find."

"..."

"Maya?"

"Yes?"

"What is your plan?"

"I don't have one yet."

*****

It was 11:37 P.M. on the wall clock. Maya was lying on her bed in her bedroom. The loud sound of the TV was coming from the hall through the partially opened door.

Maya had been wearing the same t-shirt and pajamas for the last few days. Her clothes were spread all over the room, along with her university books. Her room was messy and stinky.

Maya was not feeling sleepy, but she had no motivation to get up. Her unblinking eyes were following the movement of the second's hand of the wall clock. Her overlong nails were constantly vibrating.

Suddenly an unusual sound came from the hall. First, Maya did not pay attention. The sound came again. Maya's ears turned toward the partially opened bedroom door and heard Rita's heavy coughing sound.

'Oh, shit! It seems mom's got an attack!' She realized. She instantly got up from bed and ran toward the hall.

She saw Rita was on the hall's floor, coughing, wheezing, and gasping for air. Her whole body was shaking violently. The TV was on with its loud volume.

"Mom!...Mom!" Maya shouted. She quickly sat down and grabbed Rita's convulsing body. She supported Rita enough to sit up and held her head back. With each cough, Rita found it more difficult to breathe.

"Mom, breathe. Please try to breathe. Your Inhaler, Mom? Where is your Inhaler? Where is your inhaler?"

Rita's shaky hand pointed toward the wardrobe. Maya rushed to the wardrobe and grabbed the inhaler.

"Mom, here's the inhaler. Take a puff, quick! Hurry up!" Rita was coughing heavily and almost lost consciousness. Her eyes were rolling. She took the inhaler from Maya, but it was dropped by her shaky hands.

'It seems Mom can't hold the inhaler by herself.' Maya realized. She picked up the inhaler quickly and held it in front of Rita's mouth.

"Open your mouth, Mom, open your mouth!" Maya shouted to get Rita's attention. Rita stirred for a bit and weakly opened her mouth, but another bout of chesty coughing stopped her from keeping it open for sufficient time.

"Open your mouth, Mom!" Maya said desperately. She brought the inhaler very close to Rita's mouth. With her eyes still rolling, Rita managed to keep her mouth open for a couple of seconds. Maya put the inhaler's mouthpiece in Rita's mouth and pressed the canister on top.

"Fssst... fsssst... fsssssst!"

She shook the Inhaler and pressed it again.

Droplets from the Inhaler attacked Rita's chesty cough and broadened her narrowed throat. Within a few minutes, Rita's throat filled with life-giving air. But the chesty cough refused to leave quickly and tried to resurrect from deep throat.

"Do you feel better, Mom?" Maya asked in a soft voice. Rita weakly nodded her head and sat up straight. Her eyes were still rolled up, and she was still breathing heavily.

Maya kept observing Rita. 'Mom looks a little better now.' While lost in thoughts, Maya pressed the Inhaler. As a result, only cool air exited from Inhaler's mouth.

'Oh! The Inhaler is empty. But what if she gets another attack at night? 'Maya looked at the wall clock; it was 11:55 P.M.

'The corner pharmacy must be shut by now. I have to go to the 24-Hour Pharmacy, but they won't give me the medicine on credit. Damn!"

Rita was shaken up and torn down, like a city ravaged by a powerful earthquake. Maya took an exhausted Rita to her bedroom. She poured her a glass of water. Rita took a few sips and lay down on the bed. Though now mild and infrequent, the persistent cough was still shaking her a bit.

Maya returned to her room with slumped shoulders and sat on the bed with her eyes wide open. Her mind began spinning its web of thoughts.

'What if Mom gets an attack again later in the night? I may have to admit her to the hospital. Should I call Sarah? ...but it's too late...'

'Mom's condition is not good. I forgot where I kept the bag of money. It's all my fault. I am only the culprit here. 'The waves of negative thoughts began crashing against the shore of guilt. Maya's mind was wrapped in the sticky threads of shame and doubt.

'There must be money somewhere.' Maya suddenly stood from the bed and energetically went to Rita's room. She began searching the wardrobe without making any noise.

'Mom had mentioned about a blue plastic bag that I kept somewhere.' A thought suddenly struck Maya. 'She said I don't recollect where I kept it, but I'm sure if it's not here, then it must be in my room.'

Another sudden surge of energy flew through Maya's body. She quickly headed for her room.

She entered her room speedily. She pulled her wardrobe door harder than usual, and she keenly began her search.

The wardrobe was huge, almost ten feet tall, touching the ceiling. It had five main horizontal shelves and many small square shelves.

Maya pulled the nearby chair and stood on it. Her eyes began scanning the wardrobe like a hawk, and her hands rummaged through the shelves.

'I cannot see that blue bag anywhere. But it must be here... it has to! Let me take out all the stuff from the closet.' Maya thought while breathing heavily.

She began retrieving items fiercely from each shelf and throwing them on the floor. She opened every bag and box, scanned the contents, and quickly flung it to the floor. Her hands developed muscle memory and began working independently from her brain.

She had gone through the entire wardrobe in less than ten minutes and moved her hands through the empty shelves once more. A thin layer of sweat formed on her forehead, and she continued to breathe heavily.

After a couple of minutes, Maya took a deep breath and got down from the chair. She was greeted by the mess she had thrown on the floor. She gave one sad look at the items strewn on the entire floor.

'I must comb the entire room now. That blue plastic bag must be here somewhere.' She thought while wiping sweat from her forehead.

She energetically went to her writing table and yanked out its drawers. She looked at each item. They, too, met the same fate by being smashed to the floor. In a couple of minutes, Maya was out of breath again.

After the table, it was the turn of a smaller closet followed by wooden boxes on the floor. The same scene played out again, resulting in the pile getting more extensive on the floor.

Maya became desperate and pulled the mattress off the bed and threw it to the floor. She moved to a small bookshelf ripped the books off. She stirred the heap on the floor and opened every plastic bag. Maya looked at the wardrobe again in exasperation.

Maya stopped for a few minutes to catch her breath.

She drank some water and resumed her fanatic search through the items on the floor. She was more forceful and fiercer. She moved from one part of the room to another desperately. Slowly, she drained of energy, but she kept searching.

Finally, her hands were tired and in pain. She lost steam and plonked down on the heap. She stood up on the pile but lost her balance and collapsed.

'Shit! Where the heck is that damn bag? It couldn't have just vanished.' Maya was irritated while lying on the items.

After a few moments, she stood up wearily and tried to walk but was again struck by items lying on the floor.

"Bloody shit! Why can't I remember where I kept that dam bag??" Maya shouted angrily. She stood up in anger and began kicking the items, one after the other. Her one kick, though, connected with a heavy box, and it hit back,

"Ahhhhh... ooooouuuch!" Maya shouted in agony and crumpled to the floor.

Sudden anger went into her head. She got up quickly and dialed Sarah's number.

"What's up, Maya? It's late at night. Is everything all right ?" Sarah's worried tone came through speaker.

"No! Noting is okay Sarah! Due to an accident, I have lost a few years of memory and, because of that, lost my job. I am in financial distress. To make the situation worst, I am accused and charged with the murder of my boss! I do not remember anything due to memory loss, so I could not defend myself. "Maya's voice raised in frustration. Her eyes began emitting fire.

"On Maya! I am so sorry...but please calm down, soon you will be out of this situation." Sarah tried to condole Maya.

"I am in this mess because of either Roy or Michael. Do you find Roy's whereabouts?" Maya said in a sharp tone. Her eyes began emitting fire.

"Not yet."

"Find it, Sarah! find it! "Maya shouted. Her eyes were widened up to her forehead.

"Okay...Okay...please calm down."

"I don't have enough money to treat my mother. But I can't sit idle and watch her die. "Maya shouted again.

Maya's eyes grew tight in anger.

"I will find who did this with me, and I will teach him a lesson.. I will teach him a lesson...I will...I will..." Maya said in anger.

*****

6
Chapter 6

Michael stopped the car near Mumbai's Bazaar area. After stopping the engine he looked at Maya. She was lost in her thoughts while looking through the windshield.

"Are you sure you want to do this?" Michael looked at Maya for a moment and asked.

"Yes," Maya said in a firm voice and opened the door.

Both got down from the car and began walking in the crowded street. The area was full of old buildings. All types and sizes of shops were on both sides of the street. They were selling Tools, Furniture, Footwear, Hardware, Bronze items, Fashion items, Brassware, Cane goods, Vintage goods, Electronics, and stolen artifacts. The pavement in front of the shops was occupied with vendors and hawkers.

Michael entered one metal artifacts shop and went straight to the man at the billing counter. Michael looked at the swollen cheeks of the man and realized he was chewing tobacco. Michael murmured with him. The man nodded his head and came out of the billing counter.

The man spite the tobacco at the bottom of a nearby wall and said in his thick voice,

"Follow me."

He took Michael and Maya to the backside of the shop.

They started walking in the extremely narrow lanes. The man was walking a few steps ahead of Micheal and Maya.

After a few minutes of walk, the man stopped in front of a black wooden door and knocked on it.

In a few seconds, the door opened partially. The man slid in through it and slammed the door.

Michael and Maya waited outside.

The door opened again after a few minutes, and the same man came with one plastic bag in his hand. He handover the plastic bag to Michael.

"Check this." The man whispered. Michael retrieved one small gun from the bag. He looked at the gun carefully.

"This is a good piece. Bullets are in the bag too.." The man murmured.

Michael passed the gun to Maya.

A sweat emerged on Maya's forehead, and her standing posture shifted rigidly. She took the gun with a pondering heart and began observing the gun closely with protruded eyes. She felt the weight of that small gun in her shivering fingers.

Michael retrieved one bag from his sack and gave it to the man. The bag was full of currency notes.

"Is the amount full?" The man asked while peeping inside the bag.

"Yes.." Michael nodded and quickly closed the zip of his sack.

*****

Michael and Maya walked back to the car. They got in the car. Michael put on the seat belt, and he was about to start the car when he realized something pointed at him from the side. He looked at his left and was shocked for a second. His mouth fell open. Maya was pointing a gun at him.

"Maya, what is this?" Michael asked in surprise.

"Michael..you did not tell Sarah or me that you were present in the office when Mrs. Pinto was murdered. " Maya said with a stone face.

"What?! Yeah Okay...I was about to tell you, but you been arrested...."

"You should have told me, Michael...I know you hated Mrs. Pinto." Maya said in strong voice.

"So, what do you mean? I murdered Mrs. Pinto ?" Michael asked with bulged eyes.

Maya did not reply. She kept staring at Michael for a few seconds.

"Maya ?! what is this nonsense.." Michel irritated.

"I am not sure, Michael, what you were doing that night in the office..but soon I will find out..."

"Maya, you are not thinking straight. I understand you have been into a lot recently..and hence ...let me explain..my mom had...but first, keep the gun aside..." Michael slid closer to Maya and tried to reach for the gun.

"Stay where you are, Michael.." Maya roared.

"Maya, don't be silly ...How can I ..." Michael tried to convenience Maya. She ignored what Michael was saying and got down from the car. She put the gun in her bag and leaned down at the window, and said in a severe tone,

"I don't trust you anymore, Michael. Don't ever call or try to meet me. Stay away from me."

*****

In the morning, Roy came out from his building and walked toward his newly acquired shiny, black sports car parked in its designated spot. He was wearing a gray blazer, a blue shirt, and black trousers. He had worn expensive sunglasses and had an equally pricey leather backpack.

On the way to the car, he pressed the unlock button from the car's remote. The car responded with two quick beeps and blinked headlights.

Roy started the car. "Vroom...! Vroom...!!" The car's engine revved energetically as if it was eager to tear down the road.

The security personnel opened the gate well in time. Roy passed through the gate speedily, ignoring the saluting security guards on both sides of the gate.

In twenty minutes, Roy was at the porch of his office building. He got out of his car, and a guard took to its parking spot. Another guard promptly called the elevator. Roy got in the elevator without noticing the salute of the guard.

Roy came to his corner cabin. He proudly glanced at the nameplate on the cabin door, Roy Smith - Product Manager. 'Roy Smith - Product Manager sounds cool. Whatever I had to do to achieve this position was totally worth it.' The thought came to his mind. He entered the cabin with a sly smile on his face.

He opened his laptop, and his desk phone rang.

"Good morning, Sir." It was his secretary.

"Technical team wants to reschedule their 11 A.M. meeting to 1 P.M. Shall I reschedule? I know 1 P.M. is your lunchtime."

"No! This is the second time this week they have rescheduled the meeting. "Roy said in an agitated tone. "Tell them this is not acceptable." His narrowing eyes flicked the gaze upward.

"Okay, Sir." The secretary replied.

Roy kept the phone in a huff. He gave a nasty look to the phone and began operating his laptop.

*****

Around 9:00 P.M., Roy's car entered the porch of the famous pub- '@Banjara' at Juhu. One guard quickly came forward and respectfully opened the car's door. Roy came out of the car while keeping the engine running for the valet.

Roy was dressed in a bright purple silk shirt and black trousers. He was wearing a brown leather jacket with a big yellow sunflower picture at its back.

Roy entered the pub.

Banjara had a theme of various shades of red, yellow, and orange lights inside. The dance floor was entirely grooving to the DJ's exciting, loud music, cutting through the background of the flickering colorful bright lights.

Roy went straight to the bar. He hung his brown leather jacket on the back of the barstool and sat on it.

"Hey, Roy. What a surprise?" A female voice came from behind. He instantly turned around, and his eyes popped wide open. It was Maya.

Roy checked Maya from top to bottom. She had worn a sleeveless dark red top on tight blue denim jeans and high heels.

"I hope you remember me?" Maya asked.

"Of... off... off course, I remember you, Maya. Come, have a seat." Roy gained his composure and hand gestured Maya to sit on the next stool.

"What would you like to have?" He asked.

"Aaah..." Maya started thinking.

"I have vodka with lemonade." And without waiting for Maya's wish, he called for the bartender to order.

"You suddenly left from the company. We heard you got a good offer?" Maya asked with a smile.

"Yes, I got a good offer from HSDTecSoft. "

"Oh wow, HSDTecSoft! May I ask, how good is the offer?" Maya asked casually.

"The position of Product Manager, three times more salary than KKSwTech, plus a hefty signing bonus." Roy looked straight into Maya's eyes and said with confidence.

"Oh, my! That's impressive!" Maya said loudly. Faces from nearby tables turned at them.

"Yeah, it totally is." Roy glanced around and smiled awkwardly at the turned faces.

The vodka came around. Roy downed his glass in one go while Maya took her first sip.

"One more round." Roy gestured to the bartender with two fingers without asking Maya.

"Tell me more about your job."
Maya leaned forward, rested her right cheek on her right palm, and

looked at Roy with fake admiration.

"I am just two levels below from the CEO. The company offered me a three-bedroom apartment in a posh locality, but I opted to buy myself a four-bedroom instead. The company offered a car, too, but I recently purchased my brand-new sports car. It had been my dream for a long time to own a sports car."

"That's amazing! Look at you !! You have just been out of KKSwTech, and your life has changed dramatically, hasn't it?" Maya relaxed back into her chair and kept up the admiration in her eyes.

Roy continued boasting about the offer and how hard he had to negotiate for it. Through his conversation, he lustfully glanced at Maya's outfit on a few occasions.

"Do you mind if I ask you a question?" Roy asked.

"Sure, go ahead." Maya nodded her head while sipping her vodka.

"I heard that you met with an accident and lost your memory? Is that true? I mean, you look perfectly normal to me." He emptied his glass and kept it down.

Maya smiled, looked straight into Roy's eyes for a few seconds, and put down her glass of vodka.

"To be honest, Roy, what you heard is true."

"Oh really? That's sad." Roy said casually.

"Yeah, it really sucks." Maya looked sternly at Roy over the edge of her glass.

"And you know, after my accident, KKSwTech fired me," Maya said in an elevated tone.Maya emptied her glass.

"Because of your memory loss?" Roy asked in surprise. The next round of vodka arrived.

"No...You remember Mrs. Pinto, right?"

"Of course, I remember her...what about her?"

"They suspect that I have to do something with Mrs. Pinto's murder."

"What?! Mrs. Pinto is dead?! "Roy almost shouted. His mouth fell open. His eyebrows were raised till his forehead.

"Yes..." Maya nodded.

"Wow!" Roy roared while wiping his mouth with a napkin. He turned his head to the side for a moment. He took deep breath and asked,

"How did this happen?"

"Nobody knows the real story. One fine morning her dead body was found in my cubical. "

"Wow !" Roy said excitingly and took a deep breath.

After a couple of minutes, he asked, "By the way, who are they? who thinks you are involved in Mrs. Pinto's murder?"

"Police...and ..."

"and?"

"Maybe Kapoor Sir..."

"Oh! That's rubbish !!" Roy said in irritation.

"Yeah..they really think I am somehow involved in Mrs. Pinto's murder."

"Then how are you roaming freely? I heard you were in jail for sometime."

"I was for some time. Now currently out on bail. The case against me is going on session court." Maya finished her glass.

"Oh! That's not good." Roy sighed. ,

"But Roy?" Suddenly, Maya asked while maintaining eye contact with Roy.

"Yeah..."

"One thing still makes me curious."

"Which one?"

Maya started her next glass.

"It seems somebody tried to set me up in this. I'm curious about who could do that? And why?" Maya gave a quick stern look to Roy while sipping his vodka.

"Do you suspect anybody?"

Maya looked straight into Roy's eyes and said, "You know Roy, a sign of a real dangerous person is; initially, you don't feel him dangerous."

Roy did not reply. His shoulders were slowly bouncing on the music, and he was enjoying his vodka, sip by sip.

The DJ changed the music. The crowd dancing on the dance floor responded cheerfully.

Roy became excited. He finished his vodka bottoms up. He wiped his wet lips with his palm and looked at Maya with a happy face,

"I know who sets you up."

"What?! Really?" Maya was shocked.

Roy smiled. He put his head down and nodded. Maya's eyes were wide open. Her heartbeats were increased, and her ears were eager to hear words from Roy.

"Roy?... Who set me up?" Maya asked eagerly.

Roy did not reply. He remained seated with his head down.

"Roy?!" Maya asked again.

Roy raised his head. The smile was gone from his face. While looking at Maya suspiciously, he asked, "You said you lost a part of your memory, right? a few years' worths? How did you recognize me then?"

'Why did he suddenly change the topic?' Maya was surprised.

"Maya?"

"Yeah." Maya came to her senses. She continued drinking her vodka.

"How did you recognize me ?" Roy's eyes were gauging Maya's facial expression.

"Actually, I didn't remember you. You know, Sarah, from your team?"

"Yeah, I know Sarah."

"She showed me your picture and said, I should approach you to get a new job."

"Oh! You came to the right person. I will help you." Roy said mischievously.

Maya finished her glass quickly.

"I never saw you drinking in office parties. Since when did you start drinking?" Roy asked while wiping his palms with a paper napkin.

"Since today," Maya leaned forward and blinked her eyes. Roy responded with a meaningful smile.

The DJ changed the tempo of the music again, and it turned even louder. The people were elated by the change and cheered loudly. The lights started blinking rapidly, and it created sparkles in Roy's eyes. His feet began drumming against the floor.

Roy stood from his seat. His body was moving on the music.

"Would you like to dance?" He asked Maya while glancing excitingly at the energetic crowd.

"Aaa..no...not..."

"Come on..." Without waiting for Maya's response, he took Maya's hand in his hand.

"Let go !" He pulled Maya off her stool. Maya got off and matched his pace.

They joined the excited crowd on the dance floor. Soon, they became part of the electric atmosphere.

"This is fun," Roy screamed happily while dancing. He was occasionally touching Maya's body.

'Oh damn! What else do I have to do with this bastard?' Maya thought, making an odious face momentarily.

They danced for some time, and suddenly, the music slowed down.

Maya and Roy returned to their seat.

"Okay, Roy, don't make me wait for more. Please tell me who set me up?" Maya asked eagerly. Roy ordered the next round of vodka.

"As I had mentioned before, that thing is still stuck in my mind. I cannot get over it." Maya said in a soft tone. Roy looked straight into Maya's eyes.

"Please?" Maya urged.

Roy smiled and gave Maya a cunning look.

"What's the hurry, Maya. Let's enjoy the rest of the evening first. I have an answer to your question, but I'll give it to you once we reach my place."

"Your place?" Maya's voice raised.

"Yeah, when we are finished here, we'll go over to my house. It's nearby, and we'll have dinner. Then I will tell you the secret as we enjoy the dessert." Roy's eyes were overflowing with lust.

'Oh goodness, now I have to go to his house.' Maya thought.

Next round of vodka arrived.

Maya had started feeling relatively high and was getting worried.

'If I drink any more, I won't be able to walk, and that is not good. 'She looked at a table nearby and saw some wedges of lemons.

"I'll be right back, Roy." She stood while looking at the lemon wedges.

"Sure..." Roy said casually. He was trying to get the bartender's attention; Maya grabbed a few lemon wedges and made her way to the ladies' restroom.

*****

At 1:10 A.M., Roy's car zoomed into his building complex and abruptly stopped at its parking slot.

"Screeeeeeeeech!" The sound of sudden brakes cut through the silence of the night.

Roy and Maya got out of the car and walked toward the entrance.

"...So... I told the builder, I like the apartment, but this is my final offer, take it or leave it," Roy said.

They passed through the building security. The security guard quickly saluted. Roy, as usual, ignored the guard and pressed the elevator button.

In a few minutes, they were in Roy's apartment.

"So, Maya, what would you like to order for dinner?" Roy took out his brown leather jacket and threw it on the couch.

"Actually, I am not that hungry, Roy," Maya said while looking at the bright yellow sunflower colored image printed at the back of Roy's brown jacket. She sat on the couch.

"No... no. You must...must...have something." Roy's speech was slurring.

"No, I am fine."

"No...You need to have something. Is pizza alright?"

"Okay."

"Awesome!"

Roy dialed the pizza place's number and began giving them the order. While Roy was busy giving the order, Maya quickly dialed one number and disconnected immediately.

"Okay, 30 minutes..." Roy declared while disconnecting the call.

He came to Maya and sat close to her on the couch. He looked straight into Maya's eyes. The greed in his eyes made Maya uneasy. She moved away from him.

Roy shifted toward her and put his hand around her shoulder, and said." I was thinking, Maya; If I can get you a job in my company. I can make you...aaahhhh... a Project Manager. The salary would be two times more than what you are getting now at KKSwTech. What do you think?" Roy slightly pressed Maya's shoulder. Maya frowned. She gave sidelong glances while keeping her head still. She drew her mouth into a straight line and bit her lip.

"What do you say, Maya? Would you like to work under me? A great position, two times the salary... aahh..one sec.. let's say three times ...three times the current salary." Roy's speech was slurred. It was almost incomprehensible.

"I will think over it, Roy," Maya said pithily. She got up and sat on the opposite couch with a rigid posture. She rubbed her sweaty palms to her pant.

"Come on, why are you sitting so far? Come sit next...next...next...to... to me." Roy's speech was slurring more.

"No, I am fine here, Roy." Maya shook her head in disapproval.

"Oh, come on." Roy got up from his seat, clumsily stumbled, and dumped himself near Maya.

"Come on, Maya. I won't bite." He said with a weird smile. "Or should I?" Roy blinked his eyes and began laughing loudly.

Maya was surprised at Roy's change of mood. Her eyes became tight.

"Should I bite, no, eat you?" Roy whispered while trying to bring his face near hers.

Maya got up once more and shifted to the prior couch.

"You scared?" Roy smiled and began opening his shirt's buttons.

Maya stunned. "What are you doing, Roy? "She asked sternly.

"Nothing. It's hot in here, and that's why I'm taking off my shirt. Don't you feel hot?"

"Roy, Weren't you about to tell me who set me up?" Maya stood and asked in a raised voice.

"Yeah, yeah, I will, but first, let me take off my shirt and switch on the A.C." Roy stood up with gusto but lost his balance. He quickly grabbed the couch's armrest and steadied himself.

'Shit, this bastard will not tell me anything, and I can't wait here any longer. He is drunk and capable of doing anything now.' Maya cursed under her breath. She felt the tension in her neck and shoulder.

"Don't you don't feel hot? Come on, join me, take off your shirt." Roy began approaching Maya.

"No, Roy." Maya tried to move away, but Roy pulled her back by holding on to her sleeveless top from behind. Maya moved ahead forcibly, and Roy pulled the top. The thin top slightly tore vertically.

"Roy!!" Maya screamed. She instantly sat down on the other couch. Her heart became pondering heavily.

'Roy had gone too far. I'm going to kill this asshole right now!' Maya's nostrils flared. Her breathing became noisy.

"Come on, Maya. Don't be shy." Roy again began advancing at Maya. Maya saw a wield animal in Roy's eyes. She turned angry and leaped toward her sack on another side of the couch. She quickly unzipped her sack and retrieved the gun from it.

"Stop, Roy. Don't move," Maya pointed the gun at Roy and growled.

For a moment, Roy was surprised to see the gun in Maya's hand. But the next moment, he laughed and began moving toward Maya. He said in a casual tone, "Maya, don't be stupid, keep that gun down."

"Don't move, Roy!" Maya shouted. Her pulse speeded, and her heartbeat was pondering. Anger was on her face, and the heat was flushing through her body.

"Maya, don't be ridiculous..keep the gun down." Roy tried to calm down Maya. He moved one step toward Maya.

"Roy ! Don't move! I will shoot." Maya gave an ultimatum. Her grip on the gun tightened.

"Maya! Calm down ..Calm down." Roy ignored Maya's warning, and he advanced further toward Maya.

Maya pulled the trigger.

The bullet shoots at Roy's right leg, lower to the knee.

"Ahh..ahh...Ahh...." Roy fell down on the floor. "Oh.Sheet! Maya, you shoot me! You Bitch!" He screamed in pain. His eyes were full of pain and anger.

Soon, The lower half of his black pant turned red wet. Blood was dripping on the floor through the bottom rim of his pant.

"Maya, you bitch! I will kill you !" Roy shouted on top of his voice and crawled toward her.

Maya again fired. The bullet passed nearby Roy's ear. He suddenly stopped at his spot like a statue.

"Don't Move, Roy, don't move. The next bullet will be in your chest." Maya warned Roy with grinding teeth. Roy stunned.

The doorbell rang. Roy tried to move toward the main door.

"Don't even dare to move an inch," Maya thundered.

She went to the main door and opened it.

"Does he say anything?" Sarah asked from the door.

"Not yet, but he will," Maya said confidently. They walked back into the hall.

After entering the hall, Sarah saw Roy was on the floor with his right leg stretched to its whole. His trouser was wet under his knees, and blood had accumulated on the floor. He was in great pain. Sarah saw a gun in Maya's hand.

"Oh My God! Maya!" Sarah's mouth fell open. In disbelief, she looked at Roy's blood and quickly turned to Maya and asked, "Did you really shoot him? I thought you just wanted to scare him."

"Yes, I shoot him," Maya said in a plain tone. The calmness in Maya's words shocked Sarah.

"Tell me, Roy, who set me up? Who is trying to ruin my life?!" Maya sat on the opposite couch and asked in a commanding voice.

"I don't know what you are talking about." Roy said while controlling his pain.

"You said in the pub that you know who sets me up for Mrs. Pinto's murder? Now speak up. Who did that?" Maya yelled.

"I don't know," Roy said in a low voice, full of pain.

"Then why you said in the pub that you know who sets me up?" Maya continued yelling.

"That I just said so I could bring you over here."

"and take advantage of me ?" Maya stood from her seat and yelled.

Roy nodded. Maya's anger moved to the next level.

"You bastard. !" She went at him and kicked him at his waist.

"Oh...Ahh. Ahh," Roy shouted in pain.

"Maya..control yourself." Sarah interrupted Maya and pulled her away from Roy.

"What you want from me?" Roy asked while bearing his pain.

"The answer to my question!" Maya again stomped toward him.

"What question?" Roy raised his head asked in disbelief.

"Why did you set me up? "Maya again pointed her gun toward Roy.

"I did not frame anybody," Roy said in a startling tone.

"Why did you murder Mrs. Pinto?" Maya asked in an elevated voice with stony eyes. He pressed the half trigger. Roy heard its sound, and he became restless. Fear appeared in his eyes. His breathing became noisier.

"No..No..I did not kill anybody..pl. don't shoot me." He started making a desperate attempt to move toward the table.

"Roy, I won't ask again. Why did you murder Mrs. Pinto and put the blame on me? "Maya asked angrily.

"Maya. Please ..please..please.. believe me. I did not murder Mrs. Pinto. I just saw her body that night." Roy tried desperately to stop Maya from pulling the trigger entirely.

"Oh! You saw Mrs. Pinto's dead body in the office? What you were doing at the office that late night ?" Sarah asked.

"I will tell you but keep the gun aside." Roy pointed his shaky hand toward the gun.

Maya lowered the gun and said in an authoritative tone,

"I am listening."

"I had one urgent work deliverables on the next day. Hence I came back to the office late that evening and started working on the deliverables. Suddenly, I heard one male and a female voice. It seemed they were shouting at each other. The sound was coming from another corner of the office floor. I paid attention to voices and recognized that the female voice was of Mrs. Pinto but could not figure out the male voice. It was very brief. Mrs. Pinto had always had issues with other employees, so I thought it may be some work-related fight. Then I heard Mrs. Pinto's scream. That also did not surprise me because I had seen her losing her temper during the arguments. But there was no sound after her scream. A pin-drop silence. That surprised me. So after around ten minutes, I walked in the direction from where the sound was coming. I found Mrs. Pinto was on the floor in the pool of blood in your cubical. She had a significant injury to her head. I looked everywhere, but no one was around. "

"Why you did not tell this to the police," Sarah asked.

"I was scared. I didn't want to get involved in police matters, so I ran from there."

"But why did you kill Mrs.Pinto?" Sarah asked.

"No! I did not kill Mrs. Pinto. I swear." Roy said in a desperate tone.

"You are lying. You only murdered Mrs. Pinto." Maya roared and came forward to attack Roy. Her eyes were wide open with anger.

"No. I did not..No I did not.." Roy's eyes blinked in fear.

Maya fired one more bullet. It passed nearby Roy and stuck into the lower section of the sofa.

"Noooo..." Roy shouted in fear and fell to the ground unconscious.

Sarah ran toward Roy and checked his nerve.

"He is unconscious. we need to take him to hospital." Sarah started dialing the hospital number.

"And from there to the police station. He will definitely confess."

Maya took her mobile phone and initiated the call to Inspector Jadhav.

*****

"Advocate Deshpande, I had given you four weeks to produce the evidence of your client's innocence. Do you have it?" Judge Mathew questioned Advocate Deshpande in his usual commanding voice.

"Sorry, your Honor. We need some more time to obtain the evidence." Advocate Deshpande replied.

"As expected, your Honor, defence could not obtain any evidence because there isn't any. This is a criminal waste of the court's precious time." Advocate Patil energetically stood from his chair and argued.

"That's not true, your Honor...." Advocate Deshpande defended.

"Then where is the evidence, advocate ?" Judge Mathew interrupted and asked in a sharp tone.

Deshpande remained quiet to figure out how to convince Judge Mathew.

Advocate Patil took Deshpande's silence as an opportunity to reinforce his argument, "As I mentioned earlier, your Honor. It's all in the open that Miss Maya murdered Mrs. Pinto. The defense does not have any evidence to prove Miss Maya's innocence. I request the court to give us a favorable verdict as soon as possible."

"Please, your Honor. We have a solid lead, and we are very close to obtaining vital evidence that could change the course of this case. But we need some more time to obtain the evidence." Deshpande made a last-ditch effort to plead with Judge Mathew.

Judge Mathew thought for a few seconds and said, "Advocate, I will give you another three weeks. This, however, will be my final offering. I will not be as lenient the next time."

Judge Mathew made himself clear.

"We appreciate your support, your Honor. We will secure all the evidence and present it in the court. " Advocate Deshpande assured the Judge as he bowed a bit.

*****

Maya and Rita were waiting outside the courtroom for Advocate Deshpande.

"Did you hear what Judge Mathew said?" Advocate Deshpande asked Maya hastily while walking out. He was walking quickly than his regular speed.

"Yes... loud and clear." Maya said. She was trying to keep up with Deshpande's pace. Rita was walking behind them.

"Then do something, look harder. Find some evidence or even a single shred of evidence, however small." Deshpande said aggressively.

"Yes, we will get it," Maya assured him.

Advocate Deshpande's car came and stopped in front of them.

"Today, somehow, I managed to convince Judge Mathew, but we have to present evidence in the next hearing."

Deshpande reiterated his point and got into the car.

*****

7

Chapter 7

"Maya...Maya...Maya..." Maya woke up. Her partially opened eyes scanned all directions. She did not see anyone. She closed her eyes.

"Maya...wake up, Maya...wake up!" Voice came again.

'This is not Bhagat's voice. Who is it then?' Maya wondered. She opened her eyes again, and this time she saw a slim figure sitting on the chair near the window. Maya strained her eyes more, and her mouth fell open.

"Oh! Mrs. Pinto?!" Maya exclaimed.

The wind was guesting through the widow. Maya found it mysterious.

Maya sat up on her bed with bulged eyes as her heartbeats were thrashing in her ears. Her mouth became dry, and suddenly her entire body began sweating profoundly.

Mrs. Pinto was staring at Maya with a blank face and steady eyes. Maya noticed Mrs. Pinto was in her regular office attire, a crisp business suit. Her hair was untied, and few of them were falling on her face. Her right cheek was swollen, and there were bleeding wounds on her lips.

"Who killed you, Mrs. Pinto?" Maya asked in a soft tone. Mrs. Pinto did not respond, but she kept staring at Maya.

"Was it Roy? Is Michael anyway involved in your murder?" Maya asked again. In response, Mrs. Pinto took a deep breath and said in a low but deep voice.

"Start looking in all directions; you will find a clue."

After a few silent moments, Mrs. Pinto stood and turned toward the window. Maya saw Mrs. Pinto's back, and her heartbeat skipped. Her breathing suddenly labored. She saw a big bloody wound on the back of Mrs. Pinto's head. The injury was still fresh, and it was bleeding. The hair on Mrs. Pinto's head was matted with blood. Few bloodstreams had made their way down to Mrs. Pinto's coat.

Mrs. Pinto stood in the window and looked outside. Her hair began waving in the wind. Maya was looking at Mrs. Pinto.

After a few moments, Mrs. Pinto looked at Maya.

"You need to look in all directions. You will find a clue." Mrs. Pinto said in her deep low voice.

"Okay...I will, but first, tell me, Who did this to you, Roy?" Maya gathered her wits and asked boldly.

A sad smile emerged on Mrs. Pinto's face.

"Tell me, Mrs. Pinto, who did this to you?" Maya's voice raised in eagerness.

Mrs. Pinto slowly began leaning out of the window.

"What are you doing, Mrs. Pinto?" Maya asked in disbelief. Her face went pale.

Mrs. Pinto did not reply. She had a sad smile on her face. She remained in half-in and half-out state for a few seconds, and suddenly she was sucked outside the window like a powerful magnet attracted the tiny needle.

"Mrs. Pinto!!!" Maya screamed. She ran toward the window and peed outside.

It was pitch dark outside.

Maya's eyes began scanning in all directions, desperately. She raised her head and realized her neck had evolved stiff.

"Mrs. Pinto...where are you? Mrs. Pinto?! Can you hear me?" Maya called in the emotionally choked voice.

No reply from the darkness.

"Mrs. Pinto...where are you ?... Mrs. Pinto...Mrs. Pinto...can you hear me?... Mrs. Pinto?" Maya kept calling in her shaky voice.

Her voice kept echoing in the surrounding darkness. She did not get any response.

*****

"What brings you to the office on a rainy Sunday morning?" Sarah greeted Maya at the office's glass entrance door.

"Nothing special. Just felt like getting out of the house." Maya said while entering the office.

The cloudy weather was inducing unusual darkness on the floor. They both walked through the empty cubicles toward Sarah's cubicle.

Before sitting on her chair, Sarah pulled a chair from the neighboring cubicle for Maya.

"So tell me. Did Roy confess? "Sarah asked.

"No! Actually, he got the bail." Maya said while sitting on the chair.

"Oh.. that's bad," Sarah made an unpleasant face.

Maya kept quiet.

Suddenly, Sarah noticed Maya's wet clothes.

"Your clothes are wet. You will catch a cold. Let me get you some coffee." Sarah stood from her chair and began walking toward the cafeteria.

"Less sugar, please." Maya promptly said.

"Got it!" Sarah raised her hand without looking back.

Maya stood and walked a few steps behind the cubical, toward the glass window panel. She peered out and looked at her left. She saw one residential building at a distance. The building was nearly as tall as the Maya's office building.

'You need to look in all directions. You will find a clue.' Mrs. Pinto's words resonated in Maya's mind.

'Is this building exactly opposite to my cubicle?' Maya wondered, and she turned more at her left.

Maya scrutinized the distant building for a few seconds, and suddenly, she felt energetic. She walked with a fast-paced strut to her left, across the floor, toward her cubicle.

She came to her cubical in a rush and went straight to the window glass panel at its back.

'Yeah, this building is exactly opposite my cubicle.' Maya stared at the front building and confirmed to herself. She noticed a square-shaped opened glass window at the front building, precisely opposite her glass pane window.

Mrs. Pinto's words again echoed through Maya's mind. 'You need to look in all directions. You will find a clue.'

"There you are. I was looking for you at my cubicle." Sarah came from behind and handed Maya a mug of steaming coffee.

"Sarah...look at that building." Maya pointed her steaming coffee mug toward the opposite building.

"Which one? Lumbini Garden?"

"Yes."

"Look at that floor, exactly opposite to ours...See that opened glass window. Do you think anybody lives there?"

"I don't know, why?" Sarah shrugged her shoulders and sipped her coffee.

Maya continued to stare silently at the opened glass window from the opposite building.

"Why, Maya?" Sarah asked again.

"We must find out." Maya excited. She felt strange vibrations inside her body, and she became breathless for moments. She hastily kept her coffee mug on her desk and hurriedly began walking through the long aisle.

"Wait! Where are you going?" Sarah yelled.

"To that building." Maya pointed her hand toward the building.

After a few steps, Maya began running. She exited through the glass entrance in a great hurry and came to the elevator lobby. Both elevator icons were showing an upward arrow.

"Shit! Both the elevators are going upwards." Maya said in displeasure and ran toward the stairs.

*****

Maya rushed out of the office building. Rain was reduced to drizzling. She opened her umbrella and began walking in a small lane adjacent to the office building to Lumbini Garden. She wanted to walk faster, but the drizzle and the muddy potholes made her walk arduous.

Soon, She reached the black-colored, main iron gate of Lumbini Garden.

"Yes, madam?" The security guard came forward and asked politely.

"I need to go in."

"Who would like to meet, Madam?"

'Oh...what should I say now?' Maya was conjuring a reply when she heard a loud horn from behind. Maya turned around and saw a white van waiting at a distance from her.

"Madam, please move to the side." The guard hand gestured to Maya.

The van passed in front of Maya, and as it did, Maya read '360D Monitoring Services', written in large text, on the sides of the van. Alongside the text, various pictures of CCTV cameras, computer screens, and other equipment were printed on the van's sides.

Maya looked at the back of a van for a few seconds, and suddenly her face lit up. She walked hurriedly behind the van.

The guard quickly followed her and asked, "Madam, where are you going?". She pointed her hand to the van and said, "I am with them."

The van reached the porch of the building. A young technician exited from the passenger side with a paper in his hand in a gray uniform. He opened the backdoor of the van and climbed in. He started verifying the labels from the stack of small rectangular boxes with paper in his hand.

"Hi, can I talk to you for a minute?" Maya asked the technician from the opened backdoor of the van.

The technician glanced back at Maya for the moment,

"Sure." He said energetically and resumed his verification work.

"Do you have a CCTV system installed in this building?"

"Yes."

"On each floor?"

"No. We have one system installed for the entire building and its premises. Few apartments opted for separate CCTV system."

"So these special apartment's CCTV systems have recordings from the past?"

"Yes!"

"And does your system save the recordings for a long time?"

"Yes, Why?" This technician got skeptical.

"I stay in a nearby building. We require installing a CCTV system, not for our entire building but for a few apartments. I just want to see the CCTV installation of those special apartments. Are there any apartments you would suggest for me to take a look at?" Maya asked.

"Check with 1001, 1205, and 1302. These apartments have their own CCTV systems installed."

The technician found the box he was looking for. He picked it up and got off the van.

While closing the van door, he asked, "What is the name of your building?" But he did not get any reply. Maya had already started walking hurriedly toward the lobby.

*****

Maya's elevator reached the 10th floor. She came out of the elevator and noticed another elevator opposite hers. Two apartments were situated on both sides of each elevator. The fifth apartment was on the third side of the floor. Across the passage, a closed glass window was located on the fourth side of the floor. It was precisely opposite the fifth apartment.

Maya walked hurriedly toward the glass window. She opened the window, and a gust of wind along with droplets of rain instantly rushed inside. Maya's hair blew in the wind. She looked at her office building behind the thin transparent curtain of rain.

'Which floor of my building is exactly opposite to this floor?' Maya's eyes began scanning the glass façade of her office building. She stopped counting on the floor, exactly opposite to her.

'Hmm...it seems the opposite floor is the 8th floor of my office building. My cubical is on the 10th floor. Let me go to the upstairs.' Maya thought and took the elevator to the 12th floor.

The design of the 12th floor was the same as the 10th floor. There were five apartments on the three sides of the floor and one square-shaped glass window on the fourth side of the floor at the end of the passage.

Maya walked hurriedly toward the glass window.

The window was open, and the wind was spraying rain droplets through it, making the underneath passage floor wet. Maya stood at the window and again counted floors of her office building.

'Yes... the 10th floor of my office is exactly opposite now...and yes, yes! I can see my cubicle just behind the glass panel.' Excitement filled Maya. She jumped energetically on the spot.

She looked at the fifth apartment door, straight across the floor.

She walked toward it and read its apartment number.

'Apartment number 1205. Yes.Yes.Yes...This is one of the apartments with a CCTV camera with recording.' Maya jumped again on the spot in excitement.

She carefully inspected the apartment's main door from top to bottom. Next to the door frame, she saw a rectangular box above the keyhole and a small lens popping out from it on the wall.

'Oh! This must be the camera!" Maya's excitement grew. She stood next to the rectangular box, with her back touching the main door. She kept her line of sight parallel to the angle of the camera lens and looked straight. She could see her cubical at a distance through the glass window.

A broad happy smile appeared on Maya's face.

She quickly dialed Sarah's number and walked back to the glass window.

"Hey, Sarah... come to my cubicle."

"Why?"

"Just walk to the glass window pane behind my cubicle," Maya instructed.

Sarah's silhouette appears behind the tinted glass pane in a few moments. Maya waved at Sarah.

"I think we have found the evidence that we were looking for," Maya spoke like an excited child.

"Really?! What did you find?" Sarah exclaimed while waving back.

"Listen... there is an apartment on this floor, number 1205, with a CCTV camera installed on its main door. The camera's angle is such that it captures what is seen through this window. And I can see my cubical through this window." Maya bounced on her toe at her spot.

"Wow! That's great news, Maya!" Sarah said.

"Yeah."

"..."

"Hello? Sarah?"

"..."

"Sarah, are you there?"

"Yes... I am here."

"What are you thinking ?"

"But Maya...For the camera to record what happened in your cubicle that night, this window would have opened that night, right?"

"Yes..." Maya began thinking. In her excitement, she had not thought about that possibility. She stared at her office building for a few seconds.

"Yeah, you are right, Sarah," Maya said thoughtfully.

"and ... the only way to know that is to ask for the recording from the apartment people." Maya grew anxious. Her breathing became noisier. She walked back to the apartment and raised her hand to ring the doorbell.

"Wait, Maya! Nobody is going to show you anything just like that." Sarah shouted on the phone. Maya's stopped her finger a few inches away from the doorbell.

"Then how can we get access to those recordings?" Maya whispered intensely.

"All these recordings must have been backed up to a central location," Sarah said thoughtfully.

"Oh, got it! The recorded clips must be stored on the server of the CCTV company." Maya said while controlling her emotions.

"Yes. We need to find the location of those recordings." Sarah said.

"Yeah, good idea. " Maya's said with a wide grin. "Let me see if I can still find that technician." Maya disconnected the call and quickly called the elevator.

*****

The rain had changed the gear. It started pouring.

Once the elevator doors opened on the ground floor lobby, Maya ran toward the building's entrance.

Maya heard the sound of the vehicle's engine from the entrance. Through the curtain of heavy rain, she saw the van was still parked near the building entrance.

"Wait... wait!" Maya waved frantically and began running toward the van with manic energy.

"Is that girl calling us?" The van driver asked the technician. The technician looked through the windshield, but his view was obstructed by the oscillating wipers. He strained his eyes and caught a glimpse of Maya running toward the van.

"I think so. I spoke with this girl some time back." Technician said.

Maya reached the van window, and the technician rolled the window pane down. Droplets of rain entered the van.

"What's the matter?" He asked while looking at panting Maya.

"I need...I need....the address of your...your..your...main office." Maya completed the sentence and quickly opened her umbrella.

"Just a sec...." The technician took out his wallet from his back pocket.

"Take this card. Our company's Head Office's address is at the bottom." The technician passed a visiting card through the window. Maya held the card in her wet hand and began reading the address.

The van drove off.

Maya called Sarah while returning to the lobby.

"Listen, it seems the CCTV company's main office is in the Mahim area,"

"Okay, Mahim. Where in Mahim, exactly?"

"Sunshine Industrial complex. Near Mahim station. I need to go there as soon as possible." Maya looked at her watch.

"Don't worry, Maya, I know that area."

"Okay, great! Can we go there now?" Maya asked eagerly.

"No, no, it's not a good time. It's raining heavily. I will go there tomorrow morning."

"Why tomorrow, Sarah? We need to go there as soon as possible. "Maya continued in her eager tone.

"No, not now, Maya. I know that area very well. Rain has been pouring heavily for a long time, and there must be water clogging on the road. I will go there tomorrow morning. Now come back to the office. "

"Okay," Maya said in a low voice, and disconnected the phone.

Due to cloudy weather, dusk was settled all over the lobby. Maya stood like a statue in her wet clothes. She kept looking at the outside rain with a sad face, waiting for it to stop.

*****

The next morning, in cloudy weather, Sarah's cab stopped near the Sunshine industrial complex in Mahim.

Sarah got down from the cab. While looking at the surrounding slums area, her eyes caught the narrow lane leading to the complex's main gate.

She started walking through the lane. The rain had subsided, but it had formed countless muddy potholes in the lane.

Sarah maneuvered through potholes and reached the main gate of the complex.

Sunshine Industrial complex was a four-story, long, horizontal building. Each floor had many manufacturing units, mechanical workshops and small business offices.

Sarah entered through the main gate of the complex and walked a few steps to reach the entrance of the building.

'Where is Unit 8?' She asked the security guard standing at the building entrance.

"Ground floor, this way." The guard showed the way.

Sarah began walking in the shown direction. She passed by a few offices and came to the main door of Unit 8.

Sarah read the name on the main door, '360D Monitoring services.'

Two men were working at the main door.

While Sarah was approaching the main door, one of them said,

"Ma'am, this door is being repaired. Please use the backdoor to get into the office."

"Where is the backdoor?" Sarah looked around.

"Go through that passage, take a left and again left. You will find a small door on your left wall."

Sarah went as directed. She passed by a few more offices in the dim light and found a passage on her left. She began walking through the passage and saw another building entrance at the far end. She could see the parked vehicles in the open space through the entrance gate.

After a few steps, she took another left at the passage.

'The backdoor of the company must be here.' Sarah thought while strolling in the passage. Various boxes and sacks of goods were kept on both sides of the passage. On either side of the passage, built-in closets were on the wall. Most of the closet doors were closed, but few were open. The opened closet had different types of goods dumped in them. The cardboard cartons, along with wasted papers and other trash, were scattered all over the floor.

Sarah walked till the end but did not find the backdoor of the company.

'Where is that damn backdoor?' She grumbled.

She turned back and began walking in the reverse direction. This time, she was observing carefully at the right side of the wall. Suddenly, a narrow black door caught her attention.

Sarah pushed the door and entered the office.

"Yes, Ma'am?" One voice came from behind.

"Where is the reception ?" Sarah turned and asked.

"That way."

Sarah began walking toward the reception area. She passed several closed doors on her right. Doors had nameplates like 'Administration,' 'HR,' 'IT,' 'Marketing'.

As Sarah came close to the receptionist's desk,

"Yes, Madam, How can I help you?" The young female receptionist greeted her.

"Hi, my name is Sarah. I am interested in your company's CCTV products."

"Sure. Please be seated and go through these manuals. I will ask the salesperson to come and meet you. "Sarah sat on the couch in the reception area. The receptionist handed her a few product manuals of their CCTV system. Sarah began going through those colorful manuals.

"Can you come to the front desk? ...good." The receptionist spoke on the phone briefly.

In a few minutes, a young salesman wearing a white shirt, black trousers, and black tie came to the receptionist's desk. The receptionist directed him toward Sarah.

"Yes, Ma'am, how can I help you?" The salesman asked Sarah.

"Hi. My name is Sarah. I am interested in your company's CCTV products." Sarah introduced herself.

"Sure, Ma'am." The salesman sat next to Sarah and started giving her the product information.

After a few minutes, Sarah interrupted him and asked,

"You mentioned that all the recordings of a customer's CCTV are stored on your servers?"

"Yes."

"And where are those servers located?"

"Right here in the IT Room" The salesman pointed to the passage from where Sarah had just come in.

"Oh, here itself !" Sarah looked curiously at the corridor.

"And by the way... how long do you keep old data of each customer?"

"It depends upon the package. Minimum for three months."

'Oh...Mrs. Pinto murdered more than three months ago.' Sarah thought.

'And if a customer wants to store more than three months of data?"

"Then they need to pay extra. By default, the customer gets three months data stored."

"Oh... okay." Sarah kept listening.

"May I know, Ma'am, why are you so keen about the data storage duration ?" The salesman read Sarah's mind and asked politely.

"To be honest with you, we really need the data of one of your existing customers, Flat 1205 from Lumbini Garden. "

"Lumbini Garden? Colaba?'

"Yes. I know this sounds like an odd request, but we really need it. Can I get that data?" Sarah asked eagerly.

"Sorry, Ma'am. We don't share our customers' data with anybody. It's against our company's policy."

"Yeah, I understand, but this is really urgent. The CCTV camera on this apartment's main door might have recorded something important that we are looking for." Sarah insisted.

"Sorry, Ma'am. We absolutely cannot share our customer's data."

"But that recording, however, is really vital to us. My friend's life depends on it. We can pay to obtain the data. Please...please...please." Sarah leaned forward and urged. Her tone was desperate.

"No, Ma'am, sorry." The salesperson refused politely.

Sarah stood in excitement and asked, "Can I speak with your manager or supervisor?" Sarah asked.

"Okay, Ma'am, but that won't change anything. They too will reject your request."

Sarah sat back again. She signed heavily and lowered her head. She was lost in thoughts for a couple of minutes.

"Which package are you interested in, Ma'am?" salesman again showed her the manuals.

Sarah pointed randomly to a page on the manual without raising her head.

"This package? Okay. Give me a minute, Ma'am. I will bring the latest price list." The salesman rushed inside the office.

Sarah slowly raised her head and confirmed the salesman had gone out of sight. She stood and hurriedly began walking through the passage toward the backdoor.

"Wait, Ma'am, the salesperson, will be back." The receptionist's voice came from behind.

Sarah halted but did not look back.

"Wait, Ma'am, the salesman, will return in a moment." the receptionist insisted.

Sarah turned back and momentarily looked at the receptionist. She momentarily flashed a fake smile and resumed her walking.

"Wait .. Ma'am, wait for Ma, am.." The receptionist's voice was fading as Sarah walked toward the backdoor.

She hurriedly came out of the backdoor and almost ran toward the other entrance of the building.

*****

On Friday morning, Advocate Deshpande was on his way to court in his luxury car.

His mobile rang.

"Hello...Yes, Maya, I called you yesterday, but you did not call back. Your hearing will be starting soon."

"Yes, Sir, I am on my way to the court," Maya said.

"Do you have the evidence?"

Maya sensed the urgency in Advocate Deshpande's voice.

"..."

"Maya?"

"We may have tracked down some CCTV footage that can be admitted as evidence," Maya informed.

"That's good. Very good. Where is it? Are you bringing it to the court now?"

"Sorry, Sir, We don't have it yet," Maya apologized in a low voice.

"What?!"

"Sorry, Sir."

Deshpande sighed profoundly and remained quiet. Maya waited for Deshpande's response.

"Hello? Hello ?" Maya checked after a few seconds.

"...."

"Hello? Hello Sir, are you there?"

"Maya! Today, You were supposed to bring the evidence in the court." Deshpande resumed in a severe tone.

"I know, Sir, and we are trying our best."

"..."

Deshpande's car stopped in front of the court's main gate.

"I will try my best to defend you in court today but don't expect much."

Advocate Deshpande disconnected the phone and hurriedly got out of the car.

*****

"Well, Advocate Deshpande, today you must have brought the evidence of your client's innocence." Judge Mathew asked Advocate Deshpande.

"We think We have found a solid piece of evidence, your Honor." Advocate Deshpande stood and began his arguments.

"Good. Then submit to the court."

"Sorry, your Honor..."

"Sorry? sorry for what ?" Judge Mathew's voice raised in surprise.

"Your Honor, we have found the crucial evidence, but we don't have it in our hands yet." Advocate Deshpande explained.

"These are just tactics of the defense to kill time and delay the proceedings, your Honor." Advocate Patil stood energetically from his chair and countered Deshpande's argument.

"It looks like the defense has only one purpose, wasting the court's valuable time. They should not be dealt any leniency anymore, your Honor." Advocate Patil roared.

Judge Mathew listened to Advocate Patil and looked at Advocate Deshpande.

"That's not the case, your Honor. We are really trying hard to get the evidence." Advocate Deshpande said in a calm tone.

"Believe me, your Honor, the defense will never be able to produce any substantial evidence. I am sure..." Advocate Patil butted in aggressively.

"Why do you think so?" Judge Mathew interrupted.

"Because they don't have it, your honor. You should announce your verdict immediately ." Advocate Patil said in an elevated voice.

"Please control your emotions, and don't tell me how to do my job!" Judge Mathew reprimanded Patil.

"Sorry, your Honor. I did not intend to disrespect the court. But the defense really does not have any evidence to prove their innocence. They do not have a case here. I request you to give the verdict as soon as possible." Advocate Patil said respectfully and sat back on his chair.

Judge Mathew turned toward Deshpande and said sternly,

"You have one more week. If you don't produce any evidence, I will pronounce my verdict."

*****

Advocate Deshpande and Maya came out of the courtroom and walked outside.

"Maya, it was difficult, but I have bought you one more week," said Advocate Deshpande. He was going to go through the messages on his mobile.

"In this one week, we have to find the evidence. " Advocate Deshpande stressed on 'have to' word.

"Only in one week? That's very little time, sir. How will we obtain the evidence with such a tight deadline?" Maya shook her head.

"In next hearing, if we don't present evidence of your innocence in court, the Judge will give his verdict, and needless to say, it will be against you. You will be convicted of murder and sent to jail for a long time." Advocate Deshpande painted a gummy future.

Maya remained quiet. She kept walking along with Advocate Deshpande.

" Grab it, steal it, or do whatever. But get the evidence as soon as possible." Advocate Deshpande stressed every word.

*****

Days passed quickly as fast-moving clouds in the sky. Maya could not make any progress to find evidence of her innocence. She became restless.

"Sarah, is there any other way we can get the CCTV recording?" Maya called.

"I tried Maya. I requested. I pleaded, I offered to pay too. But they didn't budge. They said it's against their company's policy."

"To hell with their company policy. My life is at stake here. If they can't do it as per their company's policy, at least do it for humanity." Maya was frustrated, angry, and helpless.

"I understand, Maya. It's frustrating." Sarah consolidated.

"Today is Saturday; we need to produce the evidence in court on Monday. Those CCTV recordings are our only hope, now."

"Somehow, we need to get that night's CCTV footage." Sarah said thoughtfully.

"But how Sarah? How??" Maya's asked desperately.

"We need to find a way. I will check with Advocate Deshpande if we can use any legal option. But..." Sarah again thought.

"But what?"

"Tomorrow is Sunday. The court will be closed tomorrow, and on Monday, we need to produce evidence in court...We don't have much time to try for any other legal option."

"Then, what are we going to produce in the court on Monday, Sarah?" Maya asked desperately.

Sarah again thought for a few moments, looked around to make sure no one was around, and murmured on the phone.

"There is one way ..but it may not be the right way.."

"What is that?" Maya asked with bulged eyes.

"...But I think that's only our option and hope." Sarah said thoughtfully.

"What is that? Tell me fast." Maya asked eagerly.

"Listen..."

Sarah spoke for a few minutes.

In those minutes, Maya's face slowly turned nervous.

"But it's risky," Maya said in a low voice.

"Yes, it's risky, and we also do not know if there is any recording of that night. But it's our only hope. It's our only chance," Sarah tried to convince.

Maya did not reply. A few seconds passed in silence.

"Forget it, Maya. Let's drop the idea. It's too risky." Sarah said hurriedly.

Maya did not reply.

"Hello, Maya ? are you there?" Sarah asked.

"Yes, I am here,"

"I said, forget it. It's a risky idea. I shouldn't have given you the idea in the first place." Sarah said concludingly.

"No..No..you are right, it's our last hope." Maya said excitingly. Her eyes began glowing with determination.

"Are you sure you want to do it? it's too risky. "Sarah reminded.

"Yes, I know it's risky. But I will do it...I will do it."

*****

On Sunday night, around 11 P.M., Rita came from outside.

"Where you been so late ?" Maya asked. She was dressed to go out.

"I was at Hema's place," Rita answered while keeping her parse on the table.

"Why did you go there?"

"Recently, she underwent heart surgery. She just got discharged from the hospital. So I went to meet her." Rita said while going into the kitchen.

"Hmm...Okay.." Maya replied casually and looked at her wristwatch.

"And you know...It seems she had a heart attack in June itself...I asked her why she did not tell me even when you came to meet Maya.." Rita was talking non-stop. She started keeping food vessels from the kitchen platform to the refrigerator.

"She got the attack one night before you got arrested. A lot was going on with us, so she did not inform us."

Maya heard the words "one night before you got arrested" and rushed to the kitchen.

"What you just said, mom? Hema auntie got heart attack one night before I was arrested?"

"Yes..that's what she said .." Rita said while closing the refrigerator door.

"Oh! That's the night when Mrs. Pinto was murdered. Oh !..." Maya became anxious. She did not have the strength to stand. She came to the hall and sat on the couch. She bowed down and held both palms tightly on her head.

'Oh..it means...after getting Hema auntie's heart attack news, Michael hurriedly got out from the office and took a cab that night. Obliviously he must be in tension and did not wait for the change." Maya connected the dots. Sweat began pouring from her body.

"Shit...Damn of me...I misbehaved with Michael." Maya blamed herself.

"..so Hema forced me to stop for dinner. I said I will be late for home and Maya be worried...but she said Michael would drop you." Rita continued her talking.

'Michael would drop you.." words went through Maya's ears, and she stood energetically.

"What you just said? Michael dropped you?" She asked with heavy breathing and pondering heart.

"Yes, Michael dropped me."

Maya rushed toward the main door. On the way to the main door, she put her shoes and opened the door.

"Where are you going, such late night ?" Rita asked worriedly.

"I will be back in some time.." Maya opened the main door and hurriedly stepped out.

*****

Maya came out of the main gate and looked around. She saw Michael's car parked at a distance. She walked hurriedly toward the car.

Michael was busy going through messages on his mobile phone. Maya knocked on the glass window. Michael was surprised to see Maya. He rolled down the window.

"Can you please come out, Michael ?" Maya asked in a soft voice.

Michael was puzzled. He opened the door and came out.

"Michael .." Maya tried to speak. Her eyes were wet.

"Yes.."

"Michael..." Maya tried to speak, but she could not. She suddenly came forward and hugged Michael tightly.

Michael was surprised.

"I am sorry, Michael...I doubted you...Really really sorry.." Maya said in an apologetic tone. Tears started flowing through her cheeks.

Michael let Maya hug him for some time.

He looked at her and said,

"Don't apologize, Maya. You have been through a lot. If I were at your place, I would have done the same thing."

Maya again hugged him tightly. Another round of tears made their way down through cheeks.

After a few minutes, Michael looked at Maya's dress and asked, "Are you going somewhere?"

Maya took a deep breath and nodded.

"May I ask where?"

Maya did not reply. She wiped her tears and dialed Sarah's number.

"Hey Sarah, I am going to the sunshine estate now, and I am sure we will get the evidence. "Maya said confidentially.

"Are you going there alone?" Sarah asked.

"Yes!"

"Okay...but.."

"But what ?"

"There will be security guards at the main gate and also at the front entrance of the building. CCTV cameras are installed there. So once you enter through the main gate, go to the other entrance of the building"

"Other entrance? Where is it located?" Maya asked.

"It is at...." Sarah paused for a moment.

"Sarah?" Maya prodded.

"You may not be able to find it easily in the dark. I will come there to show you."

"Okay. I will be there in some time." Maya disconnected the call.

Michael got the idea of what Maya was up to.

"...Maya...." Michael said.

"Yeah?"

"Are you sure you want to do this?"

"Yes, positive! There is a CCTV camera in the apartment precisely opposite my office cubical. We guess something might have been recorded through that camera on the night when Mrs. Pinto was murdered. We found the CCTV company and the location of the recordings within that company. "Maya said in a steady voice.

"and you decided to steal those recordings?" Michael asked in a plain tone.

"Yes!"

"But we even don't know if we could find any evidence there."

"Yes, I know."

"If we are caught, we will be in huge trouble. Think again." Michael urged.

"Michael, If you are scared, you may leave. I can do it myself." Maya said in irritation.

"No. I am not scared. I am worried about you." Michael explained.

"Stop worrying about me. It won't help me." Maya was irritated and started walking toward the main road.

Michael thought for a few moments. He signed profoundly and began following Maya.

*****

After around a half-hour drive, Michael's car stopped at the entrance of the same narrow lane leading toward the Sunshine industrial complex. He looked all around through the windshield and said,

"Hmmm...these look like a slum area. Are you sure this is the right address?"

"This is what was given on the visiting card." Maya, too, stared at the lane and surrounding slums.

"The lane is very narrow. The car won't pass through it. Let's walk from here." Michael stopped the engine. They both got off the car and began walking in the lane.

Both sides of the lane were occupied with small shops of laundries, barber, tobacco, and groceries. The street lights were emitting yellow light throughout the lane. It was almost 11:45 P.M., and most of the shops were shut.

People were sleeping next to the shops' rolled-down metal doors, and many were preparing their beds outside their tiny slums. Few street dogs were roaming around for food.

After a short walk, Maya and Michael came to the main iron gate of the Sunshine Industrial complex. One security cabin was at the corner of the main gate, and one pole with tube light at its top was erected beside it. The tube lights white light was spread all over the main gate.

"What are we going to tell the security guards?" Maya whispered.

"Nothing! Let's check out the surroundings first." Michael looked at the stone wall that had surrounded the complex. He took a left at the main gate in the dark and walked parallel to the stony compound wall. Maya followed Michael, keeping a couple of steps distance between them.

After walking a few yards, Michael made a right at the crossroad and continued walking parallel to the wall in the dark.

He noticed the compound wall was broken at the top at one spot. He came close to the compound wall and peeped into the other side of the wall with strained eyes. In the limited light, he saw a few goods trucks and old cars parked inside the premises.

'We need to jump over the wall. But Maya may not be able to jump." He thought.

He again looked inside the premises. While he was observing the premises, he suddenly heard footsteps from behind. He immediately turned around and saw Maya running from the road and leap up the wall. She grabbed the top of the wall and jumped on the other side without making much sound.

"Wow! Maya !!" Michael was stunned by seeing Maya's athleticism.

"Come on, Michael, Jump fast," Maya whispered from the other side of the wall. She was bouncing on her tiptoe. Her legs were spread slightly, and her arms were state of readiness.

Michael smiled and jumped across the wall.

They bent down and jogged between the parked vehicles. They were looking in all directions and inching toward the main entrance of the building.

In a few minutes, they were near the main entrance of the building.

"You wait here. I will go ahead and make sure the guards are not around." Michael whispered and headed to the main entrance.

Maya waited between two cargo trucks.

After a couple of minutes, she heard a soft voice from her behind,

"Maya... Maya..." Maya turned around.

It was Sarah emerging from the darkness.

"Sarah! How did you get in here?" Maya's eyes were wide open with surprise.

"That's not important. "Sarah whispered in a hushed tone and pointed her hand in the dark. "Go in this direction, on your right, you will find another entrance to this building."

"Okay..Michael has gone in this direction toward main entrance." Maya pointed at opposite direction.

"Is Michael with you ?"

"Yes.."

Suddenly, Maya noticed Sarah had blood on her forehead, and her mouth was swollen. Her t-shirt was torn at the shoulder. Her jeans, too, were torn at the knees.

"Sarah! what the hell happened to you? "Maya asked worriedly.

"I followed you guys and fell down while jumping over the compound wall. But nothing to be worried about. "Sarah said casually. Her alert eyes quickly made suspicious glances in all directions and looked at Maya.

"Listen, go in this direction, and you will find the other entrance of the building. Once you enter the building, turn right at the first passage and start walking through the passage. You will see many wardrobes on both sides of the wall. Walk twenty to thirty steps, and on your left, you will see a small black door between two wardrobes. That's the backdoor of the CCTV company, and once you enter through the backdoor, you will see one passage. Start walking in that passage and keep looking at right. After a few doors, you will see the IT room's door. Recordings are located on the servers from this room."

"Okay, thanks." Maya began walking in the dark toward the other entrance of the building. After a few steps, she stopped and suddenly looked back at Sarah. Sarah's face was not clearly visible to her in a limited source of light.

"Why don't you come with me? It will be helpful." Maya asked.

"No, you go. I will wait here and give direction to Michael. Also, I will watch and make sure no one follows you. If anyone does, I will call you." Sarah said, continuing to look around suspiciously.

"Okay." Maya strolled. She walked carefully in the dark and came to the other entrance.

Maya slightly pulled the grill door at one side and sneaked into the building. In limited light, she saw the dark corridor in front of her. She slowly began walking through it. After walking a few feet, suddenly, she heard footsteps from behind.

'Oh... who is following me?' a fear gripped Maya.

She halted and turned around. She saw a lone figure approaching her through the darkness. Maya's body began shivering, and her heartbeat got faster. Her shaky fingers turned on the torch from the mobile and pointed its narrow light beam toward the approaching person.

"Shhh! Turn off the torch."

'Oh, it's Michael.' Maya realized. "Michael, You scared Me!" Maya heaved a sigh of relief and switched off the torch.

"What are we looking at here?" Michael whispered and made a few quick glances around in the dark.

"Sarah told me to take right at first passage and company's backdoor is at the left wall." Maya pointed at the corridor.

"Okay. Let's find that door then." Michael said. They began ambling, one after another. Maya's hand was sliding over the wardrobes on the left.

After a couple of minutes of slow and careful walk, Maya's hand felt the small door at her left.

'Yes, this must be that door.' Maya thought. "Michael, here..." Maya held Michael's hand and pulled him in her direction.

"Okay." Michael came forward and pushed the door open.

"The door was already open." Michael turned around and whispered.

"What do we do now?" Maya asked.

Michael thought for a second and asked, "Do you know where to find the recording?"

"Yes, Sarah said, once we entered, there is one passage. After a few doors, there is the IT room's door on the right."

"Okay. Let's go inside then!" Michael said determinedly.

*****

Michael switched on the torch on his mobile and slowly walked through the passage. He had directed his torchlight beam to the right wall.

"One..." Maya counted as they passed the first door on the right.

"Two..."

"...Three..."

"...Four..." They both looked at the door. The silver plate on the door said 'IT.'

"Yes! The recordings must be in this room! "Maya jumped in excitement.

'Shhh..." Michael kept his finger on his lips.

"Sorry.." Maya said faintly.

Michael slowly turned the doorknob. It was loose.

"This door is also already opened." Michael turned and whispered.

"Let's see what we can find inside," Maya whispered back.

Michael pushed the door and stepped inside the room, followed by Maya. The room was partially dark inside. After a couple of steps, Michael realized a spacious room with many computer monitor screens arranged on a big circular table. A faint blue glow was originating from computer screens. Behind the table, on the wall, countless green, yellow, and orange tiny bright lights were constantly blinking, indicating the activeness of the servers.

Michael carefully took a few more steps inside. As he got closer to the circular table in the middle, he noticed a person in a hoodie, wearing a dark jacket, working on the computer.

Michael walked a couple of more steps and heard the sound of the typing keys. The person was typing rapidly on the computer. Michael took one more step.

"Lumbini Garden, Apartment 1205." Michael read the letters from the screen. There was an animation of flying envelopes on the computer screen.

'Data is getting copied.' Michael thought. He looked back and pointed Maya toward the screen.

Maya took the step forward. She, too, read the screen title,' Lumbini Garden, Apartment 1205'. She quickly grabbed Michael's arm and gave him a surprised look.

The person hit two keys on the keyboard, and a message appeared on one screen, 'Do you want to delete it permanently?' The person selected 'Yes,' and the files were deleted permanently from the computer. In a few seconds, the copy animation disappeared from the screen. The person took out a pen drive from the computer's tower.

As soon as the person turned around, Michael jumped on him. They both fell to the floor. The pen-drive slipped from the person's hand and slid on the floor. Michael looked at the person and shouted.

"Maya, check the data of Apartment 1205. He was copying from that folder."

The man punched Michael hard on his face. "Ahh...!" Michael moaned in pain and was flung back. The punch was powerful. It tore Michael's upper lip, and blood immediately oozed from it. The man began searching for the pen drive on the floor in the little light.

Maya's eyes were desperately scanning the computer screen. She saw the main folder, 'Clients,' and many folders of different names.

'This seems to be the client list of this company.' Maya thought. She saw an 'open folder' icon titled Lumbini Garden.'

'Oh... looks like that guy was working on the Lumbini Garden data.' Maya saw a list of all the apartments from Lumbini Garden. She scrolled carefully through the list and opened the folder name '1205'. It was empty.

'Apartment 1205's data seems to be deleted.' Maya was stunned. She felt a knot in her stomach, and her legs were frozen. Her eyebrows furrowed, and she immediately turned toward Michael and shouted.

"Michael, the data of 1205 has been deleted."

"It must be in that pen-drive. We have to find that Pen-drive." Michael said painfully while wiping blood from his mouth. Suddenly, the man hit him once more.

'Aaaah!!" Michael reeled back in pain.

Maya frantically began searching for pen drive on the floor in the dimly lit room. She sat on her knees, her shoulders were curled, and her spine was bent. She spread both her hands on the floor and began sliding quickly on every inch of it.

The man was also looking desperately for the pen drive on the floor. He was taking small steps to search for it.

Suddenly, Michael pulled the man's leg and tripped him. The man fell but again stood quickly. Michael again pulled the man on the floor.

Maya continued her desperate search on the floor.

"Do you get it?" Michael asked desperately while tackling the man.

"No... not yet!" Maya shouted back.

Michael and man began wrestling. The man had got a grip around Michael's neck, and Michael was trying to break free from the hold. He was shaking fiercely. In his desperation, Michael kicked the man's leg forcefully, and his grip loosened. Michael pushed with his all might, and the man fell back a few feet.

"Did you find it?" Michael shouted again while breathing heavily.

"No," Maya replied.

"Search in that area...in that area!" Michael pointed toward a specified area on the floor. Suddenly, the man pushed him forcefully from behind. Michael was thrown against a wall of blinking, colorful tiny lights.

"Aaahhh!!" Michael groaned in pain. He turned around and saw the man pick something from under the table.

"Maya, catch him. Catch him!! He found the pen-drive." Michael shouted frantically. Maya tried to stop the man, but he firmly pushed her aside. She was thrown on the table. The man swiftly got out of the room.

"Michael, catch that bastard," Maya shouted.

Michael was moaning in pain. He looked at the door in anger, got up, and ran out of the room. He heard the sound of the backdoor being shut.

"He is escaping from the backdoor," Michael shouted and ran toward it. Maya followed.

They both went out of the office. They looked at left and right on the passage. Maya saw a dark figure running toward the other entrance of the building.

"Michael, there he is. He is headed to the other entrance, the one we came in from." Maya shouted desperately.

"Hey, stop!!" Michael shouted and began running toward the other entrance.

Michael's voice was heard by the security guard who was patrolling nearby. He pointed his torch at the other entrance door and quickly walked toward it.

A person wearing a brown jacket came out of the back entrance in a few moments.

"Ruko... Ruko..." Guard shouted in the local language, Hindi, and ran toward the entrance. His torchlight beam caught Michael and Maya coming out of the entrance.

"Hey, Ruko. Kaun ho tum? Yahaan kya kar rahe ho?" The guard shouted in Hindi. He quickly moved his torchlight beam at the man running toward the compound wall. Michael picked up the pace and followed the man.

"Ruko... Ruko...Rukkko!!" The guard kept shouting. The man climbed the compound wall from the same spot where Michael and

Maya jumped in.

The guard began blowing his whistle loudly. It alerted the other security guards, and they responded with their whistles. The guard from the main gate came running too, with his loud whistle. Suddenly, the whole atmosphere was filled with the loud sounds of whistles.

"Kya Hua?" One of the guards asked the first one.

"Wahaan Kuch log Kuch churake bhag rahe hai. Pakdo unhe!" The first guard pointed his torch toward the compound wall. In the yellow light beam of torchlight, the security guards saw Maya jump over the compound wall, and Michael was about to climb up behind him.

"Oye... Ruko.. .rukkko!" The security guards ran toward the compound wall. Before they reached the wall, Michael and Maya had already jumped the wall on the other side.

"Pakdo unko,unko pakdo!" One of the security guards shouted. The guards jumped over the compound but did not chase much.

*****

The man in a hoodie ran into the maze of narrow lanes in the slums. Michael and Maya started chasing him.

The man was running a few slums ahead of Michel and Maya. Maya saw the large image of yellow sunflower on the back of the man's brown jacket.

'I had seen that brown jacket and yellow sunflower before,' Maya thought. After a few seconds, she suddenly shouted, "Michael, that must be Roy!"

"Are you sure?" Michael asked without looking at her. He was chasing the man running in front.

"Roy has the same brown jacket with a yellow sunflower image on its back. I have seen Roy wearing it many times." Maya said.

Suddenly, the rain began drizzling, and the ground of narrow lanes became slippery.

"Hey Roy, stop!!!" Michael shouted.

The man zig-zagged, right, left, and right again through the narrow lanes. He navigated briskly through metal beds, water storage vessels, bicycles, motorcycles and flung them behind to slow Michael's speed. Michael dodged the thrown items tossed his way.

After few minutes, the man began panting heavily. His breathing became heavy, and his speed reduced.

Michael continued to chase after him while Maya was close behind him.

Soon, Michael came to man's proximity.

'The man seems to be slowing down.' Michael realized the slowness in man's running pace.

'I must run fast and grab him now.' Michael thought. He looked back for a moment. Maya was at a distance from him, and she was gasping for breath too.

"Roy, stop! We know you did all this." Michael shouted again. He was panting too.

The man was still trying to lose Michael through the narrow lanes. Michael took a couple of deep breaths and increased his speed. The yellow sunflower colored image at the back of the man's leather jacket was becoming more and more apparent to him.

The man briefly looked back and saw Michael was closing in. He tried to run fast but felt winded again. He was out of breath and started losing his balance.

The man came out of a lane that directly intersected the main road. He was fatigued and trying to run across the road.

Suddenly, a speeding car hit the man head-on.

"Aaahh!!" The man moaned in pain and was forcefully thrown to the side of the road.

The car came to a halt. Michael ran toward the man. The people started gathering around the fallen man.

Michael, with heavy panting, navigated through the crowd and reached near the man. He saw the man was lying on his stomach in the mud and he was not moving. The yellow sunflower on the back of his jacket was covered in mud.

Michael turned the man's body around, and shocked.

"Oh my god !" He rubbed his eyes multiple times. His mouth fell open, and he felt giddiness.

"Sam!!" Michael exclaimed in shock and disbelief.

Rain was still drizzling. A person from the crowd put his ear on Sam's chest and, after a few seconds, shouted,

"He is still breathing; he is alive!" On hearing that, few people immediately began dialing on their mobile phones.

Michael quickly searched Sam's jacket. His hand felt the pendrive in its inner pocket. He immediately grabbed it and kept it in his own pocket.

*****

Maya was utterly wet. She was following Michael, but she could not match his speed for long. She began to feel dizzy. Her breathing became labored. She stopped at one spot to breathe. She looked at a distance and could see the headlights of moving vehicles from the main road at a distance.

She saw Michael exit the lane and join the main road.

Maya resumes her run and came out of the lane. She reached the main road, and suddenly heard a car honking behind her.

"Beeeeepppp!!" Maya did not turn around. She was froze on the spot.

'I had heard this sound before,' She recollected.

Suddenly, an image appeared in her mind. In the image, she saw the main gate in the dark. The name at the main gate was 'Ruby Park.' She came out of the main gate and ran on the road in the image. She heard a car honking behind her.

"Beeeeepppp!!"

The sound of the horn was followed by the ear-splitting sound of tires under stress,

"Screeeeeeeeeech!"

Maya turned back, and her wide-open eyes flooded with yellow light from the car's headlamps.

Maya snapped into the present.

'I have seen this before,' Maya thought, and an approaching car's headlights filled her eyes.

"Screeeeeeeeech!"

'Thud!!'

The car hit Maya.

'Aaahhh.' Maya screamed in pain. She flung in the air and fell at a distance. Her head hit severely on the ground.

For the next few seconds, her eyes were opened, but a strange sound had filled her ears.

In her daze, she saw Michael running toward her.

*****

At midnight Kapoor's mobile rang. It rang a few times and stopped. After a few seconds, it rang again. Kapoor woke up. He picked up the phone in drowsiness.

"Helloooo," Kapoor answered in a heavy voice.

" Kapoor Sir, this is Michael."

"Who?"

"Michael Sir. I am your employee."

"Michael, it is the middle of the night. " Kapoor yawn.

"Sorry, Sir, but the matter is urgent. It's about Mrs. Pinto's murder for which Maya is the accused." Kapoor instantly snapped out of his sleepy demeanor. He woke up and sat straight in the bed.

"What do you know about it?" Kapoor asked in a wary tone.

"The person behind all of this is none other than Sam."

"What, Sam? Our employee? Are you sure?"

"Yes, I am sure. it's Sam, your employee."

"But Maya and Sarah firmly believe that Roy was the one who did all of this. They even mentioned that Sam had evidence against Roy," Kapoor asked surprisingly.

"No, Sir, it has been Sam all along. He created the scenes and cooked up a story around it in such a way that everyone would suspect Maya and Maya, in turn, suspect Roy." Michael said calmly.

"How can you say this so confidentially? " Kapoor asked curiously.

Michael smiled.

"I have seen the recording, Sir."

"Which recording?"

"It's the CCTV recording from the opposite building to our office building. The CCTV camera is exactly opposite to Maya's cubicle in that building."

"And what is in that recording?"

"It is a recording that clearly shows Sam murdered Mrs.Pinto."

"Oh my God!" Kapoor was shocked. "Can you please send me the recording?"

"Sure! I am also forwarding the recording to Maya's lawyer, Advocate Deshpande."

In a few seconds, Kapoor's heard the alert tone from his mobile. Michael had forwarded the recording.

Kapoor watched the recording tensely. A sweat emerged on his forehead, and he suddenly felt thirsty. He poured water into a glass from a nearby jar and drank it in one go. He kept the emptied glass on the table. He was breathing heavily.

Kapoor spent a few minutes gathering his thoughts. He picked up his phone and dialed the number.

"Hello, Colaba police station ?... this is Kapoor. I have important evidence against Sam Walker in the Mrs. Pinto murder case."

*****

It was early in the morning, and rain was pouring outside. Michael was sitting in the waiting area at a city hospital. Sam had returned from his surgery, and Maya was still unconscious.

Michael stood at the window watching the heavy rain.

'Why did Sam do all this?' Thoughts were running in his mind.

"Mr. Michael, Sam has regained consciousness. You may meet him." A nurse informed.

'Should I meet him and confront him? No, I don't want to meet that bastard. He is the main culprit. He is the mastermind... he should suffer in jail.'

'But Maya deserves answers!... Why did Sam do all this? Was it because of the grudge against Maya? Why did he murder Mrs. Pinto?' Michael started pacing back and forth fervently in the waiting area.

'Only, Sam can answer these questions. Shall I go and ask him? No, But I really don't want to meet him...but he is the only person who can shed light on the truth....but what's the guarantee that he will tell the truth?...on the other hand, what if he does? There is no harm in asking him. Who knows, he may repent and tell the truth.'

Michael went to Sam's room. He was resting with his eyes closed.

"Hi, Michael," Sam said without opening his eyes.

"I recovered the recording of your killing to Mrs. Pinto. How did you know that your killing act is recorded by CCTV camera from the opposite building?" Michael asked while entering the room.

"Maya called me asked if I knew anybody from that CCTV company. She was desperate. So, I got the clue, and I came back to Mumbai." Sam smiled sarcastically.

Michael sighed and stood in front of Sam's bed. Sam's forehead was wrapped in bandages, and his right leg was in a cast and had been kept elevated.

"By the way, You must be wondering why I did all this, right?" Sam asked in a plain tone.

"Yes!! What really happened, Sam?" Michael calmed himself down and asked.

"I thought there was nobody in the office, but Mrs. Pinto suddenly emerged in front of me and then...."

"...and then?"

"She figured out what I was up to by looking at the screen. She then threatened me to tell Kapoor. I tried to reason with her at first. Then I pleaded with her, but she was not in a mood to listen. I tried to convince her, but that stubborn lady would not give in. I lost my patience and got angry. I pushed her hard. She fell backward and hit her head hard against the concrete pillar. Believe me, my intention was only to scare her. She fell to the ground. I thought she must have become unconscious from the impact, but the following day, I came to know that she was dead. Trust me, Sam, it was an accident."

"But why do you do this, Sam? You had a good job, a great carrier, and a promising future ahead." Michael asked sadly.

Sam smiled sarcastically. Michael found it mysterious.

"Why Sam, why? Why this mess?" Michael asked again eagerly.

Sam became quiet for a few seconds and said, "I didn't want to do hardship the rest of my life. My ambition was to become rich, very rich, and very quickly. "

"Okay, but what's the connection of this with Mrs. Pinto's murder?" Michael asked.

"I told you, Mrs. Pinto's murder was an accident. "

"But on that day, you told us Roy murdered Mrs. Pinto. Now it's clear it was you. But what you sent to Maya as evidence against Roy?"

"After Mrs. Pinto fell on the floor unconscious. I created evidence to support my innocence. I took fallen Mrs. Pinto's photos and later morphed them with Roy's photos to show Roy murdering Mrs. Pinto. Those photos I sent to Maya as evidence against Roy."

"Hmm...But what were you doing at Maya's cubical? What you were up to ?" Michael asked suspiciously.

Sam did not reply. Michael waited for a couple of minutes for Sam's reply, But Sam did not reply; he kept quiet. Michael became impatient. Sam's calmness scared him.

"Michael! Tell me! What do you do!?" Michael shouted. He came close to Sam and raised his hand to punch him.

Sam took a deep breath.

"I sold the confidential documents and drawings in the black market," Sam said casually.

"What? !" Michael stunned.

"Those black market guys paid me generously. If you don't plan for big, you don't achieve big." Sam wrinkled his one eye and smiled.

"Okay, let's assume you had access to the documents, But how did you send those documents out of KKSwTech? " Michael asked with a confused face.

Sam paused for a few seconds and said, "Maya! "

"What about Maya?" Michael's face turned red.

"She was my close friend."

"Sam, what you did to her ?" Michael asked again with an elevated voice.

"I stole Maya's personal email id and password." Sam looked straight into Michael's eyes fearlessly. But Michael did not believe.

"But How did you get Maya's email id and password?" Michael asked eagerly.

"A few days earlier, in the cafeteria, I told her that my mobile battery was dead and I had to make an urgent call. That innocent girl gave me her Mobile." Sam laughed.

"And you installed malware into her mobile and stole the id and password of her personal email account?"

"Correct !" Sam laughed loudly.

"Oh...Sam! She handed you her phone with trust."Michael became angry.

"Yeah, I agree...broken glasses of trust stabs relations deeply. Sometimes it tears out the flesh of humanity...and you know Michael, trust is like a cashier's cheque. It's better to cash it on time." Sam said with a smiling face.

"..and wait a minute. Did you use her personal email id to send the documents?!" Michael almost shouted.

"Again, Correct! I came here to cubical, made one phone call from her desk phone to HSDTecSoft. I logged in her computer and sent the email through her email id with confidential documents as an attachment." Sam said excitingly.

Michael lost in his thoughts for some time. He was trying to connect the dots.

"No, Sam. I don't believe what you are saying. This must not be the reason for you to steal the documents and blame Maya. There must be something else...may be bigger than what it looks..." Michael said thoughtfully.

In a few moments, his face lit up with fear.

"Sam?! Are you a spy? " In response, Sam gave a blank look at Michael.

With disbelief in his eyes, Michael connected the dots in his mind and said intensely,

"Yes, you seem to be spying against us. You are planted here to steal confidential information. Isn't it? You did it swiftly and smartly created the evidence against Maya".

Sam smiled.

"Sam! You bastard! I will kill you! " Michael roared. His wide eyes turned red. His muscles and veins began straining against his skin. He hit a punch on Sam's face. Sam's lower lip was torn. Blood sprang oozing from the wound.

Suddenly, two police constables and medical staff stormed inside the room. Michael raised his arm to deliver another punch to Sam, but it was stopped by police constables.

"Sam! You bastard !" Michael shouted. Constable began pushing him out of the room.

"Sam, We are not going to spare you! you rat! "Michel continued scramming on the tip of his voice. He was pushed out of the room.

The nurse put cotton on Sam's torn lip.

Soon, cotton turned red. Sam's torn lip was smiling behind the red cotton.

*****

8

Chapter 8

In the cloudy morning, People were jogging on the peripheral jogging track of the park. A group of teenagers was playing cricket in the middle of the park. A small group of spectators was seated near the scoreboard placed under a tree.

Michael was on the bench, opposite the scoreboard. He was staring down at the green lawn around his bench. His face was sad, and his shoulders were down. His right knee was bouncing continually. Occasionally, He was crossing and uncrossing his arms.

Slowly, words emerged in his mind.

...You are in my deep breath,

You are in my sleepless eyes,

You are in my heavy heart,

And You are in my unfallen tears,

But my core is at peace,

Our souls are blended now... ...forever.

"Wow, what a shot!", "Great shot!", Good one!" loud cheers came from the spectators, followed by excited clapping.

Michael looked at the cricket pitch. Both the batsmen were running across the pitch toward each other. Michael put his head down again.

"Uncle, ball, please."

Michael raised his head. One teenage boy was standing in front of him, pointing toward a light green Tennis ball at a distance from Michael.

Michael unwillingly stood and walked toward the ball. He picked up the ball and threw it to the boy.

"Thank you, Uncle." The boy caught the ball and threw it toward other players. The game resumed.

After some time, Michael looked at the jogging track, and his eyes gazed. His eyebrows furrowed. The flesh around his cheeks turned red.

Maya was walking down the track from a distance. She was dressed in a white kurta, a traditional dress in India, embroidered with beautiful yellow, red, and purple flowers. Her neatly combed hair was resting over her shoulders. She had a small, brown leather bag on her shoulder and held a book to her chest.

'Wow, she looks gorgeous.' Michael stunned. His eyes brightened. He felt a sudden surge of energy in his body. In excitement, he began walking toward Maya without taking his eyes off her.

Suddenly, Dr. DeSuza's words echoed in his mind...

'It's a good sign that Maya's memories are flashing in her mind. However, we need a big event to trigger her memory. Something considerable.'

Maya was walking on the track but hadn't seen Michael yet. She was looking straight ahead with a faint smile on her face.

Dr. DeSuza's words continued to resonate in Michael's mind.

'Michael, I don't recommend you meet Maya at the hospital. Meet her outside. It will be best to appear suddenly in front of her and see if she can recollect your past memories.'

Michael stopped; he held his breath and waited for Maya's glance at him.

Maya got closer to Michael, and her mobile rang. She stopped momentarily and took out the ringing mobile from her bag. She touched it to her ear and resumed her walk. Her gaze did not connect with Michael's anxious look.

As she passed close to Michael, he smelt the smell of her perfume.

He had it in maximum goodness, but the next moment, he realized,

'Oh! Maya does not recognize me. It seems her memory is not back yet.'

Intense anguish appeared on Michael's face. He closed his eyes and covered the face with his palms. He suddenly felt the energy drain out from his feet. He sat down, dejected in the middle of the track.

*****

In a couple of minutes, Michael heard footsteps in front of him.

"Michael!" A familiar voice came. He quickly raised his head. Maya was standing in front of him with a broad smile on her face. Michael stunned. He was dumbfounded and kept looking at Maya.

"On my last birthday, what do you want to tell me ?" Maya looked at Michael with meaningful eyes.

A sweet smile appeared on Michael's face. His chest was puffing out, and he sensed warmth in his cheeks. He looked adoringly into Maya's eyes and said softly,

"Maya, I love you!"

The wave of energy enhanced Maya's emotions. She hugged Michael tightly, intensely. Michael, too, hugged her passionately.

After a while, they loosened their hug. Maya turned her head down in an acute shyness. Michael lifted her chin softly. He slowly moved his lips toward hers. Maya shook from the core. She got goosebumps all over her body. She felt a surge of electricity pass through her. She closed her eyes and allowed Michael's lips to rest on hers.

Their lips remained in an interlocked state for some time.

Suddenly, the lingering black clouds vanished. The blue azure appeared all over the sky, and the fresh green manicured lawn bathed in bright yellow sunlight.

*****

"Maya... Maya... Maya..." Maya heard the voice. The grip of sleep on her eyes loosened. She opened her eyes and saw a faint figure sitting on the chair in front of her bed.

'Oh, It's Bhagat's ghost again." Maya had tremors throughout her body. She sat up halfway with bulging eyes.

"Maya, you are not ready to leave my land. But you will...You have to...I curse you." Bhagat began moving slowly toward Maya with flushed skin. Maya noticed his eyes were wide open, showing the whites. Saliva was growing at the corners of the mouth.

"You need to learn to ignore Bhagat's ghost. Otherwise, he will haunt the rest of your life." Dr. DeSuza's words echoed in Maya's mind.

"Maya, I curse you. You will be taken far away from here. Very far..." Bhagat uttered a scream.

******

Maya's room was filling with fresh yellow light. The wall clock appeared on the front wall. Maya noted the time; it was 7:00 A.M.

"Hmmm... it's morning again," Maya murmured.

She woke up, and suddenly, she felt a pain in her stomach. She pressed her stomach with both hands and preferred to remain on the bed.

After sometime her mobile rang.

"Hello..." It was Kapoor on another side.

"I have been informed that there are emails that have been sent from your personal email account on 15th June. Those emails had an attachment of confidential documents." Kapoor continued. Maya's throat narrowed, and a sudden fear gripped her mind and body.

"I don't get it, Sir? I did not send any of those documents." Sweat appeared quickly on Maya's forehead.

The sound of paper scrambling came through the receiver.

"I am holding a list of phone calls made from your desk phone on the same day. Around the same time as Mrs. Pinto's murder, a call was made from your desk to a particular number. Do you know whose number that is?" Kapoor asked.

"No, Sir. " Maya shook her head.

"It's HSDTecSoft's number."

"Oh My God! It must be Roy who did all these things." Maya's said in a high pitch. She took a few quick breaths.

"Maya, come and meet me in the office immediately." Kapoor's loud voice came through the phone's speaker, and he disconnected the call.

*****

"Maya." Michael's voice came through the speaker.

"Yes, Michael." Maya's palm was shaking while holding her phone.

"Get ready; we need to go to Sarah's house now."

"Now? No, not now, Michael. I have to go to the office now."

"Office? Today is Saturday. The office is closed today." Michael said.

"Yeah, I know, But something happened at the office. Kapoor sir Just called"

"What happened?"

"It seems..." Maya stopped in between. "I will tell you when we meet."

"Okay..but get ready. We have to go to Sarah's house now."

"Now? I am feeling dizzy and nauseous also."

"Get ready, Maya." Michael disconnected the call.

*****

Kapoor sat down on his chair and took a deep breath. He was panting with rage. After a couple of minutes, he took out his mobile from his shirt pocket and dialed a number.

"Inspector Jadhav, this is Ashok Kapoor here. Do you have any further update on the email id to whom our documents were sent?"

"We are looking into it, Mr. Kapoor." Inspector Jadhav's thick voice came from the other end.

"Is it a fake email id?" Kapoor inquired.

"I checked with our Cyber cell, Mr.Kapoor. As per them, it is not a fake id, but that particular email id does not exist anymore."

"That email id does not exist anymore? Then to whom documents were sent?"

"The id was active only for a short while. It seems it was created only to receive those documents."

"Who created that email id?"

"No idea, all the information submitted at the time of account creation is fake. What was in those documents?" Inspector Jadhav asked.

"Those are confidential documents."

"Oh! Then, it's a serious matter." Inspector Jadhav's tone became graver. A fear appeared on Kapoor's face.

"Yes. Do you have any idea where our documents could be now?" Kapoor asked.

"No Idea, we are looking into it, but since the email id was deleted so quickly after the documents were sent, it will be tough to find its digital trail. The documents could be anywhere in the world now."

"What do you mean by anywhere in the world ?" Kapoor was astonished.

"Anywhere means anywhere, it could be with your competitor, or it could have hit the black market."

"Oh My God!" Kapoor was shocked from the core. His face was contorted with a mixture of fear and anxiety. He wiped a thin layer of sweat from his forehead.

"Our best people are working on this. I will call you once we get a breakthrough." Inspector Jadhav disconnected the call.

Kapoor did not keep down the phone immediately. In the web of thoughts, he held the phone to his ear for a long time.

******

Maya rang the doorbell of Sarah's house with jittery fingers.

"What happened to your fingers? "Michael looked at Maya's shaking fingers.

"Don't know.." Maya holds the fingers in the other palm.

After a few moments, the door opened. Sarah's father was at the door.

"Good morning, uncle, Is Sarah at home?" Maya asked with a smiling face.

"Please come in." He said briefly and went inside. Maya and Michael took out their shoes at the doorstep and followed Sarah's father inside.

Maya and Michael sat on the couch in the hall. Saraha's father sat on a chair in front of them. Maya started looking around. Many males and females of all age groups gathered in the hall. Some were seated, some were standing in groups, while others were sitting on the floor. Many were speaking on their mobile phones.

The house help gave water to Maya and Michael.

"How are you, Maya? I heard you were suffering from some mental disease?" Sarah's father asked politely.

"I'm good, Uncle. I have been taking my medication regularly. I am almost cured now." Maya said positively.

"Good." Sarah's father replied.

Suddenly, one middle-aged man came near Sarah's father and whispered in his ear.

"Excuse me." Sarah's father went toward a group of people standing in the corner of the hall.

"Let's go in Sarah's room and surprise her." Maya looked at Michael and said enthusiastically.

"Okay..." Michael said.

They both entered into Sarah's room; Maya followed Michael. Maya was halfway into the room and saw that Sarah's bed was empty. It looked as it had not been used in some time, and so did the writing table.

"Where is Sarah, Michael?" Maya looked everywhere in the room and asked curiously. Michael was standing in front of Maya. As he moved to his right, Maya's gaze shifted to the wall behind him. Maya saw a photo frame with Sarah's photo on the wall. Sarah was smiling beautifully in the photo. Maya walked toward the photo.

"Sarah looks so pretty in this photo." Maya thought. As she walked closer to the photo, she noticed a small garland of flowers and a crucifix hanging on it. Maya felt a sudden current pass through her body. She quickly took a step back and looked at Michael in great disbelief. Her eyes were wide open.

"What is this, Michael?"

Maya asked with a mixture of fear and shock in her eyes. She felt the tremors running all over her body.

"..." Michael did not say anything. He kept his head down and shook it sadly.

"Oh...No!" Maya got the answer. Her heart sank into her chest, and it began pacing rapidly. Maya thought it would explode. She looked again at Sarah's photo with intense pain on her face. She felt her energy drain out, and her legs gave way. She suddenly lost her balance, and she fell like an empty sack on the floor. Tears welled up, and her throat narrowed.

"Oh! Sarah !..." Maya started weeping loudly... uncontrollably. Michael embraced her and started patting her back softly.

On listening to Maya's loud wails, Sarah's family members hurriedly came into the room and gathered around her.

Maya kept weeping with her body throbbing and pulsing in Michael's arms. She was inconsolable. The men stood around with sorrowful faces, and the women comforted her with teary eyes.

After some time, Maya looked at Sarah's father with a face full of pain.

"How did this happen, uncle? I met Sarah last Sunday night at Sunshine industrial complex." She asked in a teary voice,

"You met Sarah last Sunday night?" Sarah's father asked in disbelief.

"Yes."

"At what time?"

"Around midnight."

Sarah's father looked at Maya in surprise and then at Michael. All of Sarah's other relatives looked at each other in disbelief. The expression on their faces clearly showed their surprise state of mind.

Suddenly, Sarah's father's mobile rang. He retrieved it from his pocket and began walking to the other side of the room.

"Maya... come here," Michael said softly but authoritatively. He gently led Maya to the wall.

"Did you meet Sarah a few days back?" Michael's hand holds Maya's upper arm. Maya saw an intense doubt on his face.

"Yeah, Michael! Remember? Last Sunday night, We went to the CCTV company's office in the Sunshine industrial complex? She met me in the premises that night and showed me the way to the backdoor of the CCTV company's office."

"What are you saying, Maya?" Michael asked with solemn eyes. His hand shook Maya's upper arm, which shook Maya entirely.

"Yeah, I even asked her to come along with me and show me the backdoor of the CCTV company, but she said she would wait there to alert me if someone follows me and also to guide you the way in case you reached there. Didn't she meet you that night in the building's premises?"

"No, she did not meet me on the premises on that night." Michael's face was full of pain and confusion.

Sudden tiredness hit Maya, and her body began sweating profusely. She sat down on the floor.

All of a sudden, Michael's face changed.

"Maya, listen to me carefully. Have you been taking your medications regularly?" Maya did not reply. She was lost in her thoughts.

"Maya?" Michael called emphatically. Maya looked at him with a blank face.

"Have you been taking your medications regularly?"

"Yes. I am taking my pills regularly." Maya said in a low voice.

"No, I don't think so, Maya. You need to check your pill bottle."

Maya did not reply. She was lost in her web of thought.

"Maya? I don't think you are taking your pills regularly. You need to check your pill bottle or ask Rita auntie about it." Still, Maya was lost in their thoughts.

"Maya?!" Michael said loudly and again shook Maya's upper arm.

"Yeah.." Maya snapped out of trance.

"Maya. I don't think you are taking your pills regularly. You need to check your pill bottle."

"No, no! I am taking my pills regularly. I am sure of it." Maya said in a melancholy but confirmed tone.

"No, you are not."

"Why do you think so?"

"Because... whatever you just said has never happened in reality."

"What do you mean?" Maya was confused further.

"How could Sarah have met you on that night at around midnight? Around 11:30 P.M. she met with a horrible car accident near her house... and... and...She died on the spot." Michael's voice shuddered.

"What?" Maya shouted. A severe pain gripped Maya's heart, and it quickly its appearance on her face. Her face turned into a blend of pain, confusion, disbelief, and surprise.

"NO!! Michael! Sarah did come and meet me that night. She was helping me to regain my memory. She knew it was important for me to regain my memory to prove my innocence against Roy's..."

Michael held Maya with both arms and again shook her intensely. "I was about to tell you, Maya; Roy did not set you up. Sam did."

"No... no... I cannot believe it." Maya said fervently but with disbelief in her eyes.

"I know you are not on good terms with Roy, Maya, but he has not framed you. Sam trapped you." Michael said in an assuring tone. Maya kept looking at him in disbelief.

"And again...Sarah did not meet you on that night. She started from her house to come and meet us at the Sunshine industrial complex, but on the way, she met with an car accident." Michael said painfully.

"So Michael, you saying, Sahara's meeting me on that night was my hallucination?" Maya's tone became fierce, with extreme disbelief in her widened eyes.

"Yes !" Michael said firmly. Maya thought for a few seconds and said,

"But Michael, on that night, Sarah really showed me the other way to the back door of CCTV company office and also their IT room...I am sure I met Sarah that night in Sunshine Industrial complex...there must be some confusion...."

"There is absolutely no confusion, Maya! Meeting Sarah on that night was your hallucination! "Michael said in a firm voice.

Maya was shocked. She started breathing heavily. She came closer to Michael and said under her heavy breath,

"Sometimes I feel Michael, our entire life is a hallucination. What if this is a hallucination, Michael?"

"No, this is real."

"I feel we all are leaving in hallucination...all the time..." Maya said intensely with a lost face.

"No, this is real, Maya! "Michael shouted. Maya came to her senses. But her face was dipped in extreme confusion. She was again pulled into her web of thoughts.

In a few minutes, Michael's mobile rang.

"Yes... yes... Maya is here with me." Michael began talking over the phone.

'According to Michael, I did not meet Sarah on that night. It was my hallucination. But that can't be true. How do I know if what is happening now is not a hallucination? This could be my hallucination. Let me go home and check my pill bottle. If Michael is right, it must be full... let me go home...' Maya thought.

"You mean for Maya? Are you sure? Oh My God!!" Michael exclaimed emphatically. He composed himself and looked at Maya, who was still in her lost state of mind.

"One second...Maya, wait here," Michael said and hurriedly moved toward the window. He resumed his speaking with a severe face.

In her web of thoughts, Maya quickly left Sarah's house. She did not put on her shoes. She began descending stairs barefooted.

*****

Maya climbed the 'Ruby Park' stairs in desperation. Her hands were shivering, and she was breathing heavily. She reached her floor and opened her bag to look for the door keys. One by one, she checked all the inner pockets of her bag with her shaky hand. She found the key to the main door in one of the pockets.

Maya tried to insert the key into the keyhole with her shaky fingers. She turned the key in the lock hole and kicked the door open with her leg.

"Open it ...Open it..." Maya thumped on the door intensely.

"Open it ..Open it...Open it... She kicked the door forcefully.

The door did not budge. She kicked it a few more times, but the door remained shut.

Maya retrieved the key from the keyhole and tried to insert it again. Suddenly, the door opened. Rita was at the door.

"Maya? What happened? Why did you not ring the bell?" Rita asked in surprise.

Maya rushed into her bedroom.

She opened her wardrobe door and took out a transparent yellow bottle of her pills. It was empty. Maya's sad face lit up momentarily.

'I know I have been taking my pills on time. Hence, I thought that I don't have the problem of hallucinations anymore." She felt relieved.

"What happened, Maya? Why do you look tense?" Rita asked from the door.

"Mom...I took these pills regularly, right ?"

"Yes, You are taking these pills regularly. But why are you asking this ?" Rita was puzzled.

Doorbell rang.

"I will get it. "Rita said, and she went toward the main door.

'But Sarah came and showed me the way to the backdoor that night? Who was she then?' Thoughts began rumbling through Maya's mind.

"Is Miss Maya at Home?" Maya heard the strong, authoritative voice from the hall.

"Yes, She is inside. Who are you ?" Maya heard Rita's voice from the hall.

"I am Brijesh Singh from 'ConfSafe' detective agency."

"Okay, Let me call her...Maya... Maya... Some people have come to meet you. "Rita said while coming to Maya's bedroom.

Rita, followed by Brijesh Singh with two other tall, muscular men came and stood at the bedroom door.

"Miss Maya, Please come with us." Brijesh Singh ordered in his commanding voice.

'As per Michael, if Sarah died before in the road accident, then whom I met in a sunshine industrial complex on that night?... Who was She?' Maya was still in her thoughts.

Maya shook from her core. Her shaky hand reached to cover her mouth.

Suddenly, Maya felt her surroundings begin to spin. Everything started appearing blurry to her.

In her daze, Maya saw Sarah appear in front of her. Sarah couldn't stand properly and had great difficulty to maintain her balance. Her face was dipped in pain. She had blood on her forehead, and her mouth was swollen. Her t-shirt had black spots and was torn at the shoulder. Her jeans were torn at the knees as well.

Maya went into flashback. She remembered Sarah's that night condition.

"Oh! Her condition was the same on that night. Torn T-shirt..wounds on lips and forehead..swollen mouth..." Maya kept looking at Sarah. Suddenly,

!.. Oh, No...No...No...No...No.' Maya realized. Her heart missed the heartbeat for a moment, and the next moment it started pondering with double speed. Sweat started pouring throughout her body. She felt sudden dryness in her mouth.

'Oh Sarah! So it was your ghost who came to show me the way?' Maya asked with bulged eyes. Her mouth was wide open.

Sarah smiled and waved at Maya for Goodbye. Maya looked at Sarah with teary eyes and extended her hand toward Sarah, but Sarah suddenly disappeared.

"It was Sarah's ghost who met me at night....Oh My God! Oh My God! It seems I can see and talk with the ghosts !" Maya was stunned. She stood like a statue. Her whole body was frozen.

Suddenly, She felt the entire room start spinning around her. The wall clock started appearing more and more blurry. The darkness enveloped her, and she collapsed on the floor.

A transparent yellow, empty pill bottle was still in her palm.

******

THE END

www.ingramcontent.com/pod-product-compliance
Lightning Source LLC
Chambersburg PA
CBHW060532160726
47991CB00001B/285